LAKE
OF
DARKNESS

LAKE
OF
DARKNESS

A NOVEL

SCOTT KENEMORE

TALOS

NEW YORK

Talos Press books may be purchased in bulk at special discounts for sales promotion, corporate gifts, fund-raising, or educational purposes. Special editions can also be created to specifications. For details, contact the Special Sales Department, Talos Press, 307 West 36th Street, 11th Floor, New York, NY 10018 or info@skyhorsepublishing.com.

Talos Press® is a registered trademark of Skyhorse Publishing, Inc.®, a Delaware corporation.

Visit our website at www.talospress.com.

10 9 8 7 6 5 4 3 2 1

Library of Congress Cataloging-in-Publication Data is available on-file.

ISBN: 978-1-945863-50-9
EISBN: 978-1-945863-51-6

Cover design by Daniel Brount
Cover artwork by Alejandro Colucci

Printed in the United States of America

LAKE

OF

DARKNESS

For Max, who liked this one

Stones have been known to move, and trees to speak.
Augurs and understood relations have
By magot pies and choughs and rooks brought forth
The secret'st man of blood.

—Macbeth (III, iv)

ONE

They came.

They came, it seemed, from every place on God's earth south of the city limits. They came with almost no money or formal education. They came never before having ridden in a train. Or a streetcar. Or an automobile. They came former slaves and sons of slaves. Some of the oldest still bore marks from leg irons or overseers' whips. They came in threadbare clothing and with shoes that were worn clean through. They came with *all* of their possessions. Everything they owned.

They came from places like Alabama and Mississippi and Texas. (And this, in an age when seventy-five percent of Americans never traveled more than seventy-five miles from the spot where they had been born.) They came from communities where segregation was so powerful, there wasn't even a word for it. It was no special way of doing things. It was the *only* way. They came having ridden up in train cars that were, themselves, often segregated. They came hoping to find relatives who had already made the trip up to Chicago. Or friends. Or mere acquaintances. And those who knew nobody had heard there were organizations with names like the Chicago League on Urban Conditions Among Negroes that existed to assist newcomers such as themselves. They had read about these organizations in the newspapers circulated by black railroad porters who worked on the trains that started in Chicago but ran all throughout the South. Many of the newcomers had never before been to a city, much less the second-largest city in the United States. None had seen a lake as large as Lake Michigan. None had seen or smelled or heard anything like the blasted hellscape that was the Chicago stockyards—where more animals were killed each day than any other place on earth.

Many had been sharecroppers. Many had not eaten properly in several days. They were—all of them—taking the biggest risk of their lives. They were wagering everything they had. It might not be much, but it was all on the table.

They came with hope. They came with desperate dreams. They came for the promise of a place less miserable than the one they had left. To some, the rumors of Chicago seemed impossible to credit. The work of a fantasist, surely. A place where black people and white people could ride in streetcars together, and enter businesses through the same doors. A place where blacks owned businesses and homes, and sent their children to proper schools. A place where you could get a job in a factory or slaughterhouse with relative ease, and begin earning a living right away. A place where you could feel free to say what you thought.

And what was perhaps *most* jarring to these newly-arrived was that the rumors were, essentially, true. This *was* happening. It *was* the case. And the sheer astonishment such knowledge instilled could be overwhelming to the point of paralysis.

The world was a different place. The world was going crazy. Going something, at least. These times were not normal. A madness, perhaps a benign one, was allowing this great migration to begin. To gather steam as though it might never stop at all.

A war consumed the world. The whole world. A terror came with that, yes. But could it, really, be *all* bad, these times of madness, if they also allowed for this change that blew on the wind? That blew across the cotton fields of Georgia and the plantations of Louisiana, and blew people north to settle in the land of Lincoln. To settle in a landscape so cold and hard and alien in the winter that it might have been another planet.

Joe Flippity was his name. He had come himself, years before. He had been among the first. Then he had watched the others who had come after him. He had watched them hard.

It was, more or less, his job.

Crespo came to fetch Joe Flippity on the first day of August. It was evening. Crespo had an idea of where his target might be, but only roughly. For a man like Crespo, that was enough.

Crespo took a streetcar to Katt's Tavern on South State Street and waited. It was like a place from a Wild West town. Little more than a broken-down house. It did not have electricity or gaslight. The men inside drank by lantern.

Crespo stood by the long wooden bar—crowded and shadowy enough that his white face was not immediately noted. Near the bar was a table. Seated at it were five Negro men, and the only other white in the place. The white man was slight and bookish, with an immaculate moustache and a yellow band around his hat. For the moment, he was doing all of the talking.

"The horses are perfectly identical, see? Actual, no foolin' *identical twins*. All the markings and mottlings alike, just as if they'd been printed from the same plates. What we'll do is take one horse and train it in secret. Out in Michigan there's a fellow I know who works cheap and won't rat. The other horse, we put it in circulation over at Hawthorne. *Never* train it. Give it a meal right before each race. Pretty soon, it has a reputation as the worst horse in Chicago. The odds on it get long. *Reeeal* long. And *that's* when we swap in the twin and bet big. We'll make a killing, gentlemen. An absolute killing! But you have to swear on your lives to keep it secret. And I need the money tonight. This owner, he doesn't realize what he has in these twin horses. He doesn't see the opportunity. Wants to split them up and sell them individual-like. What a tragedy that would be! Gentlemen, please believe me when I say that we have to act fast. . ."

As Crespo looked on, a figure stepped out from the shadows. He was tall and thin and black as jet. He wore a leather coat that fit him closely, despite the August heat. Perhaps he wore it to give the impression of being more powerfully built than he actually was. The shadow man was silent as he approached the table, seeming almost to float across the dark barroom floor.

"There a problem here?" he asked.

For a moment, only silence.

"We ain't giving this man no trouble," one of the Negro men said.

"Yeah," insisted another. "Mind yours."

"This man's not getting any trouble from *you*," said the shadow man. "But I think y'all about to receive some trouble from *him*."

The figure underneath the yellow-banded hat looked up in confusion that almost appeared genuine.

Then the shadow man opened one side of his coat to reveal a rare treasure. A Colt 1911 in an oiled leather holster. Then—slowly, deliberately—he opened the other side of his coat to reveal something rarer still . . . at least on the South Side of Chicago, at least in the coat of a Negro man. A six-pointed metal patrolman's star with CHICAGO POLICE stamped across the top and a copper badge number at the bottom. In the center of the star was the great Seal of the City of Chicago, rendered as well as it could be by a crude metal press.

The group stared wordlessly at these marvels.

"This man's business is getting *your* money . . . for something that never damn happens," the policeman said. "That horse he's telling you about? A few months from now, when you see him on the street and ask where your money is, he'll tell you it died. Or got stolen. Or died and then got stolen. He'll say he's been ruined by the whole affair, and has men he owes money breathing down his neck. He'll say he fears he is about to be killed or thrown in jail. All that will be a lie . . . but it will be enough to make you leave him alone, which will be his only purpose. And by then, you will have been took. It will already be too late."

The man with the yellow hatband opened his mouth to object. The policeman put a firm hand on his shoulder and regarded him icily.

"Mr. Weil, what'd I tell you about working my part of State Street?" the policeman asked. "You got a set of balls, coming back down here. I give you that."

"You got it all wrong," Weil said, his eyes flashing left and right, then left again. "This is the real deal this time! I'm not trying to put it over on nobody. Don't you see? I'm trying to let these fine men in on the con with me. We're going to make money *together*. These men know they're in the big city now. . . Chicago! . . . where anybody has a shot to get rich! Don't they deserve that shot, officer?"

Over at the bar, Crespo—who had apprehended Weil a time or two himself—smiled at the con man's tenacity. Even when cornered, he continued to pitch, to spin, to wheedle.

The tall, dark police officer did not seem as amused.

"Time for you to go, Mr. Weil," said the officer, helping the man with the yellow hatband to his feet. "I'm sure you understand."

"I-" Weil began.

"You nothing," said the policeman. He pinned one of Weil's arms behind his back and marched him to the door.

Weil made a show but did not really resist. As he was shoved outside, he looked back through the doorway to the men at the table. His expression told them this was all a misunderstanding. That something like this had never happened before. That it was outrageous. And that he'd be back with them at his earliest convenience.

It was clear those men still wanted to believe. They would probably try to find Weil later and ask him—plead with him, even—to let them in on the deal. The lure of easy money was just that strong. In a boomtown like Chicago—where new fortunes seemed to be made every day—there was only one true fear. But it ran deep and it consumed everyone. It was the fear of missing your chance. Of looking straight at it and *not seeing it*. And then having to watch as some other miserable son of a bitch used it to make a million dollars.

The tall police officer returned from the door, *sans* Weil. The men sitting at the table looked as though they wanted to fight. To jump the officer and beat him—maybe to death—1911 and badge be damned.

One of them pushed back his chair violently.

That was when Crespo stepped out from the bar.

"Flip!" Crespo said loudly. He made sure to let his own holster show. The men at the table thought twice, and then a third time too. For the moment, they elected to remain where they were.

"Salvatore Crespo," Flip said with a smile. "The devil brings you down to South State Street?"

"I'm looking right at him," Crespo said. "You got time to take a walk? Maybe even a ride?"

"I reckon I do," Flip said evenly. He gave the men at the table a last, long look that said they'd thank him later.

Back outside, the air was warm and the night sky was clear. It smelled a lot less like lamp oil and beer, and a lot more like shit. The police officers began to walk north.

"I start to think there's a part of town where Weil won't ply his trade, and then I see him there," Crespo said.

"You kidding?" Flip replied. "Mister Yellow loves him some black folks. He loves him some green, more precisely. Black folk ain't got as much as some others, but he'll still take it on an off night."

Crespo laughed. They passed a man selling fried pig parts on a dirty, broken cart. One of his offerings was an entire face, still smiling wide. The vendor, in contrast, failed to offer even a grin.

Beside the pig vendor was an illegal brothel that operated openly. The smell of perfume, liquor, and come eked out from its open door, as did syncopated music from a dingy band in the lobby. (The music style had recently been named after the come-smell. Or maybe it was the other way around. Flip had never been entirely clear on this point.)

"Feel like you didn't travel all this way to chat about a two-bit con man," Flip said.

Crespo nodded. He looked Flip up and down. The Italian's expression said he might be debating how to best begin a good joke.

"How long you been on the force?" he eventually asked.

They approached an alley containing a dead horse.

"You know," Flip replied, smiling to reveal bright, almost perfect teeth. "Long as I been in town, seems like."

"I thought so," Crespo said. "And how long have there been gentlemen of color like yourself on the force? Negro officers?"

Flip had not expected the interrogation to become so historical.

"While before me," he answered after considering it. "First of us due to retire soon. I heard of Negro officers as far back as—what?—maybe the seventies. Right after the war between the states."

They slowed and regarded the dead horse for a moment, then proceeded on.

"And yet they still don't let you wear a uniform," Crespo observed. "No marching in parades. No proper funeral when one of you goes down in the line of duty. Just a badge and a gun, and keep things quiet in your part of town."

Flip silently let his gaze drop to Crespo's waist, indicating that the Italian, in plain clothes, also had only these items at the moment.

Crespo grinned.

"Thing is," Crespo continued, "sometimes things can change. It builds for a while—you can feel it building—and then—*Boom!*—something happens, and the world is different. Italians didn't used to get much respect either. You know, they say we're part Negro, just a little bit."

"Italy close to Africa," Flip observed.

Crespo grinned again.

"I was a member of the Black Hand Squad," he continued. "That's a few years ago now, but it changed everything for Italian officers in this town. Some of the men from that squad are working in high places in the department now. Very high places. And *everybody's* gonna turn out for our funerals."

Flip had heard about the Black Hand Squad. Around 1900, a team of Italian extortionists had begun operating in Chicago. Mostly, they preyed on other immigrants from Italy. To dissuade those tempted not to pay protection, the extortionists—who called themselves the Black Hand—killed ten to twenty Chicagoans a year. They left the bodies at busy intersections with knives protruding from the corpses' backs and notes claiming credit. At first, the city had seemed powerless to stop them. Those who went to the authorities for assistance received little, and usually wound up dead. It started to become embarrassing. Then, in a rare show of competence, the city had created the Black Hand Squad—a contingent of twenty-five policemen tasked solely with busting the extortion ring. What made the squad unique was that every member had been an immigrant from Italy or the son of immigrants from Italy. Within six months, the squad had caught most of the Black Hand players and successfully reduced the extortions from a geyser to a trickle. (They were never stopped entirely, but had been put down to levels that Chicago could, more or less, find tolerable.) It was said the squad members had been richly rewarded for their success.

"I heard that was you," Flip allowed. "Yes, I heard all about that."

"Oh did you, now?" Crespo said.

"You'd be surprised what I hear all the way down on South State," Flip said.

"Then I'll tell you something you *didn't* hear," Crespo told him. "I know you didn't hear it because we never told nobody. And that's that we were *shit scared*. All of us. Thought we were gonna die for sure. Some of us wanted to enlist in the army rather than face the Black Hand. But in the end, we took them down. And they never touched us. We *all* survived."

"Why you tellin' me this?" Flip asked, suddenly growing uneasy.

They neared a stop where a streetcar would take them north to the Loop—the skyscrapered center of the bustling city.

"Because," said Crespo, "it's time for you to meet the man."

Twenty minutes later, Flip and Crespo stepped off a crowded streetcar and into another world. Rich men in cloaks strolled in groups, smoking and talking confidentially. Women, almost always accompanied by men, wore fine hats decorated with feathers from rare birds nearly murdered out of existence for the plumage. The buildings around them were tall and electrified. There was the smell of hot food and beer and pungent cigars.

Crespo conducted Flip down one of the only dark alleyways in sight.

"I still ain't clear on this," Flip said. "What are we doing?"

"It's better if he tells you," Crespo replied mysteriously. "He'll like to. No matter how big you get in the world, there's still some things you like to do yourself."

Halfway down the dark alley was a metal door with a brass handle. Before it loitered a lone uniformed police officer, smoking. There was a crushed straw hat at his feet. The officer regarded Crespo, who then indicated Flip. The uniformed officer squinted and screwed up his face as though trying to make himself believe that this skinny Negro was the special guest they had been awaiting.

The uniformed officer opened the door. The hinges needed oil and yelped like a sickly cat, kicked hard. It made Flip jump a little, but only a little.

"Last door at the-"

"I know where to go," Crespo said, brushing past the officer.

Flip followed.

They proceeded down a narrow wood-paneled hallway—dimly lit, but lit—which Crespo navigated without hesitation.

At the end of the hall was a single door, painted dark red, or so it seemed in the scant electric light. The mullions had been carved into long-tailed lizards. One of the stiles had been damaged by a blow, probably from a cane or gun butt. From beneath, cigar smoke poured, regular and thick. There was the sound of muffled conversation.

Crespo leaned over to Flip and spoke softly.

"I can only tell you two things about how to deal with the man. The first is that he can tell when you lie, so *don't lie to him.* The other thing is . . ."

Crespo's voice fell further, practically to a whisper.

"He, himself, will almost always lie. But you won't know it 'till-"

Before Crespo could finish, the red door was opened by a banker. Or so it might have been. Ironed shirt. Bright necktie. Diamond stick-pin. White shoes. Expensive cigar. Soft, gloved hands.

The banker looked at Crespo and Flip, then smiled a smile of genial contempt. A smile that said the two policemen were parade animals in some kind of show for children or imbeciles. Then he folded forward obsequiously—very unlike a banker, but now like a server at a private club—and beckoned them enter the smoky room.

Past the banker was a round wooden poker table with a green felt top. At the table sat a figure in a dark suit. He was hunched forward and wore a voluminous, almost flowing jacket and vest, making it difficult for an onlooker to tell exactly how large he really was. The seated figure faced away from the door, and did not turn as his guests were bid enter. His fleshy neck was exposed. Had Flip and Crespo intended him harm—to rush forward and slit his throat, for example—no one could have intervened to save his life.

Perhaps, thought Flip, offering up a naked, upturned neck was the ultimate sign of power. Or of madness.

A light bulb dangled from a thin cord above the table. It moved ever so slightly in the breeze from the door. When it swayed, it took the shadows with it. The seated figure seemed to shrink or grow with each sway.

Then the figure—slowly—stood. And turned. And in the shaky light of the small room, it seemed to Flip, and possibly also to Crespo, that, in some strange way, the city itself had stood and acknowledged their presence. And now prepared to address them.

Three hundred pounds in a day when the average man weighed half that, Big Bill Thompson—the Mayor of Chicago—was not made porcine or round-faced by his size. Instead, he managed only a genteel waddle beneath his prominent, quarterback's chin. His belt thrust far forward, as though a globe were concealed in his trousers. He was tall, but not taller than Flip. He had a small mouth that looked ready to make careful, pertinent statements. He was not yet fifty, but had the stately bearing of a much older public servant.

The mayor's most striking trait, however, was that he managed to be both handsome and repellent at the same time. Handsome from a distance, but repellent—that was the only word for it—when you got up close. When you took a second look. And Flip did.

The folds of the mayor's powerful athlete's neck concealed infected pocks and acne scars. His teeth were generally straight, but beset by rot from cigar and pipe smoke. Regarding Big Bill Thompson was like regarding a gourmet meal that had been left in an alley for a day or two. Cover the patch with the wriggling cockroaches and worms, and maybe the rest still looked good enough to eat. Maybe. But also, maybe not. And then you still knew about the worms.

"Mister Mayor," Crespo said.

Flip found that his own throat had gone completely dry. He had not expected this encounter. Nonetheless, he managed a slight bow in the mayor's direction.

"This is the one I told you about, Mister Mayor," Crespo continued. "The one I thought could help."

The mayor's small mouth stretched into a grin.

"Yes," the mayor said. "That's fine. Does he talk?"

Crespo glanced hard at Flip from the corner of his eye.

"Yes I do, Mister Mayor," Flip said through a scratchy throat. "I certainly do."

"Well that's fine indeed," the mayor said.

"Joseph Flippity," Crespo said. "Just about everyone calls him Flip. Everyone on the force, that is."

The mayor nodded, deigning that this might be acceptable.

Flip had seen the mayor before, but only from a great distance. This giant. This titan. This planet.

Thompson was a Republican, from the party of Lincoln—and Lincoln and Thompson were both names known along South State Street. Thompson had been the first mayor in the city's history to actively court the vote of black folks, and to speak of his mission as including furthering their interests. A scion of important local families, he had nonetheless killed a man with his bare hands in 1893. A career in Chicago politics had followed swiftly thereafter. His rise had been quick and straightforward. Thompson was well-liked and effective. He was plainspoken. He was not afraid to go anywhere or meet with anybody. Many already had their eyes on him as a contender for the highest office in the land. (Woodrow Wilson was an effete, East Coast college professor who had not killed anybody with his bare hands. When the political winds decided to shift back in the other direction, many felt they might shift to Big Bill Thompson.)

The mayor slicked back a loose strand of hair, then carefully tented his fingers. He opened his mouth and smiled, but for a moment did not speak. Flip had encountered precisely this kind of hesitation in the course of enforcing the law. The normally garrulous clergyman searching for the words to explain how the young girl, or boy, had come to be half-naked on his office couch. The storekeep caught with his hand in the till. The grandmother seeking to account for the stolen goods stashed in her attic or basement.

Flip knew that when a person hesitated like this, you must never speak first. You must always stay absolutely silent. Accordingly, Flip waited patiently for Big Bill Thompson to find the right words.

"Since the first settlers came here—to this river inlet beside Lake Michigan that smelled like wild onions—certain men have been asked to go, let us say, above and beyond, for the sake of the city. They have been asked to do more. To *give* more. The soldiers who manned the crude fort that grew here, beside the frozen Chicago River—how I shudder to imagine their miserable existences—were called upon to do things that were never spoken of. While starving and waiting to be killed by Redskins, they defended this honored soil. Soil they would sanctify with their own blood. They defended it against unspoken things. Things that would never be fully understood. Or known. Things the average Chicagoan need never concern themselves with, thanks be to God. And thanks to those men. Do you understand?"

"Yessir," said Flip.

The mayor flashed a lightning-quick smile with only the corners of his mouth. It was the most insincere thing Flip had ever seen. He realized, in a trice, that he had already failed one test.

"You do not understand," the mayor affirmed. "You *do not*. But you will."

The mayor turned his thick neck toward the shadows and cried: "Bring them out!"

The shadows began to move.

As a working policeman, Flip had developed some acumen for noticing when very large men might be concealing themselves behind curtains or in the dark corners of a room. But Flip was not accustomed to being so near the all-but-blinding presence of the mayor. And so his senses had been dulled, and he was utterly surprised when a strange man of tremendous musculature stepped out of the nearby darkness. The man's arms and back strained his suit almost to the point of bursting. The fedora on his head looked like a small, novelty hat placed on a bull. The man carried a fine white envelope, very large. From it, he carefully produced several photographs. He held them daintily, with the tips of his powerful fingers, gripping only the edges. He placed them face-up on the green felt table. Then he lifted his ox-like head and made eye contact with the mayor, asking if he had done this correctly. The mayor nodded, and the giant retreated back into the shadows.

Flip looked down at the table.

Immediately, he saw that the photographs showed bodies. Dead bodies. All black, and all, somehow, destroyed.

"Things are . . . happening . . . once again in our city," Big Bill Thompson said carefully. "And once more our humble prairie settlement calls for stalwart men willing to stand against the idiot hand of murder that comes in the night."

Flip swallowed hard.

The mayor's fat fingers began to search among the photographs like puffy white grubs, twitching toward a rotting morsel. Flip glanced up at the mayor's face and saw that a perverse smile had crossed the public servant's lips. The mayor inspected the images with a look of wistfulness, as if the photos spawned fond remembrances. With each reacquaintance, the mayor's strange, horrible smile grew.

"*This* photograph tells you how it began," the mayor pronounced as the grubs found their first feeding place. "The start of the summer. Just a day or two into June. An alley along 71st Street, right where it stops being Jew and starts being Negro. The Washington children. Did you hear about this incident, officer?"

Flip had not. He said so.

"A brother and sister," the mayor told him. "Both ten or thereabouts. Twins. Practically identical—except for the plumbing, of course. They'd come up from Louisiana a month before. Staying with relatives in the neighborhood—or looking for relatives who were *supposed* to have been in the neighborhood—it was never clear. Witnesses at the scene claimed no knowledge of any parents. Certainly, nobody came forward to claim the bodies. But look closely, officer! The children have been completely decapitated! You can see that, I'm sure. Yet the image is imperfect. I fear our photographer may have lost his nerve. He could not bring himself to move any nearer the corpses. So what you may fail to detect, initially, is that the heads have been switched."

Flip looked hard into the flat square image and winced. The grubs seemed to sense his discomfort and wriggled happily. The photograph showed a young black boy and girl with their heads cut cleanly off. Yet the boy's head was positioned above the body wearing the dirty white dress, and the girl's pigtailed pate had been placed upon the torso in the grimy overalls.

"They were not joined *surgically*," the mayor clarified. "Merely placed where the other ought to have been. No, it was one week later, as I understand, that the first *proper* reattachment occurred—crude though it may have been. Done with spikes from a rail fence. Here. The toppermost two photos. Look!"

The tapping grubs indicated Flip should observe a pair of photographs at the head of the table. The first displayed a pair of black boys, perhaps fifteen years old. They were supine, and had been posed beside one another. Their necks had been cut. The first picture was a close shot, but the second was even closer. That one showed the heads pulled back slightly from the necks, displaying metal spikes extending out from each of the windpipes and up into the heads.

A few paces away, Crespo puffed air from the corner of his mouth in bewilderment.

"These boys were found near the Calumet," the mayor said. "They were also siblings, and also twins—in this case, the perfectly identical kind. Hailed from Arkansas. Family name of Horner. They'd been living with a relative and looking for work on the crew digging the Calumet-Saganashkee Channel. That was the story from the work crew, at any rate. We have been unable to locate a blood relative. They say perhaps it was a long-lost uncle with whom the boys had stayed. But he has not come forward. Now . . . the next scene, Mr. Flippity, shows something that happened over one month later."

The fat grubs moved to a large photograph in the center of the table. It showed a modest living room with a fireplace, rugs, and wooden floorboards. Paintings hung on the walls and cheap heirlooms stood upon a mantle. Below, a set of fireplace tools had been disarranged haphazardly across the floor. In the center of the room were two girls, about ten years old, covered in blood . . . and perfectly identical. Their heads had been severed and crudely reattached with what looked like twine or wire. There was also a third girl in the picture, about the same age. She seemed to stand beside the fireplace, but only because she had been impaled there with a fireplace poker through her sternum.

"An informal home for orphan Negro girls," said the mayor. "Nice Christian woman runs the place. Miss Heloise, or somesuch. She came home one afternoon to find this scene, just as you see it here. The two girls on the ground with the switched heads . . . they had come to our fair city from . . . from. . ."

As if on cue, the bull of a man again stepped out. He patted his tight suit until he found a paper in his breast pocket. He removed it and handed it over. The mayor unfolded it carefully.

"Ah yes," the mayor said. "Doreen and Netty were their names. They had come from South Carolina. Nothing more is known. Miss Heloise appears to have taken them in with no questions asked. They were—as you can plainly see—also identical twins."

The photograph was grainy, but Flip could tell that the mayor was correct on this point.

"The other unfortunate," the mayor continued, pointing to the impaled girl. "I am told the responding officers do not believe she was a target. She may have walked into the room and surprised whoever—or whatever—did this. The wrong place at the wrong time, as they say. And for it, she was killed as surely as the others."

Flip looked again at the photograph. The impaled girl's eyes were open wide. She looked bewildered and overcome, but sentient. If Flip had seen the photo of her face out of context, he would have sworn she was alive.

"Then . . . finally . . . we come to it!" cried the portly mayor.

The grubs grew spastic now, as if electricity had been made to course through them. They scrambled down the green felt to the final photo resting at the bottom of the table. Momentarily, the mayor's great, equatorial belly obscured the image in shadow. Flip squinted, struggling to see. The mayor noticed this, grinned evilly, and stepped away. All was revealed in a sudden rush.

The photo showed a wooden plank floor with three figures reclining upon it. They had been placed equidistant, with the crowns of their heads nearly touching. Three Negro boys, obviously dead. Perhaps twelve or thirteen years of age. They showed what appeared to be results of the crudest surgery—as though deep wounds stretching all around their necks had been sewn up with tailor's thread. Flip understood instantly that the heads had been severed, rotated, and sewn back on.

"The Whitcomb boys," said the mayor, consulting his notes. "Discovered last Tuesday in a house on Egan Street. They . . . well, you see what has been done. This is exactly the manner in which they were found."

"Triplets . . ." Flip said softly.

"Pardon?" the mayor said.

"The Whitcomb boys were identical triplets," Flip clarified. "Couldn't they mama tell them apart."

"You knew of them?" the mayor asked, intrigued.

"A little," Flip said. "Saw them around. The family moved here from Texas a year ago."

The mayor nodded sagely.

"Good. They say you are a man with his ear to the ground, so to speak. That is why we have summoned you."

Flip did not look the mayor in the face. Instead, his eyes stayed fixed on the photographs.

"All children," Flip said. "All Negro. . . all from somewhere else . . . and every one of them a twin."

"Indeed," the mayor said with a solemn nod. "You grasp the essentials."

"I heard the Whitcomb boys died," Flip continued. "I ain't hear any details though. Nothing like this. And someone told me something about the girls at the orphanage—but again, the specifics were . . ."

"Were concealed intentionally, on my orders," the mayor confirmed. "Even within the police department, as much as was practicable."

Here, Flip arched his eyebrows and shrugged, as if to say such a goal was far from unobtainable.

"What we need now is to discover who is doing this, and to stop them just as quietly," the mayor asserted.

"No suspects?" Flip asked.

"Not a man," said the mayor. "And I use that word advisedly. For it *is* a man. No woman could have done such horrible things as these. But please, be assured . . . all that we know, all that we have—every resource—will be put at your disposal."

Silence.

Stillness.

Nothing moved.

Flip leaned closer as though he had misheard a very elderly person.

"*My* disposal, Mister Mayor?"

"Why do you think I have sent for you?" the mayor inquired rhetorically, turning his attention to the typed page in his hand. "You are, apparently, an officer of some talents. The Bruford Case. The First West Bank Robbery. The rescue of the Towson girl. They tell me there is not a more decorated Negro officer in my entire police department."

Flip did not immediately respond.

"Have I been misinformed?" the mayor pressed.

"No . . . I . . .I expect you've been informed just fine," Flip managed.

The mayor smiled.

"The city learned many lessons with the Black Hand Squad," the mayor said, his eyes flitting over to Crespo. "We learned that those inside certain communities will always have special advantages when it comes to enforcing the law *in* those communities. Yet—pleased as we were that squad's results—we were *not* pleased that knowledge of the case dispersed itself so widely. People as far away as New York now associate our city with organized crime! Can you imagine it? Chicago and organized crime?! That serves nobody. Not our citizens. Not our businesses. Nobody! So, officer, do you understand what I am asking? Do you understand what is at stake?"

Flip did not. The expression on his face showed it. Thompson sighed and took a cigar from his jacket pocket. He bit off the tip, lit the end, and took several puffs.

"The world is changing, Mr. Flippity," declared the mayor. "We stand now in times without precedent or analog. Not in this country; not in the world. Negroes will make this city, officer. And that is not election talk. Negroes from all across the former Confederacy are moving here, to this new Mecca, in numbers that will change who and what we are forever. A man can understand that . . . or he can become lost to history. How do you think I beat Sweitzer, that Democrat, to become mayor? We were not so different, he and I. Not really. But I understood the future. I grasped that immigrants to this city are a boon. A positive boon! If we continue to grow like this, we may eclipse even New York. Imagine it!—Chicago, the nation's *de facto* capital. A capital with a populace that includes men and women of race. It will be so. It must be so! I will not allow a madman to stop it."

Flip nodded seriously.

"But word travels quickly," the mayor continued. "Faster than it ever has. The telegraph. The telephone. They tell me that soon we will be broadcasting our words—*my* words—through the naked air, with receivers in every home. Our train porters already carry Chicago's newspapers to every city in the South. No . . . make that every city in the United States. There, they are read and re-read. And if word circulates that Chicago allows its most vulnerable newcomers to be killed and mutilated without consequence. . . that those who have already endured so much should find here, not sanctuary, but slaughter and horror. . . Well, it does not serve my purposes."

The mayor drew on his cigar thoughtfully. He glanced once more at the photographs on the table and smiled.

"In my idle moments—purely as a distraction, you understand—I have attempted to imagine the mind of someone who would do such things as these," the mayor said, nodding at the grisly pictures. "And all that I have been able to discern . . . is that *this* is his goal."

A beat passed.

"That *what* is his goal, Mister Mayor?" Flip asked carefully.

"Why, to kill the city itself!" said the mayor. "To reverse our growth. Our prosperity. To see that a man like me, who ran and won with the help of Negro votes—*and* woman votes, *and* Italian votes, come to't!— is never elected again. He intends that word of his murderous deeds should spread far and wide, and undo our progress. So, plainly, we are in a race against him. We must stop him. More specifically, *you* must. The city has called for assistance, officer. Will you answer?"

Flip managed a small nod.

The mayor grinned like a Cheshire cat and extinguished his cigar.

"I will expect a status report in one week," the mayor told him. "You are relieved of all other responsibilities until then. Your lieutenant has already been informed."

"Yes," Flip said, attempting to conceal the extent of his bewilderment.

"I will see you again, right here, in seven days," the mayor told him. "I expect progress. The *city* expects progress."

"I . . . yes . . ." Flip said.

With no further ceremony, the mayor threw the white envelope and the slip of paper onto the green table and walked away. He passed into the shadows at the edge of the room, and out through a door that Flip could not see. The ox-like man emerged from the darkness and began to gather the paper and photographs. He placed them into the envelope, folded it shut, and thrust it into Flip's chest. All the while, the man smiled a murderous, demented smile, his eyes gleaming in the glow of the electric light.

"We should go now," Crespo whispered urgently. "Put those pictures inside your coat. And tell this man here what you need—*whatever* you need—to get the job done."

Flip did.

TWO

The next day was Wednesday.

Flip had not slept well or extensively. In the predawn gloom, he waited on the steps of the Church of Heaven's God in Christ Lord Jesus—an imposing stone structure set back on a boulevard along South Michigan Avenue. Formerly a synagogue, in recent years it had been converted into one of the largest black churches on the South Side of Chicago. Flip smoked a cigarette as he waited, and shifted his weight back and forth on his feet. In the bluish chill of morning, it was almost cool enough for his coat.

A group of tradesmen passed. They regarded him carefully, but stayed silent. A man who appeared vagrant and insane sauntered along behind them, clearly with no destination in mind. He wore canvas bags on his legs instead of trousers. Flip stared him down hard when he began to linger, and the man moved off.

A few moments later, in the far distance at the end of the boulevard, the pastor came into view. He wore black from head to toe, and walked slowly, purposefully. He had small glasses with round, wire eyepieces. He was about fifty years old. His short-cropped hair had halfway gone to gray.

Flip, who did not regularly enjoy tobacco, quickly extinguished his smoke.

"Oh my word, it's Joe Flippity," the pastor said when he edged onto church property, as if galvanized to speech by the holy soil underfoot. "Tell me you're not here with more bad news, Flip. My flock has had about all it can take."

Flip stared straight ahead for a moment and blinked rapidly. His mind searched for alternative answers, but found none. There was nothing but the truth.

"Here about the Whitcomb boys," Flip said.

The pastor frowned and shook his head. Flip could smell the man's bergamot aftershave on the wind.

"The Whitcomb boys come into the world at the same time, and God took them away at the same time," the pastor pronounced. "What do you think of that? Coincidence? No sir. Providence. Like Jacob and Esau. Of course, Jacob and Esau would be fathers of nations. The Whitcomb boys were too young to be fathers of anything, bless them. Still pure. Still innocent."

To Flip, the Whitcomb boys had certainly looked old enough to get girls pregnant, or at least to make themselves come. But Flip did not say this to the pastor.

"How much do you know about what happened?" Flip asked. "About what *actually* happened to those boys?"

The pastor looked up and down the dark street. The sun began to peek over building-tops. Dogs barked, asking to be fed. Seagulls, hovering along the coast of Lake Michigan, pierced the air with crooked cries.

"You know I can't talk to you, Flip," the pastor said in a low voice that pled for mercy. "They said they'd shut me down. My work. My ministry. All this. We about the largest congregation on the South Side now, and they don't give a damn. White policemen said this, Flip."

"I'm an honorary white policeman this morning," Flip replied sternly. "I met with the mayor last night. Far as you know, I have blond hair and blue eyes."

As if on cue, a strange distant buzzing arose.

Flip and the pastor looked north along the avenue, now dappled in sunny orange rays. As the sound drew closer, it changed, gradually, from a buzz to a mechanical thump. A motorized bicycle appeared. It was painted army green, and had the words "Royal Enfield" stenciled across the gas tank in stark white. The device pulled to the steps of the church and fell silent. The pastor took his fingers out of his ears.

The driver stepped off and carefully removed a leather helmet, revealing a white man in late middle age. A metal star was pinned to his pocket. The man hesitated—looked back and forth between Flip and the pastor—and then took a small envelope out of his coat. Flip raised a hand, indicating to the officer that he had found his target.

"From the city," the man said to Flip, proffering the envelope. "It's everything you asked for."

"Thank you," Flip replied.

The officer lingered.

"I just want to say. . . We sure are counting on you. My cousin, she got twin girls at home."

Flip nodded seriously. The officer nodded back. Then he restarted the Enfield and pulled away.

The pastor looked back at Flip, calculating.

"They killing white twins too?"

"Not yet," Flip said, rubbing his jaw. "I expect they want me to stop it here, before it can move north."

They watched the departing motorbike until it was out of sight.

"Shall we retire to my offices?" asked the pastor.

"Please," Flip said.

"It has not even been a week," the pastor declared, easing into the high-backed chair behind his oak desk. The desk was empty save for three polished rock paperweights and a Bible. The pastor lit a series of candles. He placed some on the immense desk, and others on a window ledge beside them.

Flip put the small envelope the courier had brought into the left side of his jacket, tucking it in tight. Then, reaching into the right side of his jacket, he produced the much larger envelope from the night before.

For a moment, Flip perused the photos along with the written text, scant as it was.

"The Whitcomb boys were found at home," Flip said.

The pastor nodded sagely, his eyes magnified by his lenses and his stare given weight by the candlelight.

"In their own house, this happened," the pastor said. "Their mother. . ."

"Gladys," Flip said.

"Yes, Gladys," the pastor confirmed. "She has. . . She finds herself unable to sleep most nights. This was before the murders. A strange feeling compels her to move her legs. So she walks around her block. She does this from about one in the morning until three or four, like clockwork. I've told her it isn't safe—for a woman to be out so late—but she pays me no mind. Last Tuesday she returned home nearer to five than to four. Nothing in the house looked disarranged, she said. All seemed in order, so she returned to her own bed. Then, perhaps an hour later, she woke again and went to rouse the boys. That was when she found . . . well, it seems you have a photograph."

"I do," Flip said. "But that doesn't mean I have all the details. When did you talk to her last?"

"She came to me straight after it happened," the pastor told the policeman. "In fact, I believe I was the only person with whom she spoke . . . before the white officers instructed her to be silent. They instructed *me* to be silent as well. Insisted on it. They said silence would help the investigation."

The pastor's expression told Flip he was not sure about this.

"Maybe it will," Flip replied. "I've got to ask you some questions now, pastor. They are routine, but sometimes they help."

"Yes, of course," the pastor said.

Flip took a lead pencil and a notebook out of his pocket. He began to write, even before the pastor had spoken.

"Gladys had no enemies," Flip said. "She was loved in the community, yes? She was involved in no scandals. A good, churchgoing woman. She and her husband had moved here with the triplets around a year ago. From Texas."

"Yes," the pastor said. "All of that's right as rain."

"And the father of the boys . . ." Flip said. "He's no longer around?"

"Fell off a boxcar in a rail yard and died," said the pastor. "That was four or five months ago, though it feels like I just did the service."

Flip looked up from his notepad and squinted.

"A boxcar fall?"

"The physician said a clot of blood formed in his leg and traveled to his brain," the pastor explained. "The man had no insurance on his life. There's something of an informal railroad workers group in the neighborhood. They've been helping Gladys with money. So have we, to tell you plainly. The triplets were. . . let's see. . . they were twelve years old. Gladys knew they would need to go to work soon without a daddy. Help provide. But with what's happened now. . ."

The pastor paused a moment.

"It's going to kill her. You know that, right? Whether you catch the man who did this or not . . . It's going to literally kill her dead."

"Yes," said Flip. "I know. But—with all due respect to Gladys Whitcomb—saving her isn't what this is about."

The pastor nodded grimly.

"The boys," Flip continued. "*They* had no enemies?"

The pastor shook his head.

On the desk before them, a candle spat and sputtered, as if acknowledging a half-truth had been told.

"Course. . . folks always looked at 'em strange," the pastor added quickly, glancing down at the candle. "On account of their being so exactly alike, I mean. I always tried my best to put a stop to it— whenever I saw the gawkers—and that's God's honest truth. I told members of my flock: 'Don't you look at those boys as if they're strange. God made them that way! God has a *plan* for them, same as he does for you. *A reason.* They might look identical. They might *be* identical, down to the hairs on their head. But they've got three different souls. And God loves each one of those souls.' I told people that."

Flip nodded and wrote.

"But *some* people. . ." the pastor trailed off. "Yes, some people still made comments. Said things. I'd stop it when I heard it, but I couldn't stop it all."

"I'm sure you did everything you could," Flip affirmed, without looking up from his notepad. "Tell me, did the boys ever come to you about the gawking? Or did they ever say people might have threatened them?"

The pastor shook his head no.

"You think Gladys would talk to me?" Flip asked, putting his pencil away.

The man of God shrugged.

"She might," he said. "Talk to her soon, though. That's my advice. She isn't. . . This job, Flip. You get to know when someone ain't long for this world. And she ain't. You might not do it today, but do it tomorrow then. I won't be surprised if she passes before the end of the week."

"Thank you," Flip said, nodding. "I intend to seek her out directly. I've taken enough of your time. Good morning."

"Flip, you got to catch whoever did this," the pastor said as both men rose. "The mind of someone who could do such things . . . I can't fathom it."

The candle on the table sputtered once more.

Flip looked down at it. The pastor did too.

Then Flip buttoned his coat and departed.

Back on the steps of the church, Flip ducked behind a pillar and made sure he was unobserved. Then he carefully opened the small envelope that had come by motorbike. Inside was more money than he had ever seen in his life. Precisely what he had asked for. Ten thousand in hundred dollar bills.

Flip carefully extracted a single note and examined it in the morning sunlight. Benjamin Franklin was on the front, and some kind of Ancient Greek orgy was happening on the back. The bill was crisp and fresh. He had no doubt that it was real. Flip had grown talented at spotting forgeries and counterfeits. Some in Chicago's underworld could draw passable $50s and $100s by hand.

Flip replaced the money and put the envelope back into his pocket.

It was enough to run away with. You could head back down south and buy your own piece of land with that. Nice big farmhouse. Work for yourself. No boss. No police hierarchy. Start all over. Change your name, and probably they never catch you.

Flip forced himself not to think about the new possibilities radiating out from the firm, white envelope now only millimeters from his heart.

If anything, the appearance of the ten thousand signified to Flip that his encounter with the mayor the night before had not—at least entirely—been an imagined fever-dream. This was real and happening. The city *did* need this case solved. So much so that they had actually given him the budget to do it.

The thought was equal parts sobering and terrifying.

The sun was higher now; it was evident the day would be hot. More commuters hustled to and fro along the avenue. Some just plain hustled. Peddlers pushed carts in the direction of the Loop. Working men walked together in groups carrying lunch pails, on their ways to factories or slaughterhouses. Shopkeepers hurried to open their stores. Unattended children played or ran about aimlessly.

Flip stepped off of church property and made his way into the gathering throng.

The Whitcomb residence was a fifteen-minute walk from the Church of Heaven's God in Christ Lord Jesus, on the upper level of a slate-grey two flat. The entire block was composed of buildings so similar that Flip repeatedly had to check the address and house number to make sure he'd got it right. He did not know if Gladys Whitcomb would be awake at this hour, but he climbed to her door and hammered away—giving the loud, pitiless knock he used to rouse suspects.

The thing that opened the door—the thing that had been Gladys Whitcomb—was not alive in any real sense of the word. She was like a zombie. A creature made to walk beyond any natural ability to do so. An etherized person on a table—hung somewhere between life and death, but closer to death. A cadaver momentarily propped upright for the amusement of the medical students.

Flip knew better than to waste a zombie's time.

He flashed his badge and identified himself. Gladys Whitcomb took a few long moments to focus her eyes, her glassy stare slowly creeping up Flip's leather jacket to his face. Flip found himself dreading the full force of her gaze as one might a physical blow. When her eyes did meet his own, it was more horrible than he had expected.

For this had once been a human. Only one week ago. One week.

"Ma'am, I hope to come in and speak to you," Flip said clearly, trying not to wince under her gargoyle scowl. "We've met once or twice before, if you remember. Or maybe you don't. We're trying to catch the man who did this thing. Trying to make sure he can't do it again. Do you understand me?"

Flip swallowed hard and waited.

"I talked to the police already."

It was an automaton's voice. The voice of a recorded machine, something that no longer knew or cared what words were. A memory of an echo.

"I understand that," Flip said. "But if you could see your way to letting me come inside-"

"Why?" she suddenly cried, her features coming alive. "*Why on earth* should I do that?"

Her voice was still a patient on a table—but now it was one who had come out from the ether prematurely . . . and begged for the amputation to cease.

"Because there are clues I may be able to find," Flip explained. "Things the other policemen missed. If you let me look into these clues, it may help me catch the guilty party."

"All they did was tell me to be quiet! They ain't even look around. They just said 'Be quiet. Don't tell nobody how it happened.' Like they didn't even *care*. Even my pastor-"

"I've just come from his office," Flip said. "He is concerned for you. So am I. We only wish to help."

Gladys Whitcomb became stock still. Her eyes did not move. To Flip, it seemed as if time itself might have frozen for a moment. She stared at where his face had been positioned two seconds before, and not where it was now.

Flip realized, gradually, that this was capitulation.

He brushed past her and into the home. It was a modest apartment, with wooden floors and stark brick walls. It still smelled like a home where boys played and lived. Where they tracked in mud and asphalt and grass and horse manure. Flip saw that the floors were well scuffed, albeit recently, probably by police who had come and gone the prior week. In the kitchen was a simple stove. Room-temperature coffee rested in a metal pan.

Flip knew that if she survived until winter—which seemed doubtful—Gladys Whitcomb would almost certainly die at the first cold snap.

He found the room from the photograph—the room where the Whitcomb triplets had been discovered with their heads chopped, rotated, and sewn back on. Blood still stained the floorboard grooves in a few places. According to the notes from the responding officers, the murderer had been careful about his work. There had been little spilled. There was also no surplus of the twine that had been used to reattach the heads. Nothing left behind. The investigators had deduced that the boys' throats must have been drained over the sink, or else their blood captured in a bowl or dish. The other possibility was that the mutilations had been done somewhere else entirely, and the bodies then returned to the apartment. But to Flip, that seemed unlikely.

"Pastor tells me you walk at night," Flip said loudly. "Your legs pain you."

Gladys Whitcomb remained in the half-open doorway. She raised her head like an ancient dragon. She seemed to sniff the air.

"Pastor also says on the night it happened, you were out the house from maybe one until five. That sound right?"

The woman gave a shrug, eyes unfocused.

That gave the killer four hours, thought Flip. Four hours to kill these boys, do this *thing*, and position the bodies just so—all while spilling very little blood, and making very little noise. Flip had a hard time imagining the bodies being moved from another location. Yet that meant an almost unthinkable meticulousness on the butcher's part. Forgetting the rotation of the heads and reattachment—the mere slitting of the throats should have created more gore and chaos than anyone might have reasonably controlled. Flip tried composing scenarios in his mind in which all the blood went down into the sink. Perhaps if the boys had been drugged. Or if the boys had been willing participants.

Yet for *that* to be true. . .

Flip did not allow himself to pursue this line of thinking. He walked to the space in the center of the floor where the boys' heads had rested. He squatted and ran his gloved hands over the floorboard. A little dried blood. A little mud from policemen's shoes. And little else.

A long, thick splinter coated with blood had found its way into a small crevasse between two floorboards. Flip took off his glove and picked it out with his fingernails. He carefully placed it into the envelope with the photographs.

Flip returned to the front door.

"There anything you ain't tell the other police?" Flip asked the living dead woman. "Who the boys were friendly with? Where they spent their free time?"

Gladys Whitcomb said nothing. A single tear welled in her left eye. It slid down her cheek and fell to the floor.

At that moment, Flip determined he would reanimate this corpse no longer. Not simply because it was cruel, but because he saw he would get nothing for it.

He looked away.

It was over. She was over. The sight of her. Some things, not even Joe Flippity could bear.

He thanked Gladys Whitcomb for her time—as one might communicate ceremonially with the granite statue of an ancestor—and departed.

On his way out, Flip stopped to inquire at the first floor apartment of the two-flat. A wheezing retired millworker and his wife lived there. Had either of them heard anything the night of the murder?

The ancient man said it had been silent as the grave.

THREE

L ater that same morning, Flip made his way along 47th Street—a Negro neighborhood of private homes, small stores, and even smaller honky tonks. He reached a large brownfield left undeveloped. Empty land in the middle of a city block—several acres—strewn through with trash and animal droppings. The droppings were days old, but some still smelled fresh in the summer heat. A tall green and white sign stood at the edge of the field. Flip saw that it had been recently updated.

"Property of Singling Brothers All-Negro Circus and Shows. No Trespassing. Jos. J. Singling, Proprietor."

A week ago, "Singling" had read—in both cases—"Singer."

Beside the field lingered a boy of ten or eleven, entirely naked except for a pair of dirty brown overalls. Flip had seen him work as a kind of freelance helper for the circus when it was home. His employment arrangement was certainly unofficial, if it existed at all.

Flip tried to remember the child's name.

"Roscoe? Ralph?" Flip called, ambling over to where the boy sat.

"Rufus, sir," he replied brightly, snapping to attention.

"What happened to your sign? Who is Singling?"

"Mister Joseph changed the name," Rufus explained. "It sounds more like Ringling Brothers now."

"But it's not the Ringling Brothers," Flip said. "This outfit has got nothing to do with the Ringling Brothers."

"People don't know that," the boy said defensively. "Mister Joseph says so. Mister Joseph says people are dupes."

Flip nodded.

"Where is the circus today?" Flip asked.

"Indianapolis," said the boy. "Due back this morning. They late. Gonna show up . . . afternoon, I expect. What Mister Joseph done?"

"Nothing," said Flip. "I'm just looking to ask some questions."

"Try this afternoon," Rufus said, sitting back down on the empty curb. "Trains from Naptown always late. Then they gotta move everything from the rail yard to here. Be after lunch, at least."

"I'll check back," Flip told him, already walking away.

Deeper into the South Side, down along 71st Street, Flip found the alley where the twin brother and sister had been discovered—the first murder in the series shown him by the mayor. It was a pleasant enough neighborhood, and the day around him was becoming pleasant too. The sky was clear and blue, and a welcome breeze now cut through the growing heat.

This part of the city had become a chessboard of Negro, Irish, and Jewish pockets—with the pieces moving around every time you turned your head. Negroes moved in. Irish moved around. Jews often stayed put—and looked as though they would remain forever—then suddenly vanished without a trace for the suburbs, abandoning their country clubs and temples wholesale. It was very clear to Flip as he strolled block to block that certain businesses were designed to welcome one—and only one—sort of customer. Landlords rented to a single kind of tenant alone. In their meeting, Big Bill Thompson had characterized the spot of the murder as being where Jew gave way to Negro. As he reached his destination, Flip realized the mayor had been extremely precise.

On one side of the street there were only white faces, and mezuzahs beside nearly every door. Businesses sold clothing, baked goods, and hardware supplies, with signs partly in Yiddish, which Flip could not read. More than one passerby on this side of the street eyed him suspiciously. Whenever this happened, Flip allowed his jacket to hang open to reveal his gun and badge. This did not stop the looking, but he was not hassled or questioned.

On the other side of the street, it was entirely Negro. Not just Negro, but recent arrivals from the South. These people had the look of outsiders. It was a kind of nervous astonishment, and a resolution to make good. Some still looked up as they walked, taking in the tall apartment buildings as though they had never seen such things.

These two sides of the street seldom interacted. They did not see each other—*would* not see each other, Flip understood—until the day when they would. . .

And then all hell would break loose. Flip knew this if he knew anything.

This neighborhood—and the others like it—were unexploded bombs waiting to go off. What would finally trigger them? A misunderstanding between neighbors? A false—or accurate—accusation of shoplifting by a small businessman? A fistfight between teenagers that got out of hand?

It would be something, Flip knew. All around him was brittle, parched forest. The lighting strike was just a matter of time. This fact was known to the mayor, the aldermen, and the police force. Flip understood it was one reason why the police had concealed the murders that had occurred in this alley. Negroes saw Jews as full of strange rituals, and it would be the tiniest of steps for a film-flam journalist to insinuate their rites extended to decapitation. The Jews, in turn, viewed the Negroes as outsiders and rubes who did not understand the city, and who brought the wild conventions and proclivities of the South up with them.

These were two flints. One day, they were going to spark.

Yet on this day, it was peaceful in the alley. The blood had been carefully washed away from the flagstones. Nothing indicated that a double decapitation murder had occurred here. Or, at least—thought Flip—that bodies had been *found* here. He reminded himself that where the heads had been severed was still technically a matter of speculation.

Flip opened the envelope in his jacket and looked at the photograph of the two dead ten year olds. The girl—or rather, the body beneath the boy's head—wore a white dress. It was hardly smudged at all, and those marks were likely from mud and city grime, acquired in the course of play.

The other twins who had been killed in the photos—all had been identical. But the twins found in this alley had not been identical *precisely*. One had been male, and one female. Yet their faces looked very similar to Joe Flippity. Similar enough, he thought, to fool somebody who was looking to kill identical twins.

To the side of the alley, near to where the bodies had fallen, a stunted evergreen shrub grew from a flat strip of land that had somehow missed being paved. Flip tore off a few inches and put them into his pocket.

It would have to do.

Then he squatted on his haunches and looked again at the spot on the flagstones where the bodies had once lain. Flip looked hard. The mayor's dossier said the call had come in at 11pm, but there was no telling at what hour the act might have been committed. This alley would be a very dark place when the sun went down. The kind of place that kept its secrets.

Across the street, a Jewish woman carrying groceries paused to regard Flip cautiously.

And there, he thought, the eternal riddle. There, the thing that could not be known—could *never* be known—ahead of time. By Flip, by the city, or even by God himself.

Were these groups *right* to have a little distrust for each other? Were these two sides going to kill each other one day, just a little bit? And did they perhaps have an inkling of that? Some foreknowledge of it? A feeling for what was coming?

Those in charge of Chicago's wards seemed content simply to hope it did not happen on their watch. It would be somebody else's problem then.

Flip felt again, acutely, that all around him stood a forest of dried tinder.

Flip stood to his full height and nodded once at the Jewish woman, in a way he hoped seemed friendly.

He did not let his gaze linger to see if she nodded back, but sauntered off immediately down the block.

He'd gotten what he'd come for.

A few blocks north, Flip had lunch at a neighborhood stand that sold meat stew. It was operated by a woman whose husband worked in the stockyards. Flip knew the stew meat was likely extra trimmings that had found their way home in the man's shirt or trousers.

After lunch, he headed back to 47th Street and discovered that the circus had indeed returned. He smelled it before he saw it. It was a primal scent of animals and sweat. Singer—or was it Singling now?—kept an entire stable of horses, three manacled bears, and a tired old beast that might once have been some sort of jungle cat. (It was matted and lean, and mostly sat in its cage waiting to die. Flip believed that Singer administered a stimulant to the cat before each performance, giving the beast at least the appearance of half-life for the paying customers.)

The gutter beside the circus grounds had already begun to run with animal piss. With the great tent disassembled and loaded onto the backs of horse-drawn democrat wagons, the outfit looked less like a troupe of performers, and more like an army of grim frontier settlers encamped for the afternoon. Every person looked dog tired. There would be no unloading or unpacking of anything for a few hours. Some of the men had already made beds on the backs of carts, on the tops of crates, or simply on the ground itself.

Flip looked around for the boy, Rufus, and found him lingering at the side of a wagon. As Flip approached, Rufus suddenly took off sprinting down the street, wrinkled green bills clutched tight in his hand. Flip surmised he had been dispatched to buy the circus workers food.

Flip picked through the maze of carts until he found a man sitting on a low, three-legged stool. The man wore a white sleeveless shirt and tuxedo pants. His shined shoes and immaculate top hat had been

placed carefully on the ground beside him. He looked postprandial
or possibly postcoital. A smile of deep satisfaction spread across his
weathered face. His eyes were closed, but Flip was not surprised when
he spoke.

"Oh shit, it's Officer Flip," the man said in a jocular tone.

"Mister Singer," replied Flip. "Or should I say Singling?"

The circus owner's grin said Flip could call him anything he liked.

"We done so good," Singer said. "They love us down in Naptown.
Shows full enough we had to stop selling tickets. Did a midnight performance we ain't even planned on. Still got it full up. Madame Walker
herself came. Pulled up in her long, tall motorcar just as you say. Hell
of a sight."

"I need to have a word with one of your men," Flip told him.

"We tired," the circus owner said. "My men need to sleep. My *animals* need to sleep, Flip."

"It won't take but a moment," Flip assured him.

"My men-" Singer began.

"Police business," Flip said more aggressively. "I'm not here to jaw
at you for nothing, Singer."

The smile fell away from the ringmaster's face.

"Fine," he said. "It's always something, ain't it, with you damn
po-lice? But tell me first. Who is it this time? Who done what?"

"Nobody's in trouble, if that's what you mean," Flip told him. "I just
need a couple words with your magician fella."

The Amazing Drextel Tark had his own enclosed travelling caravan,
an arrangement which gave him the extra space he required for his
props and tricks, and also provided him with a private room for sleeping. It was a rare luxury. Most circus employees slept two or three to a
bed on the road, if they had beds at all.

Tark's caravan did not appear particularly magical to Flip. It was
covered in grime and black soot, just like all the others. The caravan
door was small and circular, almost like something a large dog would
use. Yet Tark was diminutive, so there seemed to be no issue with this

arrangement. (Flip had long ago guessed that the magician's modest apportionment was the basis for more than a few of his tricks. Tark could conceal his small legs folded backwards as a blade seemed to shear him in half, or hunch his body into a compartment built into the stage floor to momentarily disappear. Tark was like a rat or cat that wanted to squeeze underneath a door. You'd swear the beast could never shrink itself to fit—until you watched it do exactly that.)

Singer walked to the door of Tark's grimy caravan and knocked, softly at first.

"That the courtesy knock," Singer explained. "He hit the bottle pretty hard on the way back up. That boy's just skin and bones. It don't take much to get him drunk."

A beat passed. There was no sound from within. Singer and Flip exchanged a glance.

"Okay," Singer said. "Enough with the courtesy, I s'pose."

Singer laid onto the trailer door so hard Flip thought it might break. After a good ten seconds of knocking, there was a just-audible: "What . . . what do you want?"

Singer smiled at Flip. Then he did a showman's flourish with his arm extended, indicating that the feat had been accomplished. Flip could take it from here.

Singer ambled back to his top hat and sat down beside it.

Flip leaned close to the grimy caravan door.

"Chicago police," Flip said.

Another beat.

Then a voice, hoarse and mysterious as a confiding ghost.

"Flip? Is that you?"

"Yeah, Tark. Open up."

"The demon gin. It bit me hard last night. And then again this morning. You come back in a day or two, all right?"

"Tark, this is some life or death shit," Flip said. "I ain't asking you to come out and run no marathon. Have a few words with me and you can go back to sleep."

The magician seemed to consider this. Then Flip heard the noise of metal latches being undone on the other side of the door. Hinges swung and the caravan opened to reveal a desiccated young man, face down in a chaos of clothing and props. He was small and wiry and about twenty years old. He shrank back when the sunlight hit his face.

"Damn it," Tark croaked. "What time of day is it?"

With great effort, the magician forced himself to sit upright. He fumbled inside his cloak until he located an old brass pocket watch. He brought it very close to his eyes, then held it to his ear. Shook it. Then held it to his ear again.

"It's well after noon," Flip said.

"Shit," Tark said to himself. "It feels like it's next week."

"You got no magic spell for when the drink hangs over from the night before?" Flip asked.

The magician narrowed his eyes to say he was in no mood.

The interior of Tark's caravan looked like the back of a closet into which items had been thrown willy-nilly for several years. There were layers of costumes and paraphernalia representing earlier eras in the magician's career.

"It's too crowded for me to come in there," Flip said. "Why don't you come out here and sit? We'll just talk. I got something to tell you. Gonna sober you right up. Make you feel even better than magic could."

Tark raised an eyebrow and tilted his head to the side. A cure, any cure, was a cause worth fighting for. O how the magician wanted to believe! He began to inch his skinny, dehydrated body toward the opening.

After a full minute, Tark had managed to exit the caravan and lean himself against a wagon wheel. When Rufus returned from a restaurant, Flip begged a few morsels from him and fed them to the magician. The desired effect was achieved, and the conjurer perked up enough to listen.

Flip told his tale. As he did, a mask of confusion and horror crossed Tark's face.

When he had finished laying out the details of the final, triple beheading, Flip ended the recitation by saying: "So naturally . . . Tark . . . I thought of you."

For a moment, the magician did not move. Then, very gradually, he lifted his bloodshot eyes up to meet Flip's gaze. (Flip towered over the smaller man.) Tark searched Flip's features carefully—disclosing, admitting nothing.

"I think you understand why," Flip continued sternly. "But in case you don't, I'll put it like this. . . you a policeman and you want to catch a man stealing horses? You ain't just look around the empty stalls where horses used to be. You watch where there are still more horses to steal."

"The oldest of those twins was fifteen, you say?" the magician asked. "I see where you're going with this. But Flip, I'm a grown-"

The policeman cut him off.

"You can pass for twenty-one with makeup on your face, your hat pulled down, and the lighting right. Twenty-one *maybe*. Other times, Tark—when the lighting *ain't* right—you look like I should pick you up for cutting school on a weekday. Why you got to argue with me on this? I'm trying to keep you safe."

The magician pushed himself up despite the weight of the gin. He leaned against the filthy caravan and stared into Flip's eyes. His expression said that Flip had better not underestimate him. That he was a professional when it came to being underestimated. That getting others to underestimate him was how he made his living. Tark's body language invited Flip to do the same.

"What you *really* here for?" Tark asked. "What do you want from me?"

"How long we known each other?" Flip countered, having long ago mastered the policeman's secret of answering questions with questions. "How many times I help you out? Help out Mister Singer? How many times you get robbed and I get something back for you? Three times, I can think of. A year ago, another magician—a *white* magician—stole a trick from you, and I got it back. Remember that? I didn't even ask how it worked."

Tark said nothing.

"I ain't saying I know how you do it," Flip continued. "You know the one I mean. The one at the close of your act. Where you walk down into the audience, cover yourself up with a cape, and then, two seconds later, you appear all the way across the tent, back up on stage. But I've thought about it some, Tark. I've also thought how there's a young man named Ike who works as a roughneck for Mister Singer. Look about your size. Always keep his hat low over his face. Wear that eye patch. Seem to be a little slow, like he got kicked in the head. But you take away that patch and hat? Have him stand up straight? I think he might look *just like you*. And I might not be the only one to notice it, Tark. That's all I'm saying."

Tark wore the expression of a man trying to determine if he should confess or not—and, if so, to what.

"Can. . . can we go somewhere else and talk?" the magician eventually said. "A little ways away from these caravans?"

Flip lifted his eyebrows and looked around. They were already virtually alone. Every member of the circus had to be asleep or close to it. The grounds were quiet and still.

"Trust me," the magician said. "We won't go far."

Ten minutes later, they stood in an alley along 47th Street that ran between a bar and a shuttered mom and pop grocery. Tark had picked his way through the sleeping circus employees and roused a man about his size—one who wore a low hat and an eye patch. The roughneck's exposed eye seemed to rotate randomly in its socket every few moments, as though it were a constant strain for him to keep it under control.

"Ike's my brother," the magician said softly as the three men stood together in the alley. "He ain't been totally right since we were children. Fell from a high window ledge when he was a baby. I don't remember it happening, but it made him this way."

Flip inspected Ike for a moment.

Ike allowed the inspection. Said nothing.

"He can do work around the circus," the magician added. "Mister Singer likes him very much. Says he has a strong back and never complains. Plus, in addition to set up and tear down, there's one more thing Ike helps with."

Tark leaned in close and whispered into his brother's ear. Ike's eye flit nervously around the alley, then settled on Flip.

"It's okay," the magician assured his brother gently. "We can trust this man. Go ahead."

Obviously still uneasy, Ike removed his hat and coat. Then he took off the patch too, revealing an eye beneath that seemed perfectly functional, if also a bit spastic. Ike straightened his posture. He held a single finger to his nose, then slowly drew it away. As the finger moved, Ike's eyes followed. And as they did, they both became uncrossed and still.

And this man, so revealed, was a dead ringer for Drextel Tark.

Ike cleared his throat.

"Thank you, ladies and gentlemen!" Ike said in a carefully practiced voice. "You have been a wonderful audience. I am the Amazing Drextel Tark. Good night!"

Ike did a dramatic wave with his arm—manipulating an invisible cape, Flip guessed—and turned around. Then he began to walk back down the alley in measured, practiced steps.

"That's him heading offstage," the magician explained to Flip.

Tark intercepted his brother before he got too far, patting him reassuringly on the shoulder. Ike smiled. He relaxed and his eyes crossed again, resuming their random spastic ticking like the exposed guts of two separate clocks.

"You have no idea how long it took me to teach him that," the magician said, walking his brother back over to Flip.

"Can he talk normally?" Flip asked. "Like if I put some questions to him?"

"Sometimes," the magician said with a shrug.

Flip watched as Ike carefully replaced his hat, coat, and patch.

"Do you like working for the circus, Ike?" Flip said, leaning close to the man.

Ike said nothing. He tilted his head like a cat that had been addressed—noticing, but not caring.

"He takes good orders from Mister Singer," the magician insisted. "Ask him what he likes to eat, or his favorite color, and he won't say much. But give him a task, and he does it just right. He can dig a ditch. Put up a tent. Shovel shit. When it comes time, he knows how to do his work. He ain't mean to be rude to you, Flip. He just ain't know how to be around people."

Flip nodded thoughtfully.

"So you *are* identical twins," Flip said matter-of-factly, turning back to Tark. "And that's how you appear back across the tent so fast."

"Except for Ike's eyes," Tark agreed. "He can keep them still for about ten seconds. We practice. And ten seconds is all it takes to finish the show."

"How many people you think know?" the police officer asked. "Out of all the folks who work for the circus. . . how many *really* know?"

"You'd count 'em on one hand," Tark said after thinking on it. "Mister Singer, he know. A couple of the crew who work with Ike might have puzzled it out. . . . How he always goes missing when it's time for my act. But that's it. You'd be surprised by what people don't see when they're not looking for it."

Flip was not surprised at all.

"What about audience members?" Flip pressed. "People who come to see the show? Any of them ever talk to you afterwards, tell you they figured out your trick?"

"We don't have many regulars," said Tark. "Circus is based here in Chicago because it's a rail hub. The trains take us everywhere. We do homestands now and then, but not for long. If anybody besides you ever guessed how I do it, they never told me."

Flip nodded. Tark sat down on a dented metal trash can, staggering anew under the weight of his hangover. His brother toed the wall of a building aimlessly. Both men clearly wanted to get back to the circus grounds to sleep.

"And you've never heard of someone wanting to *kill* twins?" Flip asked.

Tark shook his head vigorously no, then winced from the pain of it. "Never," he managed.

"And nobody's threatened you—or your brother—in recent weeks?" Flip pressed.

"Naw," the magician said. "Nothin' like that. Do I need to worry?"

Flip put his hands into his jacket pockets and sighed.

"Not as long as you keep your secret a secret, I 'spect. You're the only identical twins left on the South Side that I'm aware of. There's no chance you know others, is there?"

Tark shook his head, more gently this time.

"I ain't seen many others, *ever*," he told Flip. "We played with a circus from New York City once. They had acrobats from China—two sisters who were identical—but they back east now. So beautiful, they were."

Tark smiled at the memory of the women. He stared up into the clouds and seemed to daydream. His grin grew wider.

Flip turned away from Tark and fingered the envelope inside his coat. The smaller one. He opened it and found a single hundred-dollar bill. Then he hesitated, and slipped a second bill between his fingers.

When he turned around, Flip saw that Tark was watching him closely. There was caution in his eyes. The magician was wondering if Flip might be about to do a trick of his own. One involving a gun.

In Chicago, all things were possible.

Instead, Flip withdrew the bills. Tark looked back and forth between the twin Benjamin Franklins, then up into Flip's eyes. They had crossed into territory that Tark had not been expecting. Flip was a straight shooter—maybe the straightest—but no straight police officer had that kind of scratch to throw.

Flip stepped forward and tucked the bills into the front pocket of the magician's shirt.

"This is for you," Flip said. "No conditions to it . . . save for one. You hear anything strange, you see anything strange—you even *smell* anything strange—you come and find me. Can you do that?"

"Absolutely," the magician said. "You can count on me."

Tark took the two bills out of his shirt pocket. He looked at them carefully, holding them up to the sunlight. Then, with a flick of his wrist and snap of his finger, he vanished them into the air.

He smiled proudly. Then he collected his brother and proceeded back across 47th and into the circus grounds.

To sleep.

FOUR

Flip caught a streetcar south as far as it would go. Then he walked until the roads ceased to be paved and there was no longer electricity or gaslight in the buildings. The men here were mostly white immigrants from Eastern Europe. There were Negroes too, but only here and there, and not many. Dust blew across the roads.

Flip found a corner saloon with swinging door. He dipped inside, flashed his star and gun at the barman, and asked where he could hire a horse. The barman rented Flip his own, and they went out back to get it. The horse looked rotten and sick, but Flip did not want to go searching for a better one. He paid the barman twice what he should have, and rode the beast southeast to the camp where the canal was being dug.

The sunlight was still bright as Flip approached the outskirts of the massive project. So many men and so much machine settled among the swampy edges of the water. Some workers lived in the city, or down in Indiana, but it was clear most had chosen simply to reside in nearby tents and makeshift hovels for the duration of the dig. Flip rode the wheezing horse to the top of a sandy dune and looked down, surveying the diggers. It looked like miserable work. The men were dusty and tired.

As they began to knock off for the day, some workingmen headed straight for the clusters of tents and outbuildings where they were camped. Some headed north, back to town. Others lingered to chat or relax. A few looked as though they would go and have an impromptu bath in Lake Michigan before they retired for the night.

Flip tied up his horse and walked toward the nearest mass of men. He heard many languages that he could not understand. Flip looked for a supervisor. Eventually, he found a bald, broad-shouldered white man in grease-blackened overalls handing out what might have been pay slips. Flip joined the crowd and waited his turn.

When he got to Flip, the bald man said: "We hire through O'Malley. You got a letter?"

Flip had some things that were even better than a letter.

"I'm here about the twin boys from Arkansas," Flip said, opening his coat. "They were called Horner. Might have had an uncle around by that name?"

The bald man just scowled.

"That's a Chicago badge," he said. "You and your horse crossed out of the city limits a ways back there."

The man folded his arms, as though he would not be of help. The men around him stared and smiled derisively. It was a pleasure for them to see their boss standing up to an officer of the law.

"These Horner boys, maybe they lived in Chicago," Flip tried. "That makes it a Chicago matter."

"Maybe *anybody* lived in Chicago," the bald man said, laughing. "That ain't no kind of answer."

The workmen laughed as well.

Flip knew effective ways of dealing with these types, but they were not quick . . . or else were not cheap. Flip remembered the mayor's request. An update in a week. Progress. And the mayor was apparently more than willing to pay.

So Flip figured it must be all right to do what now occurred to him.

Even as it churned his stomach, Flip looked into the bully's eyes and said: "Now that I think on it, I *did* bring a letter to show you."

The bald man raised a hairy eyebrow.

"It's something best kept private. You want to come see? I left it over by my horse."

"*What*?" said the man angrily.

Flip winked at him and nodded to the horse.

The man—still smiling contemptuously—left his workers and walked with the exaggerated pantomime steps of a clown to where Flip had tied the horse, lampooning him all the way. The workmen guffawed loudly.

When they reached the horse, Flip was all business.

"They lookin," Flip said low, gesturing back to the throng, "so I'm a just shake your hand."

Flip shook the bald man's hand and left a $100 bill in it.

The man closed his fist around the dough, and was immediately transformed. He gazed up at Flip as though they were long lost relatives, reunited after ages apart. His expression said that now they were forging new bonds that would *never* be broken.

Even as the man smiled at Flip like they were literally related, he also tilted his head to the side. The tilt asked if anybody throwing around hundred dollar bills really gave a fuck about two dead Negro boys from Arkansas. Was there not something *else*? Something *more important* he could do for his wealthy new friend? Wine, women, or song, perhaps? All were to be had along the dusty banks of the Cal-Sag.

"Yes," Flip confirmed, reading the expression. "The two boys name of Horner. *That's* my aim entirely. Show me whatever you got, even if you think it's nothing."

The bald man returned to his group and called aloud for a person named Salazar. Salazar—muscular, stooped, and dirty all over—soon appeared from one of the tents. Salazar squinted and rocked back and forth on his heels, wondering what was happening.

"Salazar found them," the bald man announced.

The bald man explained to Salazar that this was a police officer who wanted to know about the crime.

"Ahh," said Salazar. "You mean the-"

Salazar drew his finger across his throat and made the noise of a death rattle. Then he mimicked removing his own head. Then he laughed uproariously. The men watching laughed as well.

"Yes," Flip said. "*That*. Can you take me to where you found them?"

Salazar said he could.

The land was flat and swampy, with sand dunes every so often. They walked past the last of the diggers leaving the worksite—a final trickle of the exhausted, the lame, or the simply slowmoving. At a spot where the excavation had long since been completed, Salazar pointed to a small tin shed used to store equipment. On the ground at the back of a shed was an oil stain. Salazar looked down at it. Flip looked too. (The bald supervisor looked only at Flip, hoping desperately that his wealthy guest was getting what he wanted.)

"This where it happened, then?" Flip asked. "Where you found the bodies?"

"Some people—later—they put down oil to get rid of the blood," said Salazar. "To cover it up. I don't know why."

"Did *you* find them?" Flip pressed.

"That's right," Salazar said. "Early in the morning. I came here and saw both boys. I thought they were sleeping at first and yelled at them. Then I saw their heads were cut off. The police came and looked, only then we saw they had stakes down their necks, and the heads were switched."

The bald man stepped up.

"As I told the officers, these boys were not members of our crew—or of anybody's crew. They were just hanging around. Hoping to be hired, I guess. There's lot of people out here. Folks come and go."

"Uh huh," Flip said, turning back to Salazar. "And how did you know the heads were switched? The boys were supposed to be true identicals."

"It was little things," Salazar answered. "One boy had a scar on his lip; looked like a dog had bit him. The other one had a swollen ankle and a broken shoe. We stood there looking, and someone noticed one had *both* the busted lip *and* the broken shoe . . . and the other had neither."

"They switched the heads, and sent all the faults to the one twin," the bald foreman pronounced. "Made the other more perfect, yeah? Hahaha!"

This time, nobody else laughed. The looky-loos began to drift off.

Flip considered the oily spot in the dirt. He got down on his knees and took a scoop with his hand. From his pocket he produced an empty tin for shoe polish. He put the handful of dirt inside and sealed it.

"Anybody know their first names?" Flip asked, rising.

"We didn't truly know their *last* names," Salazar said. "Horner was a guess. Somebody's guess. I forget who. Boss man, did you know?"

The bald man shook his head.

"Well somebody said it," Salazar continued. "Somebody said the boys had an uncle around here. I never met him. I bet it was a lie. People come to Chicago and say they're related to somebody local, just to get a job."

"Is there any man named Horner on your work crew?" Flip asked.

The bald man said there wasn't.

"You know that off the top of your head?" Flip challenged him. "Without checking? You're *sure*?"

The bald man's face processed a string of emotions. The first was outrage over being questioned at all, and then a greater outrage over being questioned by a Negro policeman from the city. Then, when it seemed his anger would boil over, his face showed that he remembered his new friend had already handed him enough money for a down payment on a Model T. . . and that there might be more where that came from.

"I suppose I could take a look at the rolls," said the bald man. "Might take some time, though. Be a hell of a lot of work."

Flip diagnosed the situation perfectly, but the envelope of hundreds stayed in his coat.

"No," Flip said. "No need for that. I believe I have what I came for."

Flip headed back into the city as dusk fell. The sun turned to a savage orange fireball that hung lazily in the sky and waited there for a while, as if it had no place to go.

Flip, to the contrary, had plenty of places to visit before the evening ended.

He reached Miss Heloise's home for orphan girls just before the sun set. It was a three flat on the southeast corner of a city park. The park was strewn with trash and debris, and several bums were already settling down to camp for the night. A pair recognized Flip and worried he might have come to roust them. When he did not, they smiled to one another as if some great catastrophe had passed them over.

Decrepit, broken toys made of metal and wood littered the stone porch of the orphanage. It took Flip a while to realize they were indeed toys; most looked like rejected scraps from a carpenter's bench. The lights within the home were bright, and Flip could hear children's voices and the clink of silverware. He could also smell the unique odor of a place filled to bursting with children who did not particularly like to bathe.

Flip knocked on the thick wooden door.

For a moment, there was nothing but the continued sounds of children. Then a heavy tread came, punctuated by squeaking wooden floorboards. It grew louder, and then the door swung wide.

The woman revealed could not be bothered to look immediately at Flip.

"I said to *stay in the kitchen!*" she barked into the chaos behind her.

Down the hallway, Flip could see fifteen or twenty children seated, standing, or playing around a long wooden table. A small child who had toddled after the woman thought twice and retreated back down the passage.

"Yes?" Miss Heloise said, her eyes finally training upon the guest on her porch.

She was heavyset, light skinned, and might have been forty years old. She had black rings under her eyes—probably from a thousand nights kept sleepless by little ones—but was not unattractive. She wore a brown shawl and a flowing, stained skirt.

Flip displayed his star.

"Miss Heloise?"

"That's right," she answered.

"I'm here about Doreen and Netty," Flip said.

The woman's lips closed tight. Her eyes narrowed. Something in the expression indicated that Flip had said something distasteful. For a moment, he could not imagine what it was.

"*And Katherine*," Miss Heloise said with grim insistence. "There was a third girl too. Or doesn't she matter to the police?"

"Yes," Flip said. "She matters. Her too."

Flip noticed that Miss Heloise was holding a dishrag in her hands. She worked it back and forth anxiously between her fingers. She looked up into Flip's eyes, wondering if the police officer was being genuine.

"You all been here several times," Miss Heloise stated, working the rag. "You any closer to finding who done this? What do I have left to tell you that you don't already know?"

"I only need to take a look at the room," he told her. "Shouldn't take but a moment. I could come back in a few hours if that would be easier."

"In a few hours the children will be asleep," Miss Heloise answered, as though he was being impossible.

"Then I suppose I ought to do it now?"

She regarded Flip hesitantly, then let him inside.

Miss Heloise retreated to the kitchen, where little girls of all ages played and shouted to one another. She quickly deputized an older child to hold the fort until she returned, then conducted Flip to the foot of a winding wooden staircase that smelled like many small, bare feet. Miss Heloise heaved and groaned as she took the steps two at a time. She seemed to know them like the back of her hand. Flip, on the other hand, had to watch his footing and use the rail. At the top was a large space that might have originally been a family living room. The floor was wood and the walls were plaster. There was a large fireplace set into the wall that Flip recognized from the crime scene photo.

"The girls. . ." he began. "The *twin* girls. . .were found here and here, yes? The heads switched and reattached with barbed twine?"

Miss Heloise nodded back.

"Was there much blood?" Flip asked.

The woman thought for a moment.

"For Doreen and Netty? No. For Katherine, yes. There was a pool underneath her. It leaked down through the floorboards. Started coming through the ceiling. Scared the children something awful."

Flip walked to the center of the room. He stood in the shadow of the great fireplace, right where the twins had been found. There was nothing there. No sign that a murder had taken place. No indication that mutilated bodies had once been left in this spot. Flip ran a naked finger across the floorboard. No dirt. No grime. Nothing at all.

Flip then headed to the fireplace, to the spot where Katherine's body had been left hanging. There was a deep hole in the plaster where the poker had run her through. It would take a man of great strength to do such a thing.

Beside the fireplace was a metal container for the fireplace tools, including—it appeared—the offending implement. Across the room, Miss Heloise followed Flip's gaze.

"I had to put it back—after I'd cleaned it, of course," she said. "Otherwise the children would notice. They don't know the details of what happened. They know the girls died, but not the details. I'm hoping to keep it that way. I didn't want to leave any clues that might make little minds wander. Every child in this house has already been through enough. They understand something bad took place in this room. That's plenty."

"You yourself saw nothing, heard nothing?" Flip asked.

"How could we?" Miss Heloise answered. "We weren't home. I had taken the children to play on the beach. Kathrine wasn't feeling well, and the twins were both scared of water. But they were good girls; they knew my rules and obeyed me. I had left them alone before, with no problems."

Flip smiled and nodded.

"Of course they were good girls," he said. "How long were you away at the lake?"

"Three hours for the entire trip," answered Miss Heloise.

Flip picked up the fireplace poker and tested its weight in his hands.

"Doreen and Netty, what can you tell me about them?" he asked, swinging the poker slowly through the air.

"Showed up a couple years ago with no explanation," said Miss Heloise. "Half of the girls come that way. Someone drops them on my doorstep because they know we take care of the lost. I don't press the girls for details if they don't wanna talk, and they seldom do. Doreen and Netty said they were from South Carolina, which I told the police. Said they had no mother or father anymore. Said a man had brought them here to Chicago in a railcar, and then he disappeared. They said they were eleven years old. That was *all* they said."

"How did you tell them apart?" Flip asked, gripping the poker now like baseball player trying a new bat.

Miss Heloise paused for a moment. Flip realized her mind was processing something very terrible indeed.

"They came *branded*," Miss Heloise said soberly. "I don't know in what circumstances they were birthed and raised, but it must have been awful—a place where such things were done. You see, someone had burned a D into Doreen's back, and an N into Netty's. Just below the right shoulder. Course, I didn't have to use the marks to tell. The girls had their own personalities. Their own souls."

"Anybody ever threaten them? They make enemies?"

Miss Heloise shook her head no.

"How's a child supposed to have 'enemies' in the first place? It's a *child*."

"And you said they were good? Obeyed your rules?"

Miss Heloise nodded.

"They were some of the best," she said quietly. "Two perfect little girls. Not selfish. Played good with the others. They were a blessing. Our Father above made the one so perfect, he had to use the mold a second time. That's how I look at it."

Flip took another slow swing through the air with the fireplace tool, chasing a lazy, invisible curveball.

"Do you mind if I borrow this?" he asked, pivoting; he gripped the tool by the center of the shaft, and held it up to her face. "I can bring it back before the children notice, I expect."

Miss Heloise grew annoyed.

"Are you really going to catch whoever did this?" she said, placing a hand on her substantial hip.

Flip smiled.

"Maybe," he said. "But please . . . can I take the poker?"

"Yes, fine," Miss Heloise said sternly. "Will there be anything else?"

"No," Flip said, lowering the implement. "That should be everything."

Miss Heloise gazed at him with great suspicion.

On his way out of Miss Heloise's house, Flip lingered at the edge of the park across the street. He looked over the trees and shrubs, and at the familiar forms of the sleeping bums. He thought to himself that there would be a lot of places where you could kill somebody and not be seen in a park like that.

Places where blood could be spilled on the ground, with nobody ever the wiser.

FIVE

South State Street was fully, gloriously arrayed for the night. Every doorway of every bar was open to admit the warm summer air. All manner of sights, smells, and sounds flowed from out of those doorways to entice passersby. Electric light glowed in the tonier establishments, and mystical, seductive gaslight hummed in the rest. Musicians played. Motorcars and horses occasionally appeared, but most of the traffic was on foot—almost all men, and all of them crossing in the middle of the street without looking.

It was far from the weekend, but any visitor from the country would have sworn this was a Saturday night.

There were thirty long blocks along South State from 55th up to 25th—thirty long blocks that mattered—and Flip knew every saloon-keep and storefront proprietor by name. Yet on this night, Flip found himself pausing to stare at a group of outsiders whom he knew not at all. There was a long, somber parade of them—serious-looking people, mostly white, but with a few Negroes and other races sprinkled in—marching due south. They moved slowly and purposefully, carrying lanterns and singing dreary songs in a minor key. A few held up placards announcing they advocated for a "Capital-T Total" ban on alcoholic beverages. They wore crosses and other religious signs.

Before they got too close, Flip stopped and raised the fireplace poker. He pointed it toward the interlopers and made a sound with his mouth like a cannon firing. Then he lowered the implement and continued on his way.

Flip paused again only when he had reached the front of the Palmerton House, the finest and most expensive Negro brothel in the city. The proprietor, Sally Battle, sat in a divan on the raised front porch balcony. Beside her was a sporting girl wearing a black velvet eye patch. Set into the center of the patch were sparkling green jewels. Sally waved a familiar, unhurried hello to Flip as he avoided the brothel entrance and picked his way around the side of the building, passing into the shadows.

Behind the Palmerton, Flip found a staircase. At first glance, it seemed to lead down into utter nothingness. Few who glimpsed it in the evening hours—or even during the day—guessed that anything other than a grimy boiler room could be found on the other side of whatever door huddled in the darkness below.

Flip started down the staircase, taking each ancient step by memory. The step at the bottom was broken, and Flip avoided it, hopping down to the concrete landing. He knocked hard against the metal door.

The woman who dealt within did not advertise her services as openly as the women in the front of the building (and *they* did not exactly hang up a sign). There was nothing to indicate what visitors might hope to find on the other side . . . nothing save a single emerald stripe of paint across the door. It was haphazard and not straight, and looked possibly accidental.

When no answer came, Flip knocked even harder.

"Ursula?" he called.

No answer.

He hung his head.

"This early for her," a female voice called as Flip emerged back at the front of the Palmerton.

Flip shrugged to say it had been worth a shot.

He headed up the front steps and joined Sally Battle on the elevated porch. The sporting girl beside Sally stood, curtseyed, and headed back inside.

Sally wore an evening gown and long white opera gloves—her standard "on duty" uniform. Her age was almost impossible to guess. Flip understood that many madams (as well as their girls) often represented themselves as years younger than they actually were. This was especially true for madams who gave the impression that, for a certain price, they might still be on the menu.

Flip had no idea how old Sally Battle actually was, or if she still entertained men. On this fragrant summer evening, in this light, at this moment, he might have said she was in her early thirties.

"That patch on your girl looks fine indeed," Flip said, placing his hand on the railing and looking down into the street. "If I didn't know better, I'd say those were real emeralds. Did she lose the whole eye, or-"

"Whole eye," Sally replied, following Flip's gaze to the pedestrians below.

"You girls are some brave souls," Flip told her.

"Police are brave too," Sally answered. "We *all* stand to lose things in the line of duty. Why you got that poker?"

"Have Ursula take a look," Flip replied.

Sally nodded thoughtfully.

In front of the brothel was a hitching post for horses and, directly adjacent, a parking area for automobiles. Usually both were empty; the majority of Sally's clients reached South State by streetcar or on foot. On this night, however, there was one conspicuous exception. An enormous Pierce touring car—its black exterior polished to a gleam— sat on the street in front of the Palmerton. A liveried driver relaxed behind the wheel, reading a *Chicago Herald* and smoking a cheroot.

Flip turned halfway to Sally and lifted an eyebrow.

The madam smiled coyly.

"Adolf Graf," she said quietly, eyes never leaving the car.

"The beer baron?" asked Flip.

"Down from Milwaukee for meetings," Sally said with an almost imperceptible nod.

Flip considered this.

After great effort, the Chicago Vice Commission had, a few years prior, finally summoned the temerity shut down the Everleigh Club— the finest and most expensive brothel in Chicago, if not the world. It was a place where visiting kings and princes made sure to stop, and where the wealthiest men in the Midwest mingled. Yet even with the Everleigh shuttered, there were still many options for a man with the means of Adolf Graf that would not require him to travel all the way to South State.

"Have no doubt, the man likes Negro girls," Sally explained. "There may be other houses in Chicago *slightly* finer than mine. *Slightly.* And yes, those houses may keep *one or two* Negro girls on staff for the enthusiast. But there is no finer establishment where he can choose from twenty. Mr. Graf knows what he likes, and he knows where to find it."

"A regular, then?" asked Flip.

"Drops by every time he's in town," Sally replied with a nod.

Graf's driver lifted his head from his newspaper and looked up the street. The marching reformers had grown closer. (They had become hoarse from the effort of singing now, and transmitted only soundless expressions of disapproval. They seemed to dare any of the men on the street to spit at them, throw bottles, or take a swing. Their temerity was not surprising. They were emboldened by a string of recent successes. These were men and women who felt sure that history was on their side, not to mention holy providence. There had to be a hundred of them. To Flip, it gradually seemed less a parade, and more an invading gang.)

"I thought it would be enough for these people when they got the Levee District shut up," said Sally. "But it looks like they were just getting started. Now they want more. I never thought they would make it to *my* part of town. But here they are."

Flip rubbed his chin philosophically.

"Folks say temperance is going to solve everything," he said. "They say that if men won't drink, then they won't beat their wives. And they won't be greedy or lustful or gluttonous neither. They won't want to commit any crime at all. You combine that with this war we got going now—people calling it 'The War to End War'—it sounds like pretty soon there won't be *any* problems at all. No vice. No war. None of it. This new world is just a few months away, if you believe these people. And look at their faces. They *do* believe it."

Sally gazed down into the sea of reformers.

"You and I will be out of a job," she offered with a smirk.

Flip shook his head.

"But see. . . something tells me—something deep in the back of my head tells me—my job is completely damn safe," he said. "Yours too. Something tells me ain't a damn thing gonna change. That there's still gonna be war and drink and gambling and sporting girls. That you can move the pieces around, but you can't take 'em off the chessboard."

Sally smiled a very beautiful smile. The reformers drew nearer, their lanterns burning bright in the warm Chicago night. A few directed their gazes up to look at the Negro man and woman on the raised, railed porch of the brothel.

Flip and Sally looked right back.

"You want to come inside the parlor and wait?" Sally asked after the reformers had passed.

"All right," Flip said.

"Can I take your fireplace poker?" the madam asked.

Flip smiled as he shook his head no.

For nearly an hour, Flip sat in the gilded lobby of the Palmerton. Sally Battle's favorite color was green, and everything inside seemed to be trimmed in either glittering gold or deep emerald. Green tapestries hung from the walls. There was gold-plated piano in the lobby's center, with green ferns upon it. Gold spittoons had been placed in the corners. Flip sat on a couch hidden partially by an Oriental screen, all green and gold.

Sporting girls walked by from time to time. They were some of the most beautiful women Flip had ever seen. He smiled at them perfunctorily, but his eyes looked through them like ghosts. He understood acutely that he would not rise further in the world by flirting with any of them. And that going upstairs with any of these women —which, due to his long friendship with Sally, would have almost certainly been on the house—would only give them power over him. It would mean that he had a weakness; that they had something he wanted. And wanting—Flip understood—was the only real weakness in the world.

Flip smiled politely, sat alone, and accepted nothing more than a glass of water.

In addition to girls, Flip also watched men pass through. Some of the most powerful Negro men in the city—and a couple of whites, too—made their way inside. These were movers and shakers known not just along South State Street, but throughout Chicago. Most assumed that Flip was employed by the brothel as additional security. One very senior gentleman in a red suit wandered awestruck through the door, gazed in wonderment at the finery around him—then looked to Flip and asked "Where do I go?" Flip smiled and nodded to the lounge adjacent.

When an hour was close to up, Sally reemerged.

"Your conjure woman due to materialize soon," she said, gazing at a grandfather clock with clover hands that stood beside the door.

"I expect you're right," Flip responded, rising to his feet and snatching up the poker.

Wordlessly, he reached inside of his coat, felt around for an envelope, and came out with five hundred dollar bills. Sally's mouth opened as Flip pressed them into her palm.

Her expression of surprise was complete. Had the policeman finally, after all these years, decided on purchasing services for himself?

She vanished the bills into her décolletage with a quickness that would have impressed Drextel Tark.

"What-"

"You just keep an eye out," Flip said.

"For. . .?"

"For anything I might want to know about," Flip said to her. "You done me right for a while now, Sally. That there's long overdue."

As Flip began to exit the brothel, Sally cocked her head to the side.

"Flip. . ." she called, still confused. "Is everything all right?"

Flip saluted her silently with the fireplace poker, and closed the door behind him.

B ack behind the Palmerton, Flip made his way down the crumbling staircase, reached the basement door, and pounded on it hard.

This time, a voice came from within. A dead voice like a tear in space and time.

"Whoever knocks, open up. . . it's unlocked!"

Flip peeled back the door and ducked inside.

The shadowy, low room beyond looked and felt like an abandoned machine shop. It was a large space with no dividers, crowded-full of broken furniture—half of it covered with sackcloth, as though it would soon be moved or stored. The room had no windows, and the walls beyond the sackcloth shapes showed a perfect, utter darkness. A surreal aisle of light ran down the center; tiny lanterns with single taper candles had been carefully placed to either side of a long Armenian rug. Fifteen paces along this illuminated aisle was a wooden table. Resting upon the table was a shape about the size of a human head, covered with a thick, velvety cloth, utterly black. To one side of the table was a bare, backless wooden stool, and to the other, a very old rocking chair.

In the rocking chair sat Ursula Green.

Ursula was sexless. Genderless. Raceless. Ancient almost beyond life itself. Flip didn't like to look at her, not directly. He had to force himself whenever it came time to meet her cataract-clouded eyes. Looking at her was one thing, but hearing her talk? Up close? *That* was what he truly found near-to-unbearable. That was what physically hurt. Hurt his mind. Hurt his soul. Hurt something in his very sense of decency.

Flip made his way down the aisle. The rug crunched softly beneath his feet. Ursula said nothing and did not move as he approached. She looked dead. Another man might have felt himself practically alone. Yet Flip knew he was being carefully watched.

Flip had difficulty telling exactly how high the basement ceiling was (he had never been able to see it), and so he always ducked a little as he walked. When he reached the table, he sat carefully on the wooden stool, keeping himself hunched. At the same moment, the black cloth was pulled away. A gibbous crystal sphere was revealed underneath. Reflected tips of lantern-light swam inside it like shimmering goldfish, exploring its irregular angles.

Ursula Green seemed too inert and lifeless to have possibly moved the cloth. If Flip had not seen it happen before, he would have looked for a tripwire, a contraption, something—*anything*—to take the credit. But it was now the withered claw of the old woman that held the cloth, like a gnarled tree branch that had grown around it for decades.

Flip got himself situated.

The witch was very still; her breath detectable only insomuch as it disturbed her beard. When she *did* move or speak, however slightly, it felt to Flip, again—as with the movement of the cloth—as though the source *must* have come—could *only* have come—from somewhere else in the room. That a separate creature hiding behind one of the shadowy sackcloth shapes had jolted her. That a master puppeteer moved her. That electricity had shocked the corpse into a momentary simulacra of life. For it could not have been her own will or energy.

Could not have been.

And yet he knew, hideously, that it was.

Flip placed the heavy fireplace poker on the table in front of Ursula, directly beside the crystal ball with its swimming light-fish. Then he reached into his pocket and retrieved the long, thin splinter covered in the blood of the Whitcomb boys. He took out the few inches of evergreen shrub from the alley where the Washington twins had been found. These, too, he placed before the silent, ancient being. Then he fished out the shoe polish tin containing the oily dirt from where the

Horner twins had been decapitated. He placed this tin on the table as well, leaving it unopened.

But he was not quite finished.

Flip dipped into his coat with a thumb and a single finger. He fiddled within the envelope until he'd counted ten hundred-dollar bills. These he withdrew and carefully set on the table before Ursula.

"There is more than usual tonight," Flip said to the witch. "This is not one case; it is four. Or rather, four cases that are connected, I believe. You're going to need a bigger table, with everything I've brought."

The crone's clouded eyes moved to the objects set before her with the jerky tic-tic-tic of an automaton.

"That much money, I expect I can afford a new table," she finally pronounced, her voice like a claw down a chalkboard.

Flip looked and saw that the stack of bills had already disappeared.

Ancient and essentially dead, Ursula had still secreted them away with the same speed of Drextel Tark or Sally Battle.

Somehow.

And now the ritual began, and the old woman began to run her timeworn hands over the objects set before her. To Flip, it was like watching a department store window-dresser positioning a mannequin. The arms were stiff and did not flex as they should. The fingers did not bend. They seemed not really to feel. Ursula was rigid as though she were made of wood.

Flip watched carefully. Did the woman linger on one item longer than any other?

"These are new. . .to you," she finally pronounced, each word like a cutting dagger. "You only come here when your trail is cold, Joe Flippity. You only visit me when you've tried everything else. But you just picked up this scent. Therefore, you are in haste."

"I have a week to make progress on the case," Flip told her. "I need all the help I can get."

Flip took the envelope with the photos of the crime scenes out of his pocket. He knew they would be nearly impossible for anyone—much less Ursula—to see in this gloom, but it still felt important to make the presentation. Flip had never understood precisely how Ursula Green's gift worked, only that it did. He did not know what was necessary to show her or to tell her during these visits, so he erred on the side of everything.

The old woman never grasped a totem and spouted the name of the murderer, rapist, or thief—true—but her answers, however oblique, had an uncanny way of helping Flip to think about things he'd not yet considered. Always, it seemed, her words ultimately led him to the resolution he sought. (Would he have thought of these same case-breaking connections eventually, on his own, and without her? That was a question which haunted him, and upon which he never could make up his mind.)

Flip had been coming to see Ursula for nearly ten years. During that decade, Ursula had seemed never to age. Sally Battle said that Ursula was now 105. This would make her old enough to have known Jefferson and Adams—if not quite George Washington himself. Sometimes 105 looked about right to Flip. Other times, it seemed she could simply be a rough 80. The perspective, the amount of light in the room, it all changed his opinion from moment to moment.

Flip carefully held up the photographs and told Ursula about each one. He left out no detail. Because he did not know which notes charmed the snake, he played them all.

When he was finished, he returned the photographs to his coat and waited. Before long, an answer came.

"You don't know any twins," Ursula said. "You have no *skin* in this game, Joe Flippity. You have no skin at all."

Flip smiled. He was unfamiliar with the expression, but understood immediately what it meant.

"To the contrary, my skin is the reason I have the assignment," he told her. "This is a killer who kills Negro twins. *Child* Negro twins, Ursula. Think about that."

"A white man could stop that killer, same as you," Ursula said.

"But *I* stop this killer. . ."

Suddenly, just as the she had begun to seem—from her speech, at least—human for a moment, she fell away into the unearthly. The distorted cackles that spewed forth to interrupt the policeman were not normal human laughter, or even like a machine built to imitate human laughter. They were closer to the wild HONK HONK HONK of some giant, marine animal, whose nauseating utterances are only called "the laughter of the sea" because no other words in a terrified mariner's vocabulary exist to characterize such awful cries.

When her paroxysm had finished, Ursula drew breath like a broken bellows pulling through a wax-clogged nozzle.

"Do you really think you will change things for *anyone* in this city? Whose word do you have on that? The word of a man who always lies?"

"I. . .I. . ." Flip managed.

That was how Crespo had described the mayor, but as much could be said of any politician.

"You think you can guess what is happening here," Ursula asserted, waving a rigid stick-arm at the items on her table. "You have *no idea* what is happening here. You have no idea what *any* of this means."

Flip said nothing. He squinted unnecessarily in the darkness, trying to guess what the witch wanted him to understand—trying to guess what might bring her closer to pulling some useful clue out of the ether.

"What is a twin?" the old woman asked through a hiss and cackle.

Flip smiled from the corner of his mouth, but stayed silent.

"*Buy heck it!!!*" the crone cried so loudly that Flip started and the stool beneath him shook. (This phrase was one of Ursula's favorite expletives; Flip understood only that it indicated frustration—generally with him.) "Tell me what a twin is! Tell me!"

Flip sat straight.

"A twin is a child born at the same time as another, from the same womb," he said. "And identical twins—which most of *these* are—are ones who're born looking exactly like the other."

"And *are* they the same?" Ursula pressed.

"Not inside," Flip said after a pause. "They have their own characters. Personalities. Inside themselves, they're different people."

"But their bodies . . . are they the same?" pressed Ursula.

"It sure looks that way," Flip conceded.

The witch shifted slightly in her rocking chair.

"*You* have no twin, Joe Flippity."

Flip relaxed a bit.

"I mean, not that I know," he agreed. "Not that my mamma ever told me."

"But there are worlds where a man with your skin walks and lives," the witch insisted, raising a brittle, paralyzed finger to make her point. "There are other worlds all around you. When you saw Sally's girl tonight . . . the one with the patch. . . some part of you thought to ask if it was disease from a man's prick that had rotted the eye out of her head, or a fist that had beat it out. You nearly said something . . . but you did not. And yet, in another world, there is a man—a *you*—that did. Do you understand?"

"But I *didn't* say something," Flip maintained. "And how do you know about that?"

"There are other worlds where you have other souls, Joe Flippity."

"There. . ." Flip trailed off. "Can I meet one of these other me's? Would I like him?"

"A man may meet his physical twin," Ursula hissed. "Does it not then come that he may meet his other soul?"

Flip took a deep breath and let his eyes scan the endless ceiling of the dark, dingy basement.

Redirecting the conversation with Ursula could be something of a challenge.

Flip slumped his shoulders forward and stared at the crystal ball in the center of the table.

For a long time, he said nothing.

"Ursula, do these items tell you anything about my case?" he asked after a pause. "Is there anything I should know? Or are you just gonna talk about 'the other me' wondering if an eye was lost to violence or syphilis? If you can't see anything right now, that's all right. I don't blame you for having a bad night. Everybody does."

For a few moments, nothing more. The elderly woman was still.

"Your answer is right here," she said.

"Here, in the items on this table?" Flip asked.

The witch's eyes moved, tic-tic-tic.

"Right here," she hissed. "The one you seek. . .it is right here, in this very place."

Ursula leaned back in her chair and turned away.

After a time, Flip knew she would say nothing more.

SIX

He took the fireplace poker but left the other totems on the table in front of Ursula.

Back around the front of the Palmerton, Flip saw that the beer baron's touring car had departed. Up on the balcony, three sporting girls were relaxing and smoking, but they were none that he knew. One gave him a polite, collegial wink. Flip waved back with the poker.

Flip stepped out into the street and headed due southwest, to the top floor of the three-flat where he lived. As he walked, he asked himself the "who" questions in his head.

Who would want to kill twins in general? Who would want to kill young black twins in Chicago specifically? Who would gain from it?

Then he had a thought: Maybe it wasn't just in Chicago.

There were newsagents in the Loop where you could buy newspapers from New York, San Francisco, and everywhere in between. Maybe there were other beheadings in other cities that had *not* been kept out of the papers.

It was nearly midnight when Flip reached the dark, quiet block he called his own. It had been a long day, and he looked forward to his bed.

Forty yards out from his building, Flip detected a distinctly human-sized heap on the porch. This was not a spot where a vagrant had ever slept before, at least not that he could recall. The figure was doing nothing to conceal itself. Flip could not tell if it was alive.

Flip received very few visitors, and almost nobody outside the police department knew his address.

Flip surveyed the nearby alleys as he drew closer, but did not slacken his pace. Doing so would reveal he had seen something. One neighbor kept a pile of bricks in his yard, tall enough to conceal a man or men. Flip eyed the pile and fingered the gun inside his coat. He shifted the poker to his left hand, preparing to use it for close combat. There were still lights in a few windows, but no foot traffic that he could see.

Twenty yards from his front door, the human-sized bundle began to move. It sat up, straightened itself, and rose. Flip noticed there was a clear bottle on the ground beside it. Empty.

A voice called hoarsely: "Flip, is that you?"

Flip took his hand away from his 1911 and lowered the poker.

"Tark?" Flip said soft enough that neighbors might not awaken. "Why are you sleeping on my stoop? Are you three sheets to the wind again?"

"No," said Tark, adjusting his own voice down. "One sheet at most. What you smell is just a little hair of the dog. I was waiting for you."

Flip approached.

"For a while I sat here and practiced card tricks," Tark explained. "Then some children came and wanted to watch. But I didn't feel like having an audience, so I just put my head down and pretended to sleep until they went away. Then I guess I fell asleep for real."

"Why are you at my house?" Flip asked.

"Something bad happened after you left," Tark said, his nervous eyes rolling the moonlight. "We need to talk."

"Yes, all right," Flip said. "You better come up."

Flip unlocked the front door and they climbed the bare wooden staircase to the third floor. Flip took out a second key and unlocked the door to the private rooms where he lived alone. The residence was humble and not maintained with visitors in mind. Even so, Flip was able to wrangle some chairs around a table and move the dishes over to the sink. When Flip sat down next to Tark, he saw that another bottle of gin—as if by magic—had appeared in the magician's hand.

"Ain't a man I told to go easy on that stuff ever listened," Flip said. "But you ain't quite a man yet. Ought to try and break your taste for it while there's still time."

Tark smiled, but looked weary. His expression said that they could talk about his drinking at a later date. More pressing things weighed on his mind.

"What you got to say, then?" Flip asked. "Spit it out."

It was warm in Flip's rooms. Tark took out a handkerchief. Flip anticipated some act of wizardry, but the magician only mopped his brow.

"Well," Tark began, "broadly, I'm here because I aim to help you."

"Help me?"

"I aim to help you catch whoever is after Negro twins," Tark said.

Flip wrinkled his brow. Then he stood up. He made his way to his half-broken kitchen cupboard. He pulled out a cracked teacup emblazoned with the logo of the 1893 World's Fair. Then he ambled back to his seat. He took the bottle firmly from Tark and poured some gin into the teacup. He took a sip. It was not good. He forced himself to swallow.

"Why?" Flip said after he'd fought through the grimace. "Why would *you* want to help all of a sudden? What's changed?"

Tark stared straight ahead. His eyes became unfocused. He was remembering.

"This afternoon, after you left, a man came looking for Ike," the magician said. "I was a few blocks away, talking to a girl. I wasn't gone that long. The girl didn't want anything to do with me. When I got back, Ike was telling the story to some of the men on the crew. Trying to, anyway. Doing the best he could. He saw me, and he ran up to tell it all over again."

"And the story was?" Flip said, sipping more awful gin from the teacup, not quite knowing why.

Tark shrugged.

"Ike can be hard to understand, but I made out that a man came out of the trees—the eastern row of trees bordering the circus field—and he wore a nice suit and a homburg hat, and he was Negro . . . and he *asked Ike if he was a twin.*"

Flip nodded dispassionately from above the teacup.

"Then the man asked about Ike and *me specifically,* if *we* were twins. Then he started to manhandle Ike. I think they fought rough. Ike had a gash over his eye, and his face was bruised some. I couldn't get Ike to say if he'd fought the man, or the man had just struck him down and left. Ike knows he's not supposed to fight, so he won't talk about things like that."

"Nobody else saw this happen?" Flip asked.

"No," Tark said. "Most everybody was still asleep. Ike was only awake because you came to see us. But I believe him. He's never told a lie in his life."

"Where is Ike now?" asked Flip.

"Somewhere safe," Tark said cagily. "I put him on a train. We have some acquaintances down in Indiana. People who could take him in for a few days, and not ask questions."

"Who?" Flip pressed. "Where in Indiana?"

Tark looked down at his toes, then up at Flip—just once, very quickly—then back down at his toes.

"I don't want to tell you," Tark said. "It's better if you don't know. It's better if no one knows."

"You don't trust me?" Flip said. "After all I've done for you? You're one of my best customers when it comes to needing things returned, and you think-"

"What am I supposed to think?" Tark shot back angrily, tears abruptly welling in his eyes. "You show up and talk about this twin killer. Then my brother is beat up by a man asking if we're twins."

"But-" Flip began.

"The less anybody knows, the better," Tark insisted. "I'll tell you something that being a magician teaches you. It's that there is *never* an advantage to telling anybody more than you have to, Flip. Ever."

"If you want to help me catch this person-" Flip tried again.

"What?" Tark said aggressively. "What would Ike tell you that he hasn't already told *me*, his own brother!?"

Flip rose once more from his chair. This time he made his way over to a desk—nearly as broken as his cupboard. After some jimmying, he opened it and found a fresh notebook and a pencil.

He wrote *Male, Negro, Suit, Homburg.*

It was a start.

"I would really like to talk to Ike," Flip said.

"You're not going to talk to Ike until we figure out what is happening," Tark replied, adamant.

Flip sat back down. He tossed the notepad on the table before them. Then he took the teacup and drained the rest of its brackish contents.

"You realize you probably aren't safe either," Flip said after a final swallow. "Not in light of what you've just told me."

The magician nodded soberly.

"So what are we going to do?" Tark asked.

Flip sighed.

"I've had a busy day, and I need to think on it some. Think on everything I've seen and heard."

Tark nodded.

"I do my best thinking alone," Flip added sternly.

Tark looked down.

"I can't go back to my caravan," he said. "If they're looking for me, that's where they'll look."

"I seem to recall giving you two hundred dollars earlier today," Flip said. "You can get yourself a room somewhere for the night. Come back here at six in the morning—six sharp—and we'll have some work to do then."

Tark rose uneasily.

"Where should I-"

"I don't care where you stay," Flip said. "Just be back at six."

Tark said he would. He let himself out of Flip's apartment, and the policeman locked the door.

After the magician had left, Flip walked to his front window and looked out on the street. He watched the magician walking away in the moonlight. He had taken the gin along with him. Flip saw him tip the bottle up to his lips just as he passed out of sight.

Flip sat back down at his table and began to work.

SEVEN

The Amazing Drextel Tark knocked hard on the door to Flip's building at five-fifty the next morning. A third floor window raised, and Flip stuck his head out.

"Quiet, fool!" he whisper-shouted. "You'll wake the neighbors."

Tark shrugged to ask how else he should have approached the matter. Moments later, Flip came down and opened it for him. They walked back upstairs.

"We got a full day ahead," Flip said as they passed into his rooms.

The interior of Flip's apartment looked even more broken and disarrayed in the morning light. It also looked as though the policeman had been up for a while after Tark had left. Grisly photographs were arranged on Flip's table, and the notepad—which had contained only four words at the time of Tark's departure—now showed several pages of scribbling.

"What are we doing?" Tark asked.

Flip stepped to his stove and poured himself coffee in a tin cup like a miner might use. Then he poured a second cup and held it out to Tark. The magician accepted it.

"Someone is killing young Negro identical twins," Flip said after a sip. "He's killing them, and then mutilating their bodies."

"Yeah," said Tark. "I got that. Why's he doing it?"

"We don't know why," Flip replied, "but knowing why doesn't always matter when you're trying to enforce the law. It's enough to understand that when someone tends to do something . . .they'll tend to do it again."

"So?" Tark said, sipping his coffee and clearly finding it wanting.

"So identical twins—of any sort—don't grow on no trees," Flip said. "The first step to killing them would be *finding* them."

Tark lifted his cup to his mouth, then lowered it again without sipping. His expression said 'Yes. . . but . . .?'

"How would you do that?" Flip said rhetorically. "How would you do it if *you* were trying to find twins to kill? Would you just walk around town looking? Ask people you met on the street? That wouldn't work too well. It would also arouse suspicion. Our killer's not been caught yet, which means he's not completely stupid. Last night, did I tell you what all of the murdered children *also* had in common? The *other* thing they shared?"

"What?" the magician asked, wishing he knew a spell to make Flip's coffee taste better.

"They were all immigrants to Chicago," Flip said. "All orphans come up from the South."

"Fine," Tark said. "So what?"

"This killer looked for twins, but I think he also looked for twins nobody in Chicago would miss. Where would *you* go to try and find people like that?"

"They's places," Tark said, thinking on it for a moment.

"Yes," agreed Flip. "There are."

The Greater Chicago Negro Settlement Alliance was just south of the Loop on the first and second floors of what had once been a small garment factory. The walkway in front of the building was paved, but the adjacent lawns (formerly green and verdant) had been entirely trampled to mud. The place was close to the rail yards, and easy to reach by foot after you disembarked. There were several organizations in Chicago like it, each aimed at improving the conditions of black folks, and many with a special emphasis on assisting those recently arrived from the South. Yet this one was the most conspicuous. The first one you'd find if you got off the train and just started walking.

There were three families camped on the muddy ground in front of the former factory. Men slept on bindles that probably contained all their worldly possessions. Women slept beside the men. Children slept piled together under makeshift pup tents, with their feet protruding like cords of wood. What did these families do in the cold, Flip wondered? He thought the answer was probably that they froze.

The front door was open. As Tark watched, Flip paused in front of it to open his coat.

"Should we say I'm police too?" Tark whispered.

"What?" Flip asked.

"It's just, I ain't got no gun or badge," Tark said.

Tark wore only brown trousers, shoes, and a white dress shirt stained at the armpits.

"You don't need those things," Flip told him. "And if you got a magic wand somewhere on you, just keep it in your pocket."

"I don't use a wand," Tark shot back, clearly insulted.

"Why not?" Flip said, amused.

"Because it's not a hundred years ago," Tark said firmly, as if it were a foolish question.

"Just let me do the talking," Flip said. "Watch and listen, all right?"

Tark nodded. They went inside.

The Greater Chicago Negro Settlement Alliance had an administrative office at the front of the building, but was sizable enough that Flip could not guess what was kept in the back rooms or on the second level. Probably, on this morning, there were more people sleeping in those places. The building had the feel of a railway terminal, where many came and went.

There was a long wooden desk. A hand-drawn sign on the wall said ASK ME FOR HELP, and bore a long red arrow pointing over. There was a lone Negro man sitting at the desk. He looked half awake, but awake. He was middle aged, balding, and had a pencil-thin mustache.

When he saw Flip and Tark, he smiled and stood. Then he rubbed his eyes and stretched. A small nameplate on his desk said he was Mr. Parr.

"Two sworn officers," he said, regarding the contents of Flip's open coat. "Welcome, welcome. What *can* I do for you?"

Tark gave Flip a sideways smile, then straightened himself until he stood erect as he imagined a true policeman might.

"Those families out front. . . they have permission to be sleeping on our property," Parr added before Flip could say anything. "Alderman says it's allowable. Normally, we house folks inside, but the heat gets mighty powerful this time of year."

"I'm not here about the sleeping people," Flip told him. "I'm here to ask you about identical twins. More specific . . . I'm here to ask about *someone asking about* identical twins."

Parr smiled and stretched again. He had the look of a person whose responsibilities allowed his body remain sedentary most of the time, yet his mind was still well-exercised and lively. He seemed eager to talk.

"I *knew* that fool was up to something," Parr said thoughtfully. "He just didn't feel right. After a while, when you work with people all day, you're able to get a kind of *vibration* from folks. The man seemed all prim and proper, but he vibrated bad. Can you tell me what he done?"

"*Who* vibrated bad?" Flip said. "Start from the beginning."

"He just came in one afternoon," Parr said. "Didn't give his name. He was, oh, neither old nor young. Wore a grey suit. A fine gray suit. You know, like the Jewish tailors make?"

"He was Negro?" asked Flip.

Parr nodded.

"Did he speak with an accent?" Flip pressed.

Parr shook his head.

"But he was fine-spoken. Like. . . Like. . . A stage actor or an opera singer, I should imagine. That was the first way he set me at *dis*-ease. Something in his bearing was wrong. Was . . . fake. A man not being himself."

Flip nodded carefully.

"When did this visit occur?"

"I should say it was, oh, some weeks ago," Parr said, putting his chin into his palm like a daydreaming teenager. "Middle of June. Late June. Thereabouts. He came in and asked if we had had any identical twins come past recently. He was looking for twins as young as six or seven, and as old as thirteen or fourteen."

Flip nodded.

"He never made any small talk," Parr continued. "Never said he was anybody's relation. He just asked about twins. He asked if there were records we kept, and if our records would say somebody was a twin. He was damn-near obsessed with the idea, if you pardon my language. After he understood I couldn't help him, he still kind of hung around the building for an hour or so. Acted like he was waiting for someone. He struck up conversations with people. I could tell he was also asking them about twins. It's very quiet here at the moment—because it's so early, y'see—but this place is crowded like an Arab market most of the day."

"I'm sure it is," Flip said. "Did the man ever come again? Was that the only time you saw him?"

"That's right," said Parr. "He came only the once. I was glad when he eventually did leave. Made me uneasy."

"And *do* you?" Flip asked.

Parr smiled gently, as though he had missed something.

"Do I what, officer?"

"Do you have any identical twins coming through?"

"No," Parr said with a laugh. "No twins that I've ever seen. Not in five years working here."

"All right," Flip said.

"But I haven't even told you the most remarkable thing!" Parr said suddenly. "I almost left it out, officer! Let me tell you. . . This man asking after twins. . . He was bald headed, and he had a divot in his skull—on the right side as you regarded him, so on his own left. Looked like a war-wound. Something awful. An inch deep if it was anything. A chunk taken out, clean gone."

"I see," Flip said.

"Yes," said Parr. "You don't forget a thing like that."

"Was there anything else you remember about him?" asked Flip.

"No," said Parr, searching his memory. "I reckon that's it."

Flip thanked Parr for his time. Flip and Tark exited the settlement agency. The families sleeping out on the lawn were stirring now. One had started a small campfire for making food, even though there was likely plenty to eat inside.

The newcomers to Chicago chatted softly. Accents from the deepest South caught Flip's ear. It brought back sensations and memories so old and profound they seemed to come from the very marrow of his bones. Things he had fought for years to forget. Hard, deep things. Old things.

For a moment, he went weak in the knees.

Tark stepped in and skillfully caught the policeman under the armpit, just managing to keep him upright. Tark was immediately in awe of how little Flip weighed. It was, he thought to himself, almost like a magic trick in itself. One looked at the tall officer in the heavy leather jacket and simply assumed that he was substantial and solid. That there was something *there*.

But now Tark found that he was light and impermanent. He could be carried around like a hat rack.

Tark walked Flip away from the improvised campsite.

A few paces off of the property, Flip straightened and recovered his footing. He pushed Tark's hands away, but did not look the magician in the face.

"There you go," Tark said. "This morning air will do you good. It was stuffy in that old place. Too damn stuffy. You'll feel better out here. Say, they have bars around here? We should get you a drink. Steady your nerves."

Flip shook his head slowly. He desired no such thing.

After a few moments, as though the interval had never occurred, he returned his focus to the case at hand.

"A middle aged Negro man who shops at fine tailors and has a divot in his head," Flip said, beginning to walk once again. "You ever see anybody like that, Tark?"

"No," Tark said. "It doesn't ring a bell. And that would be a pretty big bell."

"Now I'm hopeful," Flip said. "Even if you and I have no idea who this man is, it will be hard for him to hide. People will remember a person like that. We need to visit the other aid organizations. I'm sure our suspect did. But first I want to put in a question at the station, see if they know our divot man."

"That word, divot. . ." Tark said.

"What about it?"

"It's funny. I should work it into my routine somehow. You know, about ninety percent of a magic show is just banter—talking to the audience? Only about ten percent is doing the tricks."

"Yes," said Flip. "I've seen your act, remember?"

"Then here's something else," Tark said. "That man back there working the desk?"

"What about him?" Flip said.

"He thought I was police," Tark said proudly.

Flip shook his head to say nothing could be done with some people, and steered their path deeper into the city.

They went westward, along the south edge of the Loop, passing several businesses just opening for the day. A man smoked a cigar on the stoop of a barbershop. The cigar gave off the pleasing aroma of tobacco and peach. The man had no hands, and held the cigar between small round stumps. Flip and Tark both silently wondered if he was the barber, and, if so, how he cut hair.

"You all right then?" Tark said to Flip after they had passed the barber shop. "You got faint back there, and now you ain't talkin'."

"Yes, I'm fine," Flip said, his mind working. "I'm interested in the timing of these events."

"Oh yeah?" said Tark.

"There's four of these twin killings—four that we know of," Flip said. "The first two—Washington twins in the alley, and the Horner boys by the Calumet—happen close to each other, early in June. Then there's a pause for a month, month and a half. Then twins are killed again in the house of Miss Heloise, and then the Whitcomb triplets die last Tuesday. Our man with the divot was asking around back there sometime in the middle of June."

Tark struggled to assemble the timeline in his head.

"It's almost as if our man was looking for more targets," Flip continued. "Like he aimed to kill young Negro twins, and—let's say—he knew about the Washington twins and the Horner boys. But after he killed them, he needed more. Had to go searching. So he did. Took him over a month, but he found some."

"And now he's found me and my brother," Tark said gloomily.

"Looks that way," Flip told him. "That's why we got work to do. One reason, anyhow."

In the precinct building, Flip gave his name and badge number to the officer at the desk and waited. There was a strange mix of people in the cramped, wood paneled entryway. It smelled like ten different things, most of them bad. There was a single bench completely filled with waiting petitioners. With no room to sit, Tark crossed his arms and leaned against a wall. Soon, he had fallen asleep standing.

Flip waited at the desk. After five minutes, a police matron came to greet him. She was fat and waddly, and had a crooked smile. She did not look happy to see him.

Flip gave his name a second time—slowly and clearly—and mentioned a project for the mayor. The matron's expression changed. Immediately, she suggested they could go back to a private office, but Flip said he hadn't the time and that it wasn't necessary. Flip gave her the details of the man with a divot in his head. The matron said she would have the files checked, and pass along anything they found. Flip thanked her, knocked the drowsing magician awake, and stepped back out into the street.

"My hopes aren't up," Flip told Tark. "But you never know. Maybe they picked him up for something before. Could have a name and address. Even a photograph."

"What if they do?" Tark asked.

"Then we go to where he lives and bring him in for questioning," Flip said. "And then we tell the mayor."

Flip and Tark visited seven more aid organizations before the day was out. There was the Chicago League on Urban Conditions Among Negroes, the Alliance for Orphaned Children, and the Negro Community Development Association. They also stopped at two Negro churches and two white ones that had programs for orphans. At each, they asked about a middle aged Negro man who might have come around talking about twins. They took care to mention that he might have had a part missing from his head.

The best they got were a couple of "maybes" and one "What if he wore a hat?"

As they exited a Catholic orphanage staffed by skinny French Canadian nuns, Flip announced that they would cease for the day. The sisters had seen no Negro twins. Nor had they seen a man with a divot in his head. But they *had* recently baked some cakes, and did not let Tark and Flip leave before forcing them to accept slices of cherry clafoutis wrapped in red handkerchiefs.

Outside the Catholic charity, Tark sat down on a bench and immediately began to eat his portion.

"I don't walk this much," he explained to Flip. "My legs feel like two ropes. My feet feel like flapjacks."

"It will mash your feet and toes, walking this much," Flip said unsympathetically. "You must get used to it."

"We put in a good day," Tark said, wiping his brow.

"We've discovered nothing new since six-thirty this morning," Flip pointed out.

Tark shrugged and went back to eating.

"We need to make careful notes of what we saw and heard," Flip told the magician. "Then we should formulate a plan for tomorrow."

"Are we gonna go around to the hospitals to ask doctors if they patched up a man with a scoop taken out of his head?"

Tark laughed to himself as he chewed.

Flip looked down his nose at the seated magician.

"You're joking, but that's the kind of thing that can break a case. Have you done this before, Tark? Do you have any damn idea what police work involves?"

"I know what I saw today," Tark answered. "Us asking around in a lot of stinky, crowded charity places."

There was a very long silence.

"I'm sorry," Tark said. "That's my tired feet talking. If it will get us closer to the man who came after my brother? Shit. I'll talk to every doctor in Chicago. Whatever. Let's do it."

"In that case, come on with me," Flip said. "We ain't restin' yet."

EIGHT

They took a streetcar back to Flip's neighborhood. The sun began to set. Flip thought the shadows crept oddly over Tark, seeming to linger and settle on him. Cloaking him.

Despite consuming the rich cake, Tark looked dried out and beat. Flip wondered if gin were needed, or if that would only make things worse. Whichever it was, Flip knew the tonic would almost certainly be applied vigorously within the hour.

Flip still felt alert and focused. He was thinking about the man they had to find.

When they reached the building where he lived, they saw two people waiting out front. Flip had never had so many visitors in a 24-hour period. One visitor had been his previous record, and that had been tied last night.

Curious neighbors peered furtively out at the waiting pair from behind ratty curtains or—if they didn't have curtains—unabashedly and straight through window glass. One of the visitors was a uniformed police officer. A white man, tall and broad in the shoulders. The other was a Negro woman in a fine hobble skirt. She wore no cosmetics on her face, and her hat was large and ornate. Still, it took Flip only a moment to recognize her as Sally Battle.

"Officer?" the policeman said.

Flip nodded and showed his badge.

"She came to the station," the policeman explained. "Said she had something that would help with your case. Said she knew you. Normally, we wouldn't do this, but the captain said the mayor-"

"It's all right," Flip told him. "You did right. I know her."

The officer was visibly relieved. He excused himself and hurried up the block as the shadows lengthened. Flip said nothing until the cop was out of earshot.

"You can leave a message for me at the precinct," Flip said. "I'll get it. You don't have to come to my damn house."

Sally was silent.

"And if you wanted to know where I lived, you could have just asked," Flip added.

"You wouldn't have told me straight," Sally said.

"No," Flip said. "Probably not. What do you need?"

Sally eyed the young magician.

"First of all, it is something to be discussed in private," she said. "It concerns your investigation."

"Which investigation is that?" Flip said.

"Twins," Sally said. "Dead twins."

"Which you know about *how*?" Flip asked sternly.

Sally did not respond. She glanced at the magician again.

"This man is Drextel Tark," Flip said, indicating the faded conjurer. "I don't think anybody could have a more relevant connection to this case than he does. Now tell me why you are here."

Sally reached into her purse and carefully withdrew a photograph. It was small—the kind family portrait studios produced to be placed inside a locket. She handed it to Flip. He looked it over carefully.

"I think we all need to go inside," he said.

"A re they yours, or do they belong to one of your girls?" Flip asked, tossing the photo of the swaddled twin newborns onto the table beside his notes.

Sally said nothing, and looked around his dingy apartment doubtfully.

"Yours then," Flip declaimed, and sat down at his table.

Sally and Tark also reluctantly found seats.

Tark immediately magicked a glass bottle. He took small sips straight from the mouth, and a smile slowly spread across his face. Then he looked at the photo on the table.

"Hey, they *are* twins, aren't they?" Tark said. "Took me a second."

Flip leaned back in his chair, hands clasped behind his head.

"I'll help you Sally, but first you have to reveal how you know about this," Flip said to her.

Sally sat up straight. Her jaw became hard and firm. Her eyes narrowed.

"What *don't* I know?" she said. "At the Palmerton House, we hear more than at any police station. And we keep files on customers just like the police do."

"You keeping a file on me?" Flip asked, half-serious.

"Maybe," Sally said. "We keep all sorts of information on men. What they like. What they don't. What job they have. What they'll pay extra for. Some of the Palmerton's clients work for the mayor, and maybe they heard about a special meeting between you and the big man. Maybe they even had an idea of what you talked about at that meeting. You'd be surprised what a man will tell when he's buttoning up his shirt and pulling his socks back on. It's more than he'll say when the boys in blue are beating on him down at the station, that's for sure."

Flip smiled at Sally. He did not take his eyes off her, but at the same time leaned over to Tark and made a "gimmie" motion with his right hand. Tark surrendered the bottle. Flip took it and brought it up to his lips, eyes still on Sally's. He had two good swallows, then passed it back.

"I thought I was a man who noticed things," Flip told her, "but I'll be damned if I ever noticed you were with child. And I visit with you at least once a month. Twice, probably."

"I know as many tricks as your magician," Sally said. "And just like him, a lot of mine involve costumes."

Flip was genuinely astounded. Sally had never seemed to be the slightest bit pregnant.

As Flip mulled his recent oversights, Sally took her turn motioning for the bottle. The magician carefully passed it, and the madam took a dainty sip.

"That is horrible," she pronounced. "Come to my place one day—when you're old enough and can afford it—and I'll set you up with some proper gin, like the British drink."

Sally turned back to the policeman.

"Why is he even here, Flip? You said before that he had something relevant?"

Flip informed her, in broad strokes, of Tark's connection to the case. Sally knit her brow as Flip told the tale, and her jaw became softer.

"Then I'm sorry," Sally said when Flip had finished. "My babies have me thinking a bit selfishly. I'm not the only one with something at stake, am I? You love your brother."

It was not a question.

"I'm all he has," Tark said softly. "He can't function on his own."

Sally turned back to Flip.

"Well then," she said to the policeman, straightening the front of her hobble skirt with flattened palms.

"Well then, *what*?" said Flip.

"Well then I also want to help you," Sally told him.

"You *can* help . . . by telling me how you know what you know," Flip said. "Who your leaky sources are that work with the mayor."

"You know what I mean," Sally said. "People saw you asking around today. Asking at the settlement agencies. I heard about that too! Please? I want to be a part of this."

"You got a business to run," Flip reminded her.

"My place can run itself for a while," Sally said. "If there's people aiming to stop this killer—and I *don't* help out?—I'll never forgive myself, Flip. Never ever."

Flip considered.

"I don't know what you think you can do for us," he told her. "I already have resources. If I needed more men, the department would give them to me in an instant."

"This is for me, Flip," she said, pleading now. "You don't got babies. You don't know what it is to imagine a thing in the world waiting to kill them . . .. You *can't* know Flip. You have to trust me."

"Sally, when I asked you to keep an eye out for things, I didn't mean-"

"It's too late, Flip," she said. "I'm here. I'm involved whether you like it or not."

Flip sighed.

"Sally. . . I . . . Yes, then. You can come along and help. . . if you truly want to. But. . . This is not going to be nice."

"Nice?" she said. "*Nice?* What world you think I live in?"

Flip nodded silently. He had, perhaps, forgotten just a little bit.

They sat and drank gin. Even Sally had more. At one point, it occurred to her to ask the magician: "Young man, if you can simply make this beverage appear from out of the ether—as it appears you can—then why not prestidigitate finer quality stuff?"

Tark smiled but did not reply.

They discussed what Flip and Tark had discovered so far. Flip wrote the details of every location they had visited, and all the people they had talked to. Tark and Sally conjectured further.

"You ain't never seen a customer with a lump taken out of his head?" the magician asked.

"We've seen men with all sorts of injuries, of course," Sally replied thoughtfully. "But none like what you are describing. How about you? Have you ever seen that?"

"Fewer circuses like to have a freak show these days," Tark said. "More of an east coast thing. Once, I saw 'The Man with No Brain.' His skull stopped right above his eyes. But he seemed otherwise like you or me. Could walk and talk and everything. We played a game of poker. He had a deck of cards with full naked women on the backs—real photos, not drawings. I-"

Tark suddenly clammed up, as if remembering a lady was present. Sally smiled.

"Oh dear boy, you're blushing?" she said. "How darling!"

"I think. . ." Flip said, sitting up and staring intently into his pad of notes. "I think . . . we have two stops tomorrow. One is the Illinois State Penitentiary. The other is the *Chicago Defender*. I don't have to tell you that the latter is the more dangerous."

"Former, you mean," said Sally.

"No," said Flip.

The *Chicago Defender* was the largest Negro newspaper in Chicago, and probably the United States. It was the paper Negro train porters most frequently distributed throughout the South. Its editorials urged Negroes from everywhere to move to Chicago at all costs, to come and make the city their home. Its role in fomenting the new migration to Chicago could not be overestimated.

"That newspaper office involves more danger to our investigation, and, therefore, to the city," Flip said. "We are stalking big game. One of the only advantages we have is that the killer does not know we are looking for him. But the killer *will* know if the *Defender* begins to connect the twin murders and prints something. I want to look in their archive for anything about twin murders previous to this summer. Have you two ever been there? It's run out of a converted apartment building. They don't have a proper newsroom like the *Tribune* or the *Daily News*, but they do keep an archive in a couple of closets by the back stair. They'll let you go poking around if you've got a reason."

"You think we'll really find reports of dead twins?" Sally asked.

"Or twins attacked," Flip said with a shrug. "Or twins disappeared. Though, so far, our man hasn't really tried to hide the bodies. I'd say he goes for the opposite. He goes for display."

Sally pursed her mouth and nose, as though she smelled a bad smell.

"Anyhow, Bob Abbot, the editor; he and his team are sharp," Flip continued. "They know me, and it'd be easy for them to find out what I'm sniffing for. Too easy. That's why I want the two of you to go."

"Us?" Sally and Tark said at the same time.

"Yes, and separately," Flip told them. "You'll cover more ground that way, and it will be harder for the newspapermen to guess your aim. Sally, if and when they inquire, you had a relative come up north and you're looking to see if she might have put a notice in a back issue. Tark, you don't say at first why you want to see the old issues. Then, if they press, you confide that another circus posted some ads a few months back—and you're trying to track 'em down and see if they're still hiring. Both of you, make up details as you see fit, but not too many. Go as your real selves. Give your real names. But whatever you do, don't let on that you're looking for anything about twins."

"How far back do we look?" Sally asked.

"This is an all-day thing," Flip stated. "I want you there early—arrive within an hour of one another—and stay until they kick you out."

"Or 'till we find something," Tark said.

"Even then, keep looking," Flip replied.

"What're *you* gonna do tomorrow?" Tark said.

"Ride out to the state pen and have a talk with Claude Chalifour," Flip said.

"Beef-Fist Chalifour!" Tark said brightly, to show he was familiar. "I won money on him. Lost money on him too."

"Did you bet on his fights, or on the outcome of his trial?" Sally asked.

"Both, if you gotta know," Tark told her.

Tark suddenly became thoughtful.

"But Flip. . . what you want with a crazy boxer kept people skinned-up in his basement?"

"Oh," Flip replied. "All sorts of things."

As they prepared to depart, it was grudgingly agreed that Tark—who still could not go home—would spend the evening at the Palmerton.

"I'm serious now," Flip said, taking Sally by the shoulder. "You keep the girls *away* from him. Give him a cot in the kitchen with the cooks. Something like that. If he's awake all night carrying on, doing tricks for the girls, he's useless tomorrow."

"No worries there," Sally said in a confident whisper. "I can put something in his gin . . . make him fall to sleep immediately."

Flip opened his mouth to object to this—perhaps reflexively—but then found he saw no drawback and nodded with a shrug.

The magician and the madam departed.

When they had been gone for some time, Flip retrieved the fireplace poker that he had taken from the home of Miss Heloise. He wondered what it would take to drive it—front to back—through an orphan girl, as the killer had apparently done. He wondered if he had the strength to do such a thing himself. He figured almost certainly not.

For some time, Flip held the fireplace poker, waiting for it to vibrate. Waiting for it to glow. Waiting for it to do *something*. To call to him, as things apparently called to Ursula Green. And yet the poker—near as he could tell—wished to do nothing at all.

Flip thought again of Ursula's words.

The one you seek. Right here. In this very place.

But Flip knew—Ursula being Ursula—that that 'place' could be anywhere.

He went to bed with the poker under his pillow, hoping it might infect his dreams.

The next morning—early, as was his wont—Flip rose, bathed, made coffee, and headed to the precinct station. There he requested that two telephone calls be made—one to the Illinois State Penitentiary in Joliet, and the other to a car service.

As he waited for the car, Flip looked idly for the officers with whom he usually worked. Few passed through, and those who did weren't angling for a conversation today. In fact, Flip noticed, they seemed to struggle just to meet his eyes. Flip worked for Big Bill Thompson now. That fact had become known, he realized. And it meant Flip existed in close proximity to a terrifying power. Now his colleagues were apparently nervous even to ask the details of the assignment. Better, they decided, simply not to poke the sleeping bear.

Inside of an hour, a green Hudson pulled up to the station. It had front and back seats, and a tan cloth roof blown ragged. Seeking to minimize any further awkwardness with the other officers, Flip bounded down the station steps and jumped into the back seat before the driver could kill the engine. The driver was a young man wearing aviator goggles and a long white scarf. The rear of the vehicle had been stocked with metal containers of gasoline.

Flip handed the driver ten dollars.

"State Pen?" the driver asked.

"Yes," said Flip. "You know where that is? I can draw you a map if you want."

The aviator tapped the side of his head with two fingers to say it was all up there.

The roads to Joliet were not good. Outside of cities, most thoroughfares were still not paved properly. They could be brick or cobblestone or simply dirt. Flip braced himself against the side of the car as the terrain under the wheels changed every few minutes.

The sky promised another bright morning with no risk of rain. At least they would not be pushing the car out from the mud. Flip could not say the same for ditches. The young man drove wildly, weaving in and out of traffic, swerving around carts carrying goods, scaring horses (purposefully, it sometimes seemed), and forcing pedestrians to jump back for safety.

Outside the Chicago city limits, the roar of the Hudson's engine steadied and became almost pleasant. As they neared Joliet, they passed crews putting down new asphalt mixed with hot, pungent tar.

The Wilson administration had undertaken a program to pave a single mile of road in each major American town. The thinking went that if the locals saw firsthand how much better paved roads were than dirt, they would swallow a local tax increase to pay for the rest themselves, sparing the federal government the expense.

"Another Seedling Mile?" Flip asked the driver, pointing at the giant black tar-dispenser they had narrowly missed.

"That was last year," the wild driver called with a grin. "It took! They done seeded!"

The Illinois State Penitentiary was a massive structure dating from before the Civil War. It looked shat out of limestone by workers who didn't particularly care what they were building. The architect, for his part, seemed to have been ambivalent about whether he was designing a castle or a mental asylum, and so had settled on the least-attractive elements of both. The facility had tall walls with medieval-looking tower houses at the corners, and a stern administration building rising immediately within. It held over a thousand inmates, all men.

The Hudson pulled into the gravel lot beside the entrance. Flip told the driver to wait, and got out. He took his badge from of his coat and held it up as he approached. The guard at the door looked on doubt-fully, but let him pass with a forced a smile. Most guards at the state pen wanted to be police one day. Being nice to an officer from the city was as good a place as any to start.

Claude Chalifour—known as Beef-Fist or CeeCee behind his back—was, like the first man to settle in Chicago, a Negro from the Caribbean. But unlike Jean Baptiste Point du Sable—who had only ever wanted to sell meat and whiskey and possibly opium to the area's peri-patetic trappers—Claude Chalifour had killed three people, removed their bones, and kept their skins hanging as mementoes inside his gar-den apartment on the South Side of the city. Claude had arrived in Chicago in 1902, eventually finding employment as a beef boner in the stockyards during the day, and as a boxer nights and weekends. (Nobody in Claude's neighborhood had found it odd that such a man should be seen with shoes or hands occasionally caked in blood.) Claude was large, but not a heavyweight. And when he opened his mouth, it became clear to any observer that his mind was childlike.

A deft lawyer had argued that Claude had not murdered the people whose skins had been found hanging in his apartment, but had merely *found* the bodies. (Claude's neighborhood was rough, and corpses *were* known to turn up.) Because of Claude's simple-mindedness—the lawyer further insisted—he had been unable to restrain himself from carrying out the same grisly procedures he practiced—all day, every day—in the stockyards upon animals. A judge had found this argument at least somewhat compelling, and Claude been given life without parole instead of execution.

The Joliet jailers took Flip to a bare concrete room with two wooden stools. On one stool sat Claude Chalifour. He wore manacles and leg irons connected to a steel ring in the center of the floor, adjacent to a dirty drain. Seeing the drain gave Flip renewed purpose; he thought about why he was there.

The jailers closed the metal door behind Flip, locking the two men inside together. There was natural light from the barred windows set into the wall, but no electricity. Claude smiled like a dog hoping for a treat—or at least hoping not to be kicked.

Flip reached into his coat and pulled out a red handkerchief.

"This is called cherry clafoutis," Flip said. "Some nuns gave it to me. Not but a day old. Still soft. You want to smell it?"

"I can smell it from here, mister sir," Claude said, beginning to rock back and forth on his stool.

They sat ten feet apart. Their voices reverberated in the cavernous stone room. The ceiling was curved and white, like the roof of a sewer.

"This is all yours if you talk to me," Flip said. "They tell you who I am?"

Claude shook his head no, shrugging off the question more than answering it. His eyes were now focused quite completely on the red handkerchief. His nostrils sucked up the cake-smell.

"You understand that whatever you tell me today, it don't change your sentence," Flip said. "I can't get you out, but I can't add to your time neither. Suppose you tell me you slit up a whole school full of children they don't know about? Well, it doesn't add a day to your sentence. It don't get you hanged. Understand?"

"I don't have the death sentence, but I am here forever," Claude said in what seemed a practiced recitation.

"Mm hmm," agreed Flip.

Claude's focus was like a magnet. A vein in his forehead began to bulge. It was as though he were willing the handkerchief and its contents to float across the room into his lap.

Flip understood the killer might not be able to concentrate with the treat still in sight. He placed it back inside his coat. Immediately, it was as though a blinding light had been extinguished. Claude blinked and refocused his eyes. He stared hard at Flip. Stared angrily. That was when Flip saw it. Infantile mind or no, this man had the eyes of a killer. These were eyes that had seen unspeakable things.

"Claude, you're the only person I can think of in the city of Chicago who drained a body like you did," Flip began. "Your apartment... It didn't have any special equipment. Just a tiny sink. A tiny sink that backed up easy. But you did it. You drained the bodies without spilling blood everywhere. There were only a few drops on your floor when the police came. Drops that could have come from your work in the stockyards."

Claude, for just a moment, scanned the corners of the room. Then he looked over to the locked metal door. Then he looked back at Flip. His expression wondered if this was some kind of put-on. He did not appear uneasy precisely, but rather baffled that a visitor should bring up such mundane, pedestrian details.

He inclined his head cautiously.

"You want to know... about the *drainin*'?"

"Yes I do," Flip said.

"And that get me the cake?"

Flip shrugged as though it might.

Claude smiled. His demeanor changed. He leaned back a bit on his stool and relaxed like a man at the bar about to tell a good story.

"I don't know if you done a steer before," Claude said. "Seen one slaughtered and de-boned, start to finish? But once you done a cow, a steer... Doing a man ain't nothing."

"Tell me," said Flip. "You want that cake, you'll tell me all about it."

Claude explained how a steer's throat was cut directly after it was stunned or shot in the head with a gun. He said that its legs would kick even after it was dead, and that this could result in a mess or injury, but not if you knew to anticipate it. The cries of pain would cease quickly. The breathing would cease too, but the legs were always the last thing to go.

Claude said if your goal was to avoid making a mess, slaughtering on the ground outdoors was always preferred—if it was a summer day and you had a grassy spot that would soak up the blood, or if you could do it in a river or lake, that was fine—but if you had the means to hang your subject by its feet over a drain, that was also acceptable. Claude told Flip about a hook he had positioned inside his apartment, just above his own modest sink. And how a subject knocked unconscious could be placed upon it with relative ease.

"So how did *you*. . .?" Flip interjected.

Claude laughed a horrible laugh and clapped his hands. He explained that he had killed his victims outdoors, always. Behind his building, in the darkness, over grass. Then he had moved the bodies inside. But he waited until they had been secured above his sink before properly opening the throats.

"You didn't cut off the heads off of your victims," Flip pointed out. It was a statement, not a question.

Claude spun his eyes in a circle, searching the dingy room for an explanation.

"The heads," Flip said.

"I heard you," Claude said. "I took out the skulls. Yes, I did that."

"But. . ." Flip pressed.

"No, you right," the killer allowed. "I didn't properly cut the heads off. With a beast in the slaughterhouse, you got to cut off the head right away. And if it's a steer, the dick and balls. They got to go immediate. Meat gets tainted otherwise, and it don't taste right. I heard a dead man can come. You heard that? I heard a dead man can get a stiff cock. I ain't know if that's true, but a dead steer's dick sure as hell can do some things."

"Let's stay on heads," Flip said. "You ever meet anybody who wanted to cut off heads—heads of *people*—for fun? Maybe switch around heads of two people as a joke? Put the head from one on another's body?"

"Why would anybody do that?" Claude wondered. "That's strange. Wouldn't work neither. You take off a head, it ain't gonna work on another body. Strange, strange."

It was hard for Flip to resist pointing out to Claude that he had kept the whole, dried skins of three humans inside his home—something most people might find 'strange' if anything was.

Instead, Flip said: "You ever hear of Doctor Frankenstein and his monster?"

Claude shrank back in his seat.

"No doctors!" he called. "I don't need one! I feel just fine."

"I only wondered if you knew him."

"Well, I don't," Claude snapped. "Why? What'd he do?"

"He did something very bad," Flip said absently. "Now how about this: You ever hear of a man who had a divot taken out of his head? Like had dent in his head, up by his temples?"

"No," Claude said. "Is that what Dr. Frankenstein look like?"

Flip shrugged to say it was possible.

A few moments passed while Flip thought.

"What else you want to know, then?" the killer said impatiently. "I want that cake."

Flip stared at him hard.

"You're *certain* you never heard of anybody who wanted to cut off a person's head and switch it with another body?" Flip pressed. "Maybe even with a twin brother or sister? Keep it in the family?"

"No," Claude said. "Like I told you, that's strange."

"I see . . ." Flip said.

"So now give it to me," Claude said. "Give me that cake. I done what you asked."

"One more answer first," Flip said.

The killer motioned with his hand to say Flip should bring it on.

"Did the people *you*. . . the people *you* drained. Did they ever . . . *cooperate*?"

"Did they *what*?" said Claude.

"You know," Flip said. "Did they *agree* to let you kill them? Maybe they walked outside with you, so you could stab them before you hung them over your sink? Help you not make such a mess?"

Claude's demeanor changed. He looked Flip up and down disbelievingly. Then he shook his head with a violent series of jerks. Flip realized, astonishingly, that the killer was registering disgust.

"What kind of a man would *agree* to it?" Claude asked.

Flip turned up his palm to say 'You tell me.'

"Naw," Claude said. "They ain't agree to nothin'. They fought me every inch of the way. Fought the whole damn time. That's what made me smile. That's what gave me the hardness in my nether parts. Not so much the killing itself, y'see. Not the draining afterwards, if I'm honest. Nor even the breaking down of the body. But the *fighting*. Watching 'em fight me. Feeling it. Better than boxing by tenfold. I think about it every night in my cell. And that's the one thing they can't take from me. Even though I'm stuck here, in my mind I get to be *there* every night and make them fight for it. And they always lose and I always win. Get to keep that in my head forever."

Flip stood up from the stool. He brushed himself off, arranged his coat, and headed toward the door.

The stark betrayal registered full on Claude's face.

"You gonna give me that cake!" he commanded. "I can smell it! You gonna give it to me!"

Flip knocked hard on the metal door with his bony, Abe Lincoln knuckles.

"We're done!" he called to the guard. "Done in here!"

"You gonna *give* me that cake!" Claude screamed.

The killer stood from his stool and charged forward, seemingly forgetting his leg irons and manacles. After a few feet, the chains went taut and he slammed face first into the concrete floor. He pulled wildly against the irons. The chain itself seemed sure to hold, but the bolt in the floor looked less reliable. The killer's wild tugging scraped the chains hard and kicked up silica dust. It hung in the air, catching the light streaming in through the barred windows.

Flip fingered his 1911. He knew the sound of a gun's report in the cavernous room would be deafening, but stood ready to fire if the killer broke free. Something told Flip their both being Negro would at least make the aftermath go smoothly. There would be paperwork, but not too much.

Before anything could happen, a guard opened the door. It was an old man with a harelip and a single silver eyebrow.

"Y'all done then?" he asked.

"Surely," Flip said, reaching into his coat.

The killer stopped tugging. A glimmer of hope.

"This some fine cake my wife made," Flip said, handing it over to the old man. "Wonder if you wouldn't accept it with my thanks. I appreciate you men arranging this."

The guard took the red handkerchief with a smile.

Claude's howl was like a dog's.

"What'd you do to *him*?" the guard asked through a trifold grin.

The guard's tone said that *whatever* it was, it was just fine.

"Damned if I know," Flip replied. "Some people are a mystery."

Heading back to Chicago in the Hudson, Flip regularly forgot to brace himself when the car took a bump in the road. He was too deep in thought about Claude Chalifour. How there had been so little blood. How it had been a simple thing.

Flip's years on the force told him the mutilation of a person already-dead arose only from one motive, one emotion. . . and that was *hatred*.

Anger—mere anger—faded, usually in the time it took to strangle someone, or in the sobering instant after the stark, sharp cry of a gun. Anybody could kill in anger. But you had to properly *hate* someone to tear off their face afterwards. To mutilate their genitals. Or, Flip assumed, to decapitate them. Maybe you hated them because they had abused you. Maybe because they had stolen your woman or man. Or because they had shamed or embarrassed you. Whatever the case, hatred was what it took.

Then Flip got to thinking about Crespo and the Black Hand.

The Black Hand never mutilated anybody's body. To the contrary, they wanted the victims recognizable. When the Black Hand killed—by poison, a slit throat, or, as was most common, several stab wounds to the back—the victim had always stayed recognizable, because the bodies were the calling cards of the organization. If the Black Hand tapped you, you were either going to pay, or you were going to become *advertising* for them. Either way, they won. Either way, you were useful. You could provide something they wanted.

Flip thought about how the dead twins had been positioned. He thought carefully about each of the murders. The boy and girl in the alley. The boys beside the canal. The pair in the orphanage, with their friend pinned to the wall. The triplets at home. The killer had taken no pains to conceal them, but he *had* taken pains. He had mustered the effort to switch the heads—and in some cases to reattach them—and to make no mess as he did so.

This was a kind of a show, Flip thought. It was like the Black Hand in that respect. It was meant to be seen by someone. But . . .who was the audience? Who was supposed to see what the killer had accomplished? Was it the families that would discover these stomach-churning mutilations? The cops like him who would be called in afterwards? Or some entirely unknown audience, perhaps a private one?

Flip's history was spotty, but he knew Egyptians had once mutilated their dead. He knew of mummies. Organs in jars. Skins dried with salt. Ornate tombs that took armies of slaves to build. Flip wondered if his killer could be operating on an extension of this thinking. Did he believe he was preparing his victims for an afterlife? Helping them? That was one possibility. But simple punishment seemed a possibility too. If ritual mutilation could whisk someone up to paradise, surely it could also ensure you found your way to the other place. Flip knew certain religions held that a stained body could render you irredeemable. That a tattooed man was cursed if he was a Jew. That a Mohammedan could not find paradise if he had eaten pork. That a follower of the Buddha could not reach true enlightenment if he consumed garlic.

And there—just as the road under the Hudson's tires began to firm, and the skyline of Chicago came back into view—Flip began to wonder if he had found it. A hate for these twins that went beyond the moment of death. A hate intended to ensure they would find no peace in the afterlife. A hate that hoped to confuse god or the devil with switched heads. Who was who, and how should they be judged?

The Hudson pulled up in front of the precinct station where Flip had begun his day.

"This is good?" the driver asked. "I can drop you somewhere else. For what you paid me, that's no problem. I can even wait and take you home after."

"That's not necessary," Flip told him. "Thank you."

The driver nodded and replaced his goggles. The man seemed to relish his job. With his eyewear and scarf, he looked as though he already fancied himself in an aeroplane, cruising high above European fields.

The way things were going, Flip wondered if he might soon get his wish.

NINE

For the rest of the day, Flip made queries and calls, checked files and logs, but his department had no arrest record of a man with a divot in his head. That trail was cold.

Flip stopped at a grocery on his way home, then found Tark and Sally Battle sitting out on his porch. He could tell from their faces that their own searches had been likewise fruitless.

"Come on in and tell me about it," he said to them. "I'll make us some supper."

"I came up empty, Flip," Sally told him. "Tark believes he found something that's *maybe* related, but I think he's seeing things that aren't there."

"Oh really?" Flip said as they began to climb the stair.

"Yes, really," Sally affirmed.

"And what do *you* think you found," Flip asked Tark.

"I didn't find any articles about decapitated twins," Tark began. "But I *did* find articles about decapitations—a couple of them. I was thinking that maybe our killer could have wanted to practice on *one* person before he moved on to *two*."

Flip set down his groceries beside his stove.

"It's possible," Flip said. "He could have wanted to start with just one person. That's not out of bounds to imagine."

"But he kills *twins*," insisted Sally.

"Yes, he does that *now*," Flip told her. "But he's going to want to make sure that he does it right. Does it *correctly*. If that means a practice run back in the day, I think he'll do it."

"What did you learn in Joliet?" Tark said, a bottle of gin suddenly resting on the table before him.

"That the roads are getting good," Flip said, slicing vegetables and meat. "Better, anyway."

"And that boxer?" Tark pressed.

Flip thought for a moment as he sliced up a carrot.

"He didn't tell me who our man is," Flip said. "But the conversation made me think on some things. For example, I think our killer has some knowledge of anatomy, or has worked in the stockyards like Chalifour. I think our killer knows how to drain a body—either outside, or over a sink. Two of the killings happened indoors, and there were sinks and pipes to carry the blood away. I think our killer is taking care to do these things. I think we know that much."

Tark opened his mouth to say something, but then thought better. Flip continued to chop vegetables.

"Often, I find I am able to crack a case when I review all the small steps a criminal must take in order to complete the deed," Flip said. "I am trying to take myself through how our man did these murders. I am trying to imagine his actions so I can imagine *him*. The last two killings—the orphanage girls and the triplets—were indoors and clean. I am thinking about why. Maybe the draining made the reattaching easier. I am also interested in how he has switched the heads and tried to reattach them in *different ways* each time. In the first crime scene, he places one where the other ought to be. Just places them there, on the ground. In the next, he uses a spike to hold them fast. Then barbed wire. Then a proper needle and thread. It is almost as though he is attempting something. . . He is experimenting. Getting closer each time."

"You don't think he believes he can switch heads. . . and the people keep on living?" Sally asked, putting her hand to her mouth.

"Even Claude Chalifour dismissed that idea," Flip said. "I think everybody knows that wouldn't work. Well. . . almost everybody."

Flip tapped a wooden spoon hard against a pot where water boiled. Sally and Tark jumped.

"Tark, why don't you tell me what you think you found in the *Defender* archives?" Flip said.

Tark quickly produced notes from his pocket and began to read.

"Wendell Wentworth, a Negro, aged 32, was found with his head separated from his body on Western Avenue, behind his cart. It is believed his neck may have become entangled in horse tacking, and his mare started unexpectedly, pulling long and hard enough to cause the fatal injury."

Tark smiled triumphantly, took a slug of gin, and set this first note on the table. Then he held a second handwritten card up to his eyes.

"Mary Jo Hall, 15, a Negro girl, died tragically in a fall from the roof of the Masonic Temple at the corner of Randolph Street and State Street, where she was employed. The young girl died instantly from the fall, as was apparent immediately to any onlookers, the force of the impact detaching her head from her body. Her head was found several feet away in the median landscaping. Her mother said the girl had been sad and despondent."

Flip put a lid on the pot and let his stew begin cook. Then he joined Tark and Sally back at the table.

"Neither of those are very good, Tark," Flip said. "How far back did you get?"

"I tried to go as far back as 1912," Tark said. "And Sally took 1912 to 1910. We divided up the work, to be more efficient."

Sally nodded to say that this was true.

"You say you 'tried to. . .'" pressed Flip.

"It's hard to read every newspaper," Tark said. "Even if you are just looking for headless twins."

"And *you* found nothing at all?" Flip asked Sally.

The madam shook her head.

"I expect I found as much as Tark. Only I had the sense to ignore the horse accidents and suicides."

"Hey!" Tark objected. "What if someone made them *look* like accidents? Maybe that's what he *wanted* people to think."

"It doesn't seem likely," Flip told him.

Flip suddenly paused and his eyes went to the open window—the one all the way across the apartment that looked down on the front stoop and street below. Tark and Sally had never seen a man's ears prick up quite like a dog's, but they were seeing that now. (Tark would have sworn Flip's ears actually moved.)

"Tark, make sure my pot don't boil over," Flip said softly, already moving toward the window.

Flip reached the window, saw something immediately, and then raced to the staircase.

Sally and Tark looked at one another and followed after him. (Sally tarried long enough to move the stewpot off the stove.)

At the bottom of the staircase, Flip threw open the front door to his building. An envelope had been placed on his door with his name scrawled across it. On the steps leading away were two people. One was a man in trousers and wrinkled shirtsleeves, and the other a boy no more than eleven years old.

Flip smiled and cleared his throat.

Joseph Singer and his unofficial assistant turned back around.

"See, Mister Singer," Rufus said. "I *told* you this was where he lived."

Flip's own smile fell away quickly. He plucked the sealed envelope from his door and approached the pair.

"You got my magician in there?" Singer asked. "That note really for him."

Flip considered bluffing, or failing to answer the query. Yet this option collapsed entirely when Tark and Sally arrived at the bottom of the staircase, excited and curious.

"Mister Singer, there he be!" the youngster pointed out.

"I see him," the ringmaster assured the child.

Tark pushed past Sally and Flip, storming up to his employer.

"My brother all right?" the magician asked. "You need to tell me."

"I ain't heard otherwise," said Singer. "But it's plain there are those who still have an eye on finding him. And you."

"Why?" said Flip. "What's happened?"

Singer paused a moment and nodded to himself. The expression said that he would get straight to the heart of the matter.

"Now I didn't see it firsthand," Singer began, "but that man came around again asking after Ike. The same man from before. Nobody seen where he come from, and nobody seen where he go. Wore a suit. Wore his homburg low."

"I talked to him!" Rufus announced proudly, shifting from foot to foot with excitement.

Singer nodded.

"What did you talk about?" Flip asked, crouching down in front of the boy.

"Where Ike was," Rufus replied. "I said I didn't know, because that's the truth. Then the man said he wanted to see the caravan of the Amazing Drextel Tark. I showed him. The man knocked on the door, but there wasn't anybody inside. Then the man said he would come back another time. Then he went away."

"And when did this happen?" Flip asked.

"Near to sunset yesterday," said Rufus.

"Could he have been a friend of Ike's?" Flip said. "An acquaintance?"

Flip already knew the answer, but wanted to gauge Singer and the boy.

"Ike didn't—doesn't—know anybody other than his brother," Singer said. "Drextel can vouch for that. And I never saw this man before. Drextel has his admirers—much as I hate to admit it—but nobody ever comes around to ask for *Ike*."

Tark looked anxious. He put his hands on his hips and glanced from Rufus to Singer to Flip.

"We thought you would want to know," Singer said. "That's all. Whoever he is—whatever you done—that man still looking for you."

"Tark hasn't done anything," Flip said sternly. "And also, how did you find me? Nobody used to know where I lived. This week I seem to have become the easiest man to locate in Chicago."

"We just asked at the station," Singer said, not seeing what the fuss was about. "We just gave your name."

With an eye to helping the mayor, it seemed the cops on the South Side would let anybody know where to find Joe Flippity. And Flip knew that door swung both ways. If the killer wanted to come at him, well. . .

Flip sighed in frustration.

"Is there anything more?" Flip asked, turning back to Singer. "Any details you aren't telling me? Anything else this man did?"

Singer looked defensive and squinted.

"No. . . I . . . Damn, son. I thought you would *want* to know. We only tryna help. I tryna get my magician back."

Singer's voice fell to a whisper.

"I ain't like to say this in front of him—because he'll want a damn raise—but the kid is a draw. One of the best acts I got."

Tark heard every word.

"If I'm one of the best, then how come you pay me what the horse trainers make?"

"See what I mean?" Singer said. "See? And you get paid what you get paid cause you still a boy, Tark. Damn! Have a little patience. It's coming. That's coming."

"Who else saw the man in the homburg, other than Rufus?" Flip pressed.

"I. . . uh. . . maybe a couple of my roughnecks," Singer said. "The man didn't really talk to them. Not like he talked to Rufus. And all he said to anyone is he's looking for Ike and the Amazing Drextel Tark."

Flip nodded seriously.

"Did he ever take his hat off?" Tark asked. "Did you see a hole in his head?"

Singer's neck jerked back in surprise.

"A hole? What do you mean? Rufus, you see a hole?"

"No sir," Rufus said. "I didn't see any hole."

"You've given us a great deal to think about, Mr. Singer," Flip said. "I want to thank you for taking the time to come here. Tell me, how long will your circus be town?"

"We're off for a week," Singer said, scratching his neck. "Little more. Then we do a couple of shows here in the neighborhood. Then we go on up to Milwaukee."

"In that case," Flip said, "you can plan on hearing from us sooner rather than later."

Singer and Rufus departed. Back in Flip's modest rooms, the trio sat around the table and ate second-rate stew.

"Damn," Tark said. "This why you so thin? There ain't nothin' to this. Too many carrots. Hardly any meat at all."

Sally Battle ate silently and politely. Flip had never been taught how to cook. Books from the library had only taken him so far.

Flip looked at Sally without appearing to. This woman ran the most successful Negro brothel in the city, which meant it was nearly the most successful brothel, period. She could afford to eat at fine restaurants every night of the week—and maybe she *did*, for all he knew—yet she was here. In these modest, reeking policeman's quarters, eating soup made from old vegetables and beef scraps from a tin bowl with a measuring spoon.

He thought again of the photograph of her twins.

"You're *sure* that Ike is safe where you put him?" Flip asked the magician.

"As sure as I was before," Tark said. "He's still somewhere across the border, if that's what you mean."

Tark said the word 'border' as though Indiana were a distant and savage land.

"He's with people I trust," Tark continued. "There's no reason to think he could be found."

"Is there any chance that Ike will return—or *be* returned—before tomorrow night?" Flip asked.

Tark considered this carefully, looking like a card-player wondering whether to raise, fold, or call.

"No," he eventually answered. "You don't need to worry about this so much, Flip."

"In that case, I have determined what we should do next," the policeman declared.

Sally and Tark looked on intently. Flip finished his soup silently before explaining himself.

"Tomorrow morning I will go and do some things alone," Flip said to them. "Then I'll have to prepare for what we're going to do tomorrow night . . . together."

Tark and Sally looked at one another.

"With *your* day, Tark, you will go out and buy an eye patch and a floppy Irish hat like your brother wears. Use the money I gave you. Then you're gonna spend time practicing. You know how to practice. If he can be you, then you can damn-straight be him. Buy yourself a mirror to practice in front of."

Tark cocked his head to the side.

"You intend to-"

"To use you as a lure?—as bait?—yes," Flip said. "We'll tell Singer what we're going to do, and position you at the edge of his circus camp. Isolate that part of the field. Make it feel like it would be easy for our mystery man to come and find you. To prey on the one who is slower and duller. And then when he makes his move . . ."

With a glance, Flip indicated his 1911.

"I suppose I could do that," Tark said thoughtfully.

"What I don't fully know is . . . if our killer will want to murder just *one* of you," Flip said in a tone of distant, academic conjecture.

Tark swallowed hard.

"That's to say, does it have to be both at the same time?" Flip continued. "So far, he's killed people who looked identical *together.* I don't know if that's important. If he can kill Ike, but not you—or you, but not Ike—will he do it? Or, if he's in a situation where he can kill both of you—*but not cut off your heads*—would he act *then*? I . . . I'm trying to figure these parts out."

Tark looked at Flip nervously and had a swig from his bottle.

"Now Sally, what would be helpful from you-" Flip began.

"Tomorrow is Saturday, yes?" Sally interjected.

Flip nodded.

She sighed.

"I can help in the morning if you need, but. . . I will have to spend tomorrow night at the Palmerton. There is an upcoming engagement I cannot break."

"Fine," said Flip. His tone, in that single word, reminded Sally that this was her choice. All of it. Sitting here, eating terrible soup in his apartment, drinking tenth-rate gin with a magician, was not something he needed her for. She could come and go as she pleased.

"What else then?" asked Tark.

"I suggest you go take a walk," Flip replied. "Find a bed. There's nothing else to be done. Prepare for tomorrow night. Get your mind right."

The next morning Flip skipped up the steps of the apartment complex that housed the *Chicago Defender* at seven o'clock sharp, and made his way inside. The interior smelled like newsprint and tobacco and coffee. He asked the first person he saw if Robert Sengstacke Abbott was yet in his office. The receptionist—young and new—nodded yes and waited for Flip to identify himself. She became alarmed when he merely brushed past into the crowded newsroom. Only the intercession of Abbott himself—opening the door to his office, coffee cup in hand—prevented her from raising her voice.

"Bob!" Flip said brightly.

"Hey, there he is," Abbott said, a genuine grin stretching ear to ear. "Number one lawman on the South Side."

Robert Sengstacke Abbott, the editor and publisher of the *Defender*, was about forty-five years old. He wore a tidy mustache and was round-faced. He favored felt bowlers and straw fedoras, and was seldom seen outside of a three-piece suit. He had short hair, very dark skin, and piercing eyes.

"Step into my office," Abbott said. "My warm-up can wait."

Flip followed Abbott back inside the converted bedroom that served as his office. Every inch of the large desk within was covered with typewritten pages, newspaper clippings, or handwritten notes. Manuscripts and copies of the *Defender* were stacked against the walls in piles tall as a man. Behind his desk hung a framed photograph of Booker T. Washington. On the wall opposite was a print of W.E.B. Du Bois.

The front page of the Saturday issue was laid out on Abbott's chair. The headline screamed: *PHOTO-PLAY BOUND TO AROUSE RACIAL HATRED!*

"You seen this nonsense?" Abbott asked, catching Flip's glance. *"Birth of a Nation,* they call it. A three-hour movie designed to make the audience feel in favor of clansmen."

"Must've missed it," Flip said. "I go to comedies mostly. Charlie Chaplin. Fatty Arbuckle good too."

"Harold Lloyd, then?" Abbott asked, always enthusiastic to talk about the cinema. "If you like those two, you must like Lloyd."

Flip shook his head.

"Naw. Not Lloyd. Face looks too much like a ghost. Makes me uneasy."

Abbott shrugged. Each had his tastes.

"What can I help you with, Flip?" Abbott asked, moving aside the fresh issue of the *Defender* and plopping down in his chair.

Flip understood Abbott was a busy man.

"Were you here in the office yesterday?" Flip asked.

"I was," Abbott said.

"And did you notice a pair asking to root through your archives?"

Abbott smiled.

"*Uncommonly* good-looking woman, if I recall. . . and then—if my memory also serves—a young man I've seen do tricks in Singer's circus. Though, did you hear they've changed their name?"

"I did hear that," Flip told him.

"Everything is positioning in the marketplace," Abbott declared.

"Would it surprise you to know that that woman was Sally Battle?" Flip said. "Of the Palmerton House?"

Abbott nodded slowly and carefully, as if struggling to remain neutral about such a person and place.

Abbott was that most uncommon strain of man—most uncommon in Flip's world, at any rate—who seemed genuinely to have no vice. There was no battle going on inside of Robert Sengstacke Abbott. The endless, epic war between pleasure and temperance was not being fought on his soil. In fact, he seemed numb to just about everything not to do with publishing his newspaper.

Flip did not necessarily see this as indicative of any moral merit. If you avoided vice simply because you lacked the receptors for it, did that really set you up to claim virtue? The fact that over on South State Street there was a building filled with the most beautiful Negro women in the world—and you could fuck them for money—might have registered for Abbott in the same way a cat would appreciate the architecture of a cathedral, or a dog might consider a Rembrandt.

"I came here to tell you that they were working for me," Flip told Abbott. "*With* me, I should say."

"What's going on?" the editor asked.

"I'll tell you," Flip said. "But do me a kindness. Let's skip the part where I remind you of all the favors I've done you over the years. All the times I gave you information you needed for your stories. When I tipped you on who your reporters could press for answers, and where to find them. Not to mention all those times you've used me as an anonymous source."

"I feel such favors have been fairly repaid," Abbott said stoically. "I don't need to remind you of *those* instances, either."

"Good," the policeman said. "Then we both have good memories. I sent them here because I hoped they would find things quietly, and I wouldn't have to tell you what is happening in the city. What is *truly* happening. . ."

There! Lo and behold!

A spark shone in Abbott's eyes. The hunger. The *want*. The way other men might have looked at a woman, or a tall glass of beer, or a steak dinner—now Abbott looked at Flip.

The newspaperman *did* desire. He desired stories. He desired that things kept secret and safe from prying eyes should be neither. Yes, thought Flip. Robert Sengstacke Abbott now would come truly alive.

"I'm surprised," Abbott said thoughtfully, trying to conceal his evident interest. "I'd have thought I'd have earned that. We are fair and honest in our representations of law enforcement. We portray the Chicago Police in a sympathetic light whenever it is warranted. We have been careful to outline the unfairness endured by Negro officers, for example. You know what we do here, Joe Flippity. We're not a mystery."

"No, you're not," Flip said. "But you didn't let me finish. I said I hoped I wouldn't have to tell you . . . Not that I'm not going to."

As Abbott sat back in his chair, like a king in a paper-filled throne room, Flip described carefully the case before him. He included his personal meeting with the mayor, and even the budget he had been given. He discussed his conversation at the settlement charity, and the search for the man with the divot in his head. The lone detail omitted—as ever—was his consultation with Ursula Green.

"You want it bad, don't you Bob?" Flip said as he concluded. "I see it in your eyes."

"These *are* remarkable goings-on," Abbott admitted, drumming his fingers very rapidly on his desk. "A Negro officer placed in charge of a case of this magnitude . . . with the potential to impact all Negro policing in the future. And . . . at the same time . . . Mutilation! Murder! An emergency in our community. An immediate risk to the welfare of citizens. Something that would be *immoral* to keep away from the public. . ."

There he went.

Flip sighed and shook his head.

"Bob, first of all, he only kills identical twins. Second of all, if you run a story, it will make it more difficult for me to catch him. He'll understand he is being pursued. *That* would be the immoral thing to do."

"Then. . . why have you come here?" Abbott asked, seeming genuinely puzzled.

"Because you know better than anyone what is happening on the South Side of this city," Flip said. "You have information nobody else does. You got more feelers than the Chicago Police for damn sure. There have been four killings of Negro twins, Bob. Four that I know of. I want to make certain there haven't been others. To catch this beast, I have to know as much about him as I can."

Abbott rubbed his chin with fingers that were almost entirely covered with pen and printing ink.

"Off the top of my head?" Abbott said. "No. Nothing. I can think of no story we've ever done about twins being mutilated, and my memory is what they call photographic. I can recall with great clarity from the present back to, oh, 1910 or thereabouts. Before that, if it's not photographic, it's still very good. And I tell you, I surely would have remembered something like this."

"What about twins, generally," the policeman pressed.

Abbott considered it.

"Yes," he finally pronounced, "I do seem to recall something involving twins and murder once upon a time. It does not meet the exact profile you are looking for, but. . ."

"Good," said Flip. "That's something, anyhow. I'm going to need that information. Whatever you have."

A rapid and frantic knocking erupted at Abbott's door. It was summarily thrown open before an answer could come. A young man stood on the other side. He had a pencil behind his ear and excitement seemed to pulsate out from him.

"Mr. Abbott!" the young man cried. "The mayor's forged an agreement with the rail workers. There will be no strike!"

"He did *what*?" Abbott said, rising to his feet. "That strike was a sure thing."

"They met in secret—all night at the Congress Plaza," the reporter said. "My source tells me the mayor didn't let them leave until they'd hammered it out. Kept them there like prisoners 'till morning."

"Very good," said Abbott, as though praising a star pupil. "This is tomorrow's front page. I want you to get in touch with Oscar De Priest and get a quote about what this will mean for folks on the South Side who take trains in to work."

No sooner did the reporter begin a retreat from Abbott's office, than a middle-aged woman stuck her head into the doorway to replace him. She held up a newspaper.

"Bob? The *Tribune*'s done it. In today's edition."

"Done what, Cheryl?" Abbott asked.

"Called the mayor 'Kaiser Bill,'" she said. "You told us we had to wait for the *Tribune* to do it first, if we wanted to do it. Well they have. And *I do*."

The publisher rolled his eyes and shifted in his chair.

"The mayor loves him some Germans," Abbott said to Flip. "Won't rightly say which side he supports in this war, leastways."

"We could do our own variation," Cheryl suggested. "What about 'Wilhelm Thompson'? Something like that."

"I'll think about it," Abbott said. "But try to come up with something better than that, eh?"

"Fine, but you should read this," Cheryl said, and tossed the *Trib* with practiced motion onto the mountain of paper on his desk.

Abbott turned to Flip.

"I should really attend to things," Abbott said. "It's like this all day. And once it gets going, it doesn't stop 'till the sun goes down."

"That's fine," Flip said. "We may have a line on this man—this killer—tonight. I have a plan. If it works, you'll hear from me. You'll get the full scoop. But in case it doesn't, can you have somebody write up what you know about other twins? Have it delivered here."

Flip took out his notepad and jotted.

"Surely, surely," Abbott said, placing the note in the pocket of his vest.

Flip thanked the publisher and turned to leave. Outside, other members of the newsroom had their eyes on Abbott's door, waiting for a chance to pounce.

"Should I leave it open?" Flip asked.

"Might as well," said Abbott. "And Flip?"

The policeman bent an ear.

"You will owe me. For not printing this now? Something this big? This wipes out all the other favor-accounts we ever had. We start over, with you in debt to me big. You got it?"

"Fine," said Flip. "Just send over what you have. And let me know if that 'photographic' mind of yours remembers anything more."

Flip left the offices of the *Defender* and headed down the block to a store called Percival's Dry Goods. The sun rose above him. The morning, yet again, was unfolding stultifyingly clear and hot. As he walked, Flip allowed himself to consider the benefits of a position like Abbott's. Namely, all of the thrill, and none of the risk. It was a safe job. Newspaper publishers had been shot in the Wild West, but *never* in Chicago. Never east of the Mississippi. If Abbott were to be assassinated for something he exposed, it would be a citywide scandal. If a policeman like Flip were to be shot, it would be nothing.

Nothing at all.

Flip reached Percival's Dry Goods as it was opening and went inside. It was the worst, most disreputable store of its kind that Flip knew. Almost everything it carried was both dirty *and* stolen. (If you had stolen something in good shape, you didn't take it to Percival.)

The moment the proprietor behind the counter saw the lawman, he began to protest in a thousand different, simpering ways of his innocence.

Flip waved a hand.

"Ain't here for that," Flip said, not even bothering to look at the man. "You show me your dirtiest dungarees. Worst ones you got. If I look too tall for 'em, don't you pay that any mind."

The proprietor moved cautiously, still searching for the trick or trap.

He walked around his counter to help Flip find the clothes he needed. There were some thin choices on a crooked shelf in the back.

Flip selected what he wanted, paid, and left the store.

That evening, Flip and Tark arrived together at the fallow lot that held the Singling Brothers circus. Singer himself was waiting to receive them, Rufus by his side.

"Holy cats!" the youngster said. "I thought you really *was* Ike when I seen you comin'. You got the eye patch, the crazy-eye, and even the walk!"

"It is a fine counterfeit," Singer offered, looking the young man up and down.

"Wasn't that hard to figure," Tark said. "I been watching my brother all my life."

"And what are *you* supposed to be?" Singer asked, turning to Flip.

Flip wore a pair of soiled blue jeans with the pockets straight in the front like a cowboy. He had ancient work boots that looked ready to sit up and start talking on their own; they were covered in mud and blood, and had almost certainly been worn in the stockyards. Flip's workshirt was nineteenth-century, like something an Amish person would wear. It was also covered in mud.

"I'm supposed to be precisely nothin'," Flip told Singer, as if this should be obvious.

"You early," Rufus said. "He ain't come 'till past sunset."

"He could be watchin' us now," Flip cautioned. "I don't think he is, but you never know."

Rufus looked around nervously. Flip smiled.

"Show me where you saw him yesterday," Flip commanded. "The very spot."

Rufus did, walking them to the side of the circus grounds.

"Came out of those bushes and trees over there," Rufus explained. "Then he walked directly up to me."

"All right," said Flip, rubbing his jaw, guessing at the trajectory of it. "He must have approached through the empty lots past the trees. What we're gonna do . . . Tark? There you are. What we're gonna do is position 'Ike' by the edge of the bushes. Give him a stool to sit on. Maybe have him close his eyes—his eye—and look like he's asleep. If the man comes again, he'll see he doesn't need to interact with the rest of the circus. If his goal is to get to Ike, he can do that without taking but a few steps out into the field."

Tark cocked his head to the side.

"I'm waiting for the part where you say you're gonna stop him before he kills me."

"I'll be right over there, by the edge of the caravans," Flip said.

"What you gonna do if he makes a sudden move on me?" Tark asked emphatically. "What if he tries to cut my head off? Can you shoot him from there with your gun?"

Flip looked from the edge of the field over to the circus caravans.

"Probably not," he said. "Liable to hit you just as soon as him."

Tark crossed his arms to show this was not satisfying.

"But here's the thing . . ." Flip continued. "I don't think he's going to attack you. From what I've seen, that's not how he works. What I think he'll do is try to talk to you. I think he'll ask if he can come back later in the evening, when Drextel Tark is also around. Or maybe he'll ask if you and your magician brother will go meet with him somewhere. He might even offer you money to do it."

"So he can cut off our heads," Tark said.

Flip looked left and right in a way that said this should be obvious.

"How long until sunset?" Tark asked.

"A while still," said Flip. "Couple hours at least."

"Can I drink gin while I wait?" asked Tark.

"Does your brother drink gin?" Flip asked.

"My brother drinks *everything*," Tark said.

Flip indicated it would be acceptable.

Tark produced a clear glass bottle from his brother's clothes and took his first sip of the evening.

They waited for hours. Tark found a small circular podium—like a lion might sit on in an animal act—and placed it near the edge of the field. He took a seat upon it, partook heavily of his juniper beverage, and appeared to fall into an authentic doze. Heavy, crepuscular rays cut between buildings and lit up the brownfields orange and red. The sun moved low and large in the sky.

Flip sat in the shade of a broken wagon wheel. It was the furthest from Tark that he could sit and still trust his eyes on the trees and scrub. He would not, at this distance, be able to rescue Tark from an assailant with any surety, yet he felt unconcerned for the magician's safety. His killer was a man who planned carefully and who struck only when the stars were right. And these stars were decidedly wrong.

If the killer approached from the wooded place as he had before, he would hesitate at the treeline upon encountering Tark (so unexpectedly close and vulnerable). It would be startling. Then, probably, he would sense that something was off and back away. (He was smart. Flip knew this if he knew anything.) But by then it would be too late, and Flip would move on him easily. The sleeping magician, though? No, he was safe. Hundreds of people in Chicago were at risk of being assaulted or worse this night. Flip did not think Drextel Tark was one of them.

Flip watched the treeline carefully. He looked hard and unerringly, but saw not so much as a city rat. Certainly, Flip glimpsed no man with a fine suit and a divot in his head peeking through the trees.

As the sun dipped lower, Flip sensed footsteps approaching from behind. The circus workers had been warned to stay away, but had not been told precisely why. Flip glanced back and saw Singer approaching. The ringmaster held a thermos.

"Thought you might like some soup," Singer said.

Flip accepted the metal container.

"We takin' bets on what gon' happen," the circus proprietor informed him.

Flip raised an eyebrow as he sucked down hot broth.

"Two to one is he falls over," Singer explained. "But Tark falls over all the time when he's in his cups. That's easy money. Three to one is somebody shows up—anybody. Five to one, the man from yesterday shows. Ten to one, there's some kind of rumpus—a fistfight, like. And twenty to one is . . . you shoot somebody."

Flip lowered the soup.

"Only twenty to one?" he asked.

Singer nodded and smiled.

"I didn't say shoot him *dead*," Singer clarified, looking out across the darkening field to where the magician dozed. "Just that you shoot him. Truth is—between the animals and the men—violence tends to go down on this here corner. And it's been quiet for a while. Too quiet. We due."

Flip handed the thermos back to Singer.

"'Course, the other half of it is—a lot of my people would like to see some violence on Tark. Not too much, now. . . Just a little. He don't do no heavy lifting, and he gets his own caravan. Lot of folks jealous of that. I don't know that I'm exempt."

"I thought you liked Tark," Flip said.

"He's a draw. Good at magic, and only gonna get better. But. . . Damn. I don't know. Something about somebody that *good* that *young*. . . It just make you want to see them get knocked around. Nothing fatal. But if Tark could end the night with a black eye, there'd be lots of smiles around here tomorrow, I tell you that."

"I don't think anyone is going to visit us tonight," Flip said, repositioning himself beneath the wagon wheel. "I think the only way your boy gets a black eye is if he falls off that animal stand."

"So you're saying it *could* happen?" Singer said with a grin.

Flip smiled back.

"I'd give it even money."

Tark did not fall, and neither did a strange man appear. The closest Flip got to excitement was when a cluster of seagulls from the lake swooped down and buzzed Tark. Yet the magician was in too great a stupor even to notice.

When the sun had set completely and the stars began to come out, Flip resigned himself fully to the operation's failure. He stood from under the wheel and stretched his legs. His right knee gave an audible crack, as it sometimes did when the weather changed. He stalked over to where the magician sat.

Tark looked dead asleep, but opened a careful eye when Flip drew near.

"Nothing?" Tark asked.

"Nothing," Flip answered.

Tark relaxed and let his legs dangle off of the stand.

"I ain't sure he's real."

"What's that?" Flip replied.

Tark stood up and began to do his own stretching and bending. He winced several times, probably just from the gin.

"I don't know for certain," the magician said to the policeman. "I just get this feeling, now, that maybe he's not real."

"You're not making sense," Flip told him. "People saw him. He talked to Rufus."

Tark waved this detail away as if it were inconsequential.

"I had a dream just now," Tark said. "Scary one. I was sitting right here in the dream—just like I done—and you were right over there underneath the wagon wheel."

"Are you sure it was a dream?" Flip asked, giving the line of trees one last, hopeful scan. "Because if the next part is a bunch of birds flew in your face, then it wasn't."

"I'm sure it was a dream," the magician insisted. "There was a thing in it, like a monster. It looked like bugs you see crawling through the grass—the little critters—only it was a hundred feet high. Two hundred. Real tall, Flip. Standing over me. It was coming in from the lake, walking on land."

"That's a big critter," Flip said.

"Yes," agreed Tark. "With its head like a triangle pointed down. And triangle eyes, too. And it was doing what you were, Flip. It was looking at me. Watching over me. And it was hoping the man with the divot in his head would show up."

"It was hoping?" Flip said. "You could tell that?"

Tark nodded.

"Maybe you shouldn't drink so much," Flip told him.

"Why that got to be the first thing people say whenever I have a dream? Or my back hurts? Or my tooth aches? Shows what people know. A drink will make a dream like that go away, not the other way around."

From the corner of his eye, Flip noticed Singer sauntering out onto the field. The circus owner sensed that the evening's affair was at an end.

"No bites?" he asked as he drew near the pair. "Didn't catch your fish? My magician's kind of puny. Maybe you need bigger bait."

Tark sneered.

"No, we didn't see him," Flip conceded. "I don't know how you wagered, but I hope you won."

"You kidding?" Singer said with a toothy grin. "The house always wins. Just a matter of how much."

Tark paced about like a long-legged bird, getting the blood back in his extremities. Flip surveyed the horizon intently. Singer shook his head, as if this were all very strange.

Then, suddenly, Singer grew still. His eyes locked onto something. Without warning, the circus owner raced to the edge of the treeline.

The spot to where Singer galloped looked dark and filthy—but, most importantly, empty. Flip wondered if the man would be bitten by rats.

"Now what's *this*?" Singer called.

Flip and Tark jogged over.

There were no rats, but there was, lost in the high grass, a half-crushed hat. A homburg. The crown looked trampled by a single foot-fall. Singer bent down to pick it up.

"Let me," said Flip.

"There could be rats underneath," Singer warned. "These trees are full of them."

"I know that," said Flip, carefully grasping the hat.

The policeman examined the homburg in the small light there was left. No maker's mark. It was fine but old. Well-worn. Plenty of dried sweat on the band inside.

"That's him," Singer said. "That belongs to the man who came by yesterday."

"You sure about that?" asked Flip.

Singer nodded enthusiastically. He went for Rufus, and a moment later returned with the boy. Rufus was keen to make the identification.

"That's the man's hat!" Rufus adjudged. "Sure as I know anything!"

"Thank you," Flip said.

Flip tucked the hat under his arm for safe keeping.

"I bet he was watching from the trees tonight, and a rat came up and scared him," Rufus opined. "His hat fell off and he couldn't find it again."

Flip tried to gauge the position of the hat in relation to the wagon wheel. A blind spot, perhaps, where Flip could not have seen a visitor? He could not be sure. Had the killer come after all?

"What if the hat fell off earlier?" Flip wondered. "Remind me, where did he leave—the strange man—when he went away yesterday?"

"Right though here," Rufus said. "Right where we're standing now."

"Man could have left his hat before," Flip said. "Or tonight."

Singer looked around.

"Hmm," Singer said. "Let's keep this between us then, yeah? I ain't sure how it affects the betting pool."

They began to head back toward the circus tents.

"You think I'm gonna get my magician back anytime soon?" Singer asked.

"Too early to tell," Flip answered. "Way too early to tell."

TEN

The feeling stayed with him. The feeling that Ursula Green was animated by something larger and stronger than herself. Something that existed outside her small, frail body. Something that hid in the darkened rooms, and waited alongside her. That the tentacles of a powerful leviathan extended up into her dress or shawl (or whatever the matted rags she wore had once been), and that only their slithering manipulations allowed her to speak and move and perform her magicks.

Something other. Something beyond.

Flip counted out another thousand dollars and put it on the table. He lifted the crystal scrying ball, using it like a paperweight, and brusquely slid the green bills underneath. Then he exhaled in a single, frustrated sigh.

Ursula's marine-animal laughter began almost immediately.

"It's only been three days!" she croaked.

"A man with a divot in his head," Flip said. "Start talking."

He looked back down to where he had placed his money. Money which, he now saw, had already vanished. Because of course it had.

Ursula could not have had the strength to lift the ball, much less to do so deftly and silently.

But something had.

"Divot right *here*," Flip continued, pointing to his own pate. "He's Negro. He's middle aged. He shops at fancy tailors. Yeah?"

"There are men like *that* all over this city," Ursula stated.

"I suppose," Flip told her.

"But perhaps there are not *so* many," Ursula said mysteriously. "One is two. Two is one. How many men can there be, really?"

"You tell me," Flip said. "This is *your* racket, remember?"

"O Joe Flippity . . . you have no idea," Ursula croaked distantly.

"Don't start with that again," Flip said sternly. "I might have more of an idea than you think."

The rocking chair moved slightly underneath Ursula. Her head lolled like an automaton losing power.

"Why has this muddy, cold place beside Lake Michigan been the site of so much murder, Joe Flippity? Why are there so many secrets here? Why so much blood? Why will there be so much blood a hundred years from now? And a hundred years hence, and a hundred years after that too?"

Flip was silent.

"Relax yourself," Ursula said. "You're not the only one who knows *nothing*."

Flip opened his mouth to object, but thought better of it.

"One man can be confused for another," Ursula continued. "The living can be confused with the dead. But what does it matter? All humbug. All mirror. All nonsense."

Flip waited a moment longer.

When Ursula did not continue, he said: "What have *I* confused, Ursula? The woman upstairs, the one who runs this building where you live, she has twin babies. You don't start to be precise with me, something could happen to them one day. This isn't street criminals killing each other. This involves a woman we both know. Your damn landlord."

Ursula's chair rocked once more.

"This place—only for a *moment* is it a city—is part of a cycle of things. That is what you fail to understand. What has happened here has already happened, and will happen again. The mayor who called for you—he is mayor now, and, later, he will be mayor again. This war in Europe—it will be now, and then later, it will be again. The killer who takes these people. . . He kills now, and then later he will come again. And again. And all because you cannot see behind the mirror. You can see only your own face in it. But to another, it is a window. And he reaches through. He reaches through and searches for what has been taken."

Flip's stark frustration mounted.

"I have brought you *the man's hat*," Flip said loudly and deliberately. "It is stained with years of his sweat. Other times, I've brung you something a man only touched once or twice, and your words have told me where to find him. And those times, I paid you a whole lot less than I just did."

Again, Ursula Green laughed like an ocean beast with something stuck in its blowhole.

"O it's got you now, Joe Flippity," she cackled with amusement. "It's too late for you. You stuck in the jaws and don't even see it. You just squirming back and forth. And the pity of it? You ain't even what it's tryna eat! You're just the only one dumb enough to wander right into its mouth!"

Flip tried to be patient with the teetering old woman. They sat in silence for some time. Flip heard the ticking of his pocket watch. Occasionally, the cry of a reveler on the street outside could be heard. Flip looked up into the dark ceiling above them. It was unseeable and might go to infinity.

"You don't even know what he did. . . " Ursula eventually whispered. "Even that, you have not puzzled."

Flip's eyes flit over to the conjure woman, though he hated to look straight at her. He took a deep breath, summoning all his resolve.

"All right," Flip said, staring straight into her face. "What did he do?"

"This is different," Ursula said. "It searches for *him*. It searches for what was taken. You must see that. It is old. Older than Chicago. I remember, because *I* am older than Chicago. It is older than the Indians, even. It searches for what *he* took."

Flip put his chin in his hand.

"You're not going to shoot straight with me tonight, are you Miss Green?" he said.

"To the contrary, Joe Flippity," she croaked. "This is the one night when I have said much more than I ought."

Flip walked immediately home. Two things were on his stoop.

The first was a small paperboard box from the *Chicago Defender*, with what sounded like news clippings inside when you shook it. Abbott's people had worked fast.

Placing the box under his arm, Flip turned to the second thing—a note pinned to his door. The script that said "Joe Flippity" was in a flowing hand—almost womanly.

Flip knew that hand. Salvatore Crespo.

He opened and read.

Flip,
Some people need to meet you. Come tomorrow noon. Grand Army of
the Republic room in the downtown library. Dress presentably.
Crespo

Flip laughed. Then he frowned. He could not think of any way this summons could be good.

In his rooms, he opened the package from the *Defender*. Inside, carefully organized by date, he found every issue of the *Defender* containing stories about or relating to twins. Birth announcements. Awards and scholarships. Death notices. All the salient parts had been marked to bring them immediately to the reader's attention.

There was also a note. It read:

Flip,
I got you one. June 1, 1910.
Bob

To this note had been appended a single newspaper clipping, separated from the others. Flip unfolded the newsprint and read.

NO MOTIVE IN HAYMORE CASE

Police Fail to Find Clew in Slaying of Twin Brothers

The Murder is a Mystery

After a week of investigation, police say they are no closer to solving the murders of Cornelius and John Haymore—negro men aged 24—at their home at 32nd Street and Prairie Avenue. The men were identical twin brothers employed at the Johnson Foundryworks. It is reported that the bodies were mutilated, but police would provide no further specifics.

Two of the three suspects taken into police custody on the day of the murder have been released. One, a demented man, remains in custody held on connection to a separate charge of public lewdness. He has not been found to have any involvement in the murders. No witnesses have come forward. A police precinct captain confirmed to Defender reporters that the other men taken into custody had been seen fighting with the Haymore brothers in Dirk's Alehouse on 59th Street one week prior. However, the suspects have been able to confirm their whereabouts on the night of the murders.

"Are you any closer to finding the killer of the Haymore brothers?" a police inspector was asked by a Defender reporter.

"We are still hunting for a clew that will bring this case to resolution," the inspector replied.

"Is it true that nothing was taken from the Haymore brothers' home, and that their wallets and personal effects were not disturbed?" the inspector was asked.

"Yes, that's correct," the inspector told the reporter.

"Are there theories behind the mutilation of the dead bodies?" the inspector was further asked. "It is said unspeakable things were done to them."

The police inspector declined to answer this or any further questions.

The killings of the Haymore brothers are the ninth and tenth reported murders of negro men in the city this year.

Though multiple conjectures exist regarding the ways in which the twin brothers were allegedly mutilated, they are unprintable in a family publication.

Flip put down the newspaper clip and tried to think.

He had heard nothing of these brothers or their killing, but the location was very near his beat. He racked his brain to remember anything of it.

When nothing came, he went into his bedroom, opened the broken armoire that leaned permanently in a corner so that it did not topple over, and began to assemble his nicest suit of clothes.

ELEVEN

The next day at half past eleven, Flip and Drextel Tark hopped on a streetcar and headed up to the Loop.

In truth, they hopped on several.

In an appeal to the votes of workingmen, Chicago politicians had passed laws mandating that no streetcar ride—from one end of a company's line to the other—could cost more than five cents. The streetcar companies had responded by swiftly breaking themselves up into several smaller companies—all, ultimately, owned by the same people—so that now any commute worth making involved transferring lines at least two or three times.

Flip and Tark stepped off their final streetcar in front of the public library, a tall limestone monolith that seemed to take up an entire city block. Flip told Tark to wait outside and not to get into trouble. Then he walked up the steps of the great, grey building, carefully adjusted his necktie, and slipped inside. Flip had been to city libraries before, but never to one this far north. Or this grand. It was the finest library in the city, if not the entire United States.

The lobby was all stone and brass, like a poor man's imagining of a rich man's house. Flip did not know where to go. He asked a receptionist behind a desk where to find the Grand Army of the Republic room, and was directed to climb several flights of stairs past walls covered in tiled mosaics. When he reached the uppermost landing, Flip saw an open doorway. Seated on a bench beside the doorway was Salvatore Crespo. There were also three other men—hired muscle, it looked like—milling in the hallway. They wore tight, ill-fitting jackets.

The Italian rose.

"You look like you just came from a wedding," Crespo said.

"Only suit I got," Flip answered.

The men shook hands.

"What's going on?" Flip asked.

"I don't even know how to tell you," Crespo said. "The mayor wants you to meet some more people; I guess is the shortest version. You ready?"

Flip shrugged to ask if that mattered.

They walked through the high open doorway. The room beyond was marble, wood, and tile. The ceiling held the largest stained glass dome in the world, oppressive in its sheer magnitude. The room was conspicuously empty—like a large ballroom between events—with the exception of a small cluster of well-attired men. They stood close to one another, like bums huddled for warmth in the winter. Despite being inside the finest room of one of the city's finest buildings, they looked uncomfortable and out of place. Flip immediately noted that one of the waiting men, the largest, was the mayor. And the others, he gradually realized, were the most powerful men in Chicago.

Wrigley, McCormick, Marshall Field, Oscar Mayer. And those were just the ones with faces Flip recognized from the newspapers.

Flip felt his gorge rise. Butterflies suddenly seemed to be flapping about in his stomach. The mayor was one thing, but this? This was fighting in a whole other weight class.

Crespo placed a hand on Flip's shoulder to steady him.

"Come on," the Italian whispered low. "They shit and piss just like you do, champ. Just like you do."

Flip wanted to add that—while this might be true—their ancestors had also likely owned his ancestors. That one word from them could still end a man's career (in virtually any industry, but certainly in law enforcement). And that most of them were wearing clothes that—even if you didn't count the gold watches and diamond stickpins—cost more than a Chicago police officer made in a year. (Some of them, just the pants would get you there.)

"This is the officer in charge of the investigation," Flip heard the mayor saying as Crespo walked him over.

Flip felt like a bride being conducted to the altar, or maybe a man being led to an execution. Perhaps they were the same. The feeling was a total loss of control. It seemed to Flip that he floated rather than walked. Crespo pulled him like a child's toy balloon.

They reached the mayor and joined the orbit of his awesome girth. Crespo patted Flip twice on the shoulder and released him. He had done all he could. Now Flip was sailing under his own power.

Instinctively, Flip straightened himself, standing rigid and at attention. Yet in a trice, he realized this made him the tallest man in the room. Concerned that the all-powerful might not enjoy being overshadowed, Flip slowly, imperceptibly began to lower his shoulders and spine until he was only eye-to-eye with the tallest of them.

The rich men smelled like ten different colognes. Their clothing did not fit like clothes most men wore, but had been cut custom to give them shoulders and conceal their bellies. Their teeth were clean and mostly straight. Their fingernails had no dirt underneath.

"Mister Mayor," Flip said.

"Officer, these gentlemen are some of my best friends," the mayor announced with a wink.

Flip was relieved that Big Bill Thompson—at least outwardly—was not made nervous by the presence of these captains of industry.

"And my friends have taken an interest in the case you are pursuing," the mayor continued. "In fact . . . they believe they may be able to be of some assistance to you."

"Mister Mayor," Flip stuttered. "When we met, you asked me to give you a progress report in a week. With all respect, that gives me two more days. And I *am* making progress."

The mayor smiled as though Flip's terror was amusing.

"Of course, officer," he said. "We are not here to force a premature update, or to question your methods. You were selected precisely because your methods seem to be the best on the South Side of Chicago. Perhaps the best in the city! No. . . We have only asked for the pleasure of your company because my friends have some information that they believe may. . . make your job easier."

The mayor nodded to the rich men, and one stepped forward. It was the youngest. He looked no more than thirty. Flip recognized him as one of the several Marshall Fields. A man with Roman numerals after his name and unspeakable reams of wealth.

As he approached, Flip wondered why the others had made Field their spokesman. Perhaps speaking to a policeman was an unpleasant task—a vulgarity—and the others had avoided it through simple seniority.

The young man opened his mouth, but—suddenly, before he could get his first word out—a different man in a cloak raised a hand and cleared his throat. This senior man looked to the mayor, then at the many doors set into the walls of the GAR room. Flip realized the man was embarrassed . . . or frightened.

"Ahh yes," the mayor said. "Of course."

The mayor motioned to Crespo, and the Italian made a quick circuit of the room, closing every door and locking them whenever they had locks. When he'd finished, he returned to the mayor and stood at attention. The mayor tilted his head to the side, testing the silence like a chef might sample a broth. When no sound came back, the mayor yielded the floor once again to the young Marshall Field.

"First of all. . . officer . . . it is a pleasure to make your acquaintance," Field began awkwardly, extending a gloved hand. Flip shook it.

"All of us—we all appreciate very much what you are doing."

Flip wondered why any of these men—much less all of them—should give a second thought to Negro twin murders in the south part of town.

"And, ah," the young man continued, a quiver in his voice, "as the mayor says, we have some information that we believe may be useful to you, in helping to stop these crimes."

Flip said: "More information never hurts."

The Field nervously looked back at his compatriots. Most were not actually paying attention to what was happening. They looked down at the carpet or up at the enormous dome of glass. One of them—the one Flip recognized as Wrigley—gave Field a scowl that said 'Get on with it!'

Field turned back to the policeman.

"There was a man named Durkin who used to work for us," Field said. "He performed . . . *certain tasks* on our behalf."

"He worked for all of you. . . together?" Flip asked. "As an employee?"

"That's right!" Wrigley called sternly, as if to say Field should be allowed to continue uninterrupted.

"Yes, he worked for all of us," Field affirmed. "He did a variety of things, but usually he was reserved for jobs requiring discretion. You might say we employed him so as not to waste the time and resources of the Chicago Police Department. If there were matters that he could handle for us, then we did not need to take an officer such as yourself away from an important investigation. Say, if you were solving a murder—such as you are now—or catching a defiler of women, that would be more important, frankly, than the private concerns of wealthy men. So we employed Durkin as a sort of courtesy to the department."

"A generous act of municipal charity!" boomed Big Bill Thompson, patting Field on the shoulder. "The equivalent of a most generous donation to the city's coffers. And Chicago thanks you for it!"

Wrigley rolled his eyes.

Field continued nervously.

"But, while on business for us, Mr. Durkin, we believe. . . unfortunately. . . became involved in inappropriate things. Frankly, horrible things. Because of this, he was dismissed from our service. In a very permanent way. Yet, apparently . . . he still persists."

Flip thought for a moment.

"What did he do to warrant this dismissal?" Flip asked.

There was moment of silence. Big Bill Thompson coughed.

And in a trice, Flip knew and the breath nearly went out of him. Crespo was standing on the other side of the room now, and would not catch him if he fell. Flip spread his feet wide and shifted his weight on his heels, hoping he would not tumble forward onto the carpet.

A moment later, he felt steady once more.

"I see," Flip told the men evenly. "Then this is *indeed* important to my investigation. Central, in fact."

Field nodded.

"We thought it might be."

"So. . . Durkin is. . . *dismissed*?" Flip asked carefully.

"Yes," Field said. "But. . . Ah. . . As I said. . ."

Suddenly, Wrigley pushed his way forward. He was all stern and hard. He towered beside Field and gave the younger man a look that said he was done. Pulled out of the game. Field slunk back to the group. Wrigley shook his head in frustration. It was clear that—as perhaps with so many other things in Wrigley's life—if he wanted it done right, he would have to do it his damn self.

"We think our man—Durkin—is the one who killed your twins," Wrigley said. "He went rogue. Went insane. The problem is that once we realized this, we had Durkin *taken care of* on or about the ninth of June. . ."

"And there have been at least two twin murders since then," Flip told him, completing the thought.

Wrigley's expression showed that they were finally getting somewhere.

"The people who 'took care of' Durkin for you. . . For, I am guessing you did not do this personally?"

Wrigley smiled.

"The men who did the job are not contactable. They wanted it that way. Required it, in fact. They were hired through an outfit in New York. Came to town special, and cost us an arm and a leg. And, it appears, they were not worth even that. They said it was handled. They even gave us a photograph of the body. But they would not say *where* they had disposed of it. Against policy, they told us. Now, we believe the entire thing may have been forged."

"A forged photograph?" Flip asked.

"We suspect Durkin fell into league with them," Wrigley said. "He could have bribed them to fake the photograph instead of killing him—lord knows, we have all given him enough money over the years that he is quite well-to-do in his own right. He could have pretended to be dead while they took the picture, and then high-tailed it. Promised to disappear and not to kill again. And our friends from New York? They would get paid twice."

"May I see the photograph?" Flip asked gently.

Wrigley nodded so vigorously that the age lines in his forehead bounced up and down.

"Who has it?" Wrigley called. "McCormick?"

One of the wealthy men came forward and produced an envelope from his jacket. He handed it to Wrigley, who in turn proffered it to the policeman.

Flip carefully extracted the photo inside.

It showed white man. Middle aged. Wiry but tough-looking. Beginning to bald. Lying on his back in a rocky shoal that might have been somewhere along Lake Michigan. He was wearing a white tuxedo and had been shot twice in the chest. His eyes had rolled back in his head and his mouth gaped unnaturally. To Flip, it looked real. The bullet holes. The man's expression. Even the pallor of his skin. It looked completely real.

Flip handed the photograph back.

"This appears to be the correct man?" Flip asked. "To be Durkin?"

"It does," Wrigley confirmed. "His face is bit different dead, but I think it is him."

Flip took a step away from Wrigley. He began to pace slowly around the room as he thought.

"If Durkin is dead, then why do the twin murders in my neighborhoods keep happening? Either he is not dead, or someone else is committing these crimes. Any other explanation doesn't make sense."

Wrigley nodded as he watched Flip pace.

"When he was in your service, and when he was. . . functioning correctly. . ." Flip said carefully. "Did he ever have cause—in the course of this *correct function*—to do the kind of thing-"

Wrigley cut him off.

"No. At least. . . not like this. We may have asked him to 'solve problems' for us before, yes, but we never instructed him to. . . nor would we have allowed him to. . . and never, ever children. . . with such ghastly disfigurement. . ."

Flip glanced over at the group of rich men. Their faces said that Wrigley was telling the truth. Discreet problem solving was one thing, but mutilation quite another.

"He has become a devil!" one of the rich men cried. "He is a literal devil from the pit! I rue the day that you introduced me to him, Wrigley. For when you dance with the devil, he will eventually choose to lead the dance. And then God help you!"

Wrigley shot back a look that said such words were not constructive and could wait for a different time and place.

"Do you know if Durkin had anything to do with the murder of two brothers named Haymore?" Flip asked. "Passed in a similar way, some years back."

Wrigley considered.

"I don't know anything about that," he said. "But if there was another case where identical Negroes were beheaded—and you're asking me if it could have been Durkin—I'm not here to say it wasn't."

"Did Durkin ever work in the stockyards," Flip asked. "Ever work around cutting or draining meat? Deboning? Slaughter?"

Wrigley looked to the group. The gentlemen exchanged shrugs.

"We have recently—upon consultation with one another—learned that Durkin provided each of us with a different history of himself," Wrigley said. "They are inventive tales, I'll give Durkin that. But, apparently, all lies. From safari guide in Africa, to decorated veteran of the Spanish War, to a man who rode horses in Hollywood movies, to an accomplished jewel thief. Probably, none of them are true. If you're

asking if it's possible that Durkin once worked in the Chicago stockyards, your guess is as good as ours."

Flip considered this silently.

"What else?" the gum baron pressed. "What else have you got?
You must have more, yes? You have been on the case for several days
now. . ."

Here, Big Bill Thompson intervened.

"William, the processes of our most effective law enforcement
agents must be respected. Interrupting an investigation still underway-"

Wrigley raised a hand. He turned back to Flip, put his other hand
on his forehead, and sighed. A mask seem to come off.

"Officer, do you believe it is possible for a man to kill from beyond
the grave?" Wrigley asked. "Your colleague, Mr. Crespo, has told us
your expertise may extend to such extra-natural matters. Those of us
here. . . *some* of us. . . have concerns that this may be what is occur-
ring now. Every day, we learn more. With each passing moment, the
advancement of science tells us more about the hidden world. That
world which is there—just there—beyond our seeing or hearing. But
now, finally, we are beginning to hear and see it. You are familiar
with spirit photography, yes? And with the disruptions in phono-
graph recordings that experts think may be attempts by the dead to
communicate with us? We stand at the beginning of a new age, officer. What I would give—my entire empire, assuredly—to have been
born one hundred years hence. That will be an age of marvels we can
only but ponder. So much will be revealed. As it stands, we are like
men fumbling in the dark, only beginning to detect the first variations between shades of gray. But a floodlight is coming. It is coming
most assuredly."

And Flip suddenly understood that his reputation for relying
upon clues from a soothsayer—something he did not advertise, and
had shared with few beyond Crespo—was probably why he had been
selected for the assignment. For *this* as much as for his superlative
track record of closing cases.

He also understood that these rich men were scared. And they were men accustomed to fearing nothing. Now, fear united them. Fear had brought them here in person. It was fear of a danger that might come from the beyond. More specifically, thought Flip, it was fear that even though they'd had their rogue fixer executed, he could still reach out from the beyond and kill them back.

Little wonder that they employed guards at the door.

It was not the lives of twin Negro children that concerned them. They feared for their own skins. (And, Flip supposed, at an outside shot, the skins of their immediate families.) Nothing more, nothing less.

From the back of the group, McCormick spoke up.

"I daresay, if there are additional resources you require—officer—beyond what the city has been able to provide, you shall have them. Anything at all."

"I have always made it a point to employ Negroes in my processing plants!" Oscar Mayer enthusiastically chimed through his heavy German accent. "The Negro community is practically *my* community. And if there are ways I could serve it *further. . .*"

"The city has been very helpful," Flip assured them. "At the moment I have everything that I need. Leads are being followed. Some identifications are being made. There are certain things that are consistent between descriptions. And I am close—I believe—to making a break in the case."

"You have a suspect then?" another of the rich men cried, all mustache and monocle. "Who? Where? Does he look like the man in that photo?"

Again, the mayor piped up.

"The officer's methods are trusted, and he will make an arrest at the correct time. Not before or after. However well intentioned, prompting the police to act hastily can cause the criminal to get wind and flee. I've seen it too many times, gentlemen."

Big Bill Thompson had seen nothing, and Flip knew it. Yet the industrialist appeared mollified by the mayor's words, and nodded until his mustache-ends shook.

Then Wrigley spoke again.

"You see the gravity of what is happening here. Alive or dead, Durkin must be stopped. Too many lives stand to be affected by this madness. Whoever he is—*whatever* he is—you must put him down."

Flip nodded somberly and reiterated that he believed there would be a resolution very soon. Then he looked over to the mayor with an expression that asked if there would be anything else.

"But we have taken you away from your investigation for too long," the mayor said. "It is the Lord's day, after all. But villains do not pause to observe it, and so neither may we."

The mayor looked up, heavenward, into the largest glass dome in the world.

"May I have a picture of him?" Flip asked as they prepared to depart. "It doesn't have to be the one of him dead."

Oscar Mayer reached into his coat pocket and pulled out a different photo of Durkin. He held it out to Flip. In this image, the henchman wore a fine pinstripe suit. His hair had been oiled and slicked back. He smiled rakishly.

Flip accepted it, and thanked the man.

The mayor raised his arm, almost like a Roman saluting. His expression said that they should understand that—voila!—it was now well in hand. Being taken care of by an expert. Only a matter of time.

Then, as Flip turned to depart, the mayor's eyes flit in his direction for the quickest instant.

And in that instant, Flip understood wholly and completely, that, if he failed, it would surely mean his life.

"Never seen him before," Tark said as they rode in the first trolley that would take them back to South State.

He returned the photo to Flip, who tucked it into his coat.

"Neither have I," Flip said. "I know a few high-level operators in this city, but I've never heard of this one. 'Durkin.' No. I don't know him. Then again, that's how you get to work for all the wealthiest men. You keep your name out of policemen's mouths."

"They were all really there?" Tark asked. "Every one you said? All in one room?"

"Yes," Flip confirmed.

"I only know those names," Tark admitted. "I can only imagine how they'd look in person."

"Keep imagining," Flip told him. "The real thing would disappoint you."

The streetcar left the Loop and passed a group of feral dogs, starved and barking so loudly for scraps that the men were forced to raise their voices.

"Strange kind of position for a man to have!" Tark said as he leaned against the side of the streetcar.

"What is?" Flip asked, looking at a snapping, brindled mutt, all ribs and teeth.

"You know!" Tark shouted. "Someone who works for so many rich men! Kills people for them!"

Flip was silent for a moment. The busty woman reading a newspaper beside them turned her page noisily, as if it would retroactively cover the magician's unsavory words. Tark looked around in a tight circle and hung his head. The sound of the barking dogs fell away.

After a moment, Flip cleared his throat.

"What a man like that is, really, is a man who can go between worlds," Flip said softly, just audible above the trolley's clatter. "Beyond any specific service he provides, *that* is how he is useful to them."

"Between worlds?" asked Tark.

"Between rich men and poor men," Flip said. "Between the law abiding and the lawless. Between those protected by politicians and police and lawyers . . . and those who are hunted by them. *That* is the rarest kind of man. If you can do that—go between worlds on someone's behalf, and sell that service—you can become almost as rich and powerful as those you serve."

Flip adjusted his voice down further. Tark had to lean in close.

"If Mr. Wrigley or Mr. Rosenwald, say, want somebody killed— well, they have the money to pay for it a few thousand times over, don't they? But what they *don't* have is the first clue about how to find somebody to do it. And if they *do* chance to talk to a hired killer? They won't even speak the same language. Not really. They won't be able to connect, to trust each other. It will be awkward for everyone. Rich men don't like to feel awkward."

"So a guy like Durkin does it all for them," said Tark, nodding.

"Yes, he does. But of course . . . there's a problem with a man who can go between worlds. And that is: you never know in which world you're going to find him. A man like Durkin could be anywhere. Anywhere at all."

An hour later, Flip and Tark arrived back in front of the Palmerton House.

"Sally been putting you up all right?" Flip asked. As was so often her custom, Sally was standing on the front balcony, relaxing with a pair of her girls.

"It's a nice place, I suppose," Tark said as they approached. "She gives me a little room to sleep in, up on the top floor. Makes me stay up there, though. I can't go down to the lounge. I think she doesn't want me looking at the girls."

"Yes," said Flip. "She also doesn't want any of the guests thinking they can fuck you."

Tark's expression revealed that this possibility had not occurred to him.

As Flip and Tark climbed the front steps of the Palmerton, Sally sent her girls back inside. Flip saw immediately that Sally had a strange glow about her. A sheen. She wore a thin robe of spun silk. It tied in front and went all the way down to her toes. She smoked from a long jade cigarette holder. A thin gloss of sweat covered her forehead. Her makeup was slightly disarranged. Flip could tell that she had been awake most of the night.

"This okay?" Flip said, meaning their visit.

"Yeah, come on," Sally said, turning to conduct them inside. "Why are you dressed like that?"

"Police business," Flip told her.

Sally steered them straight to the lounge. Even this early, even on a Sunday, the Palmerton was not empty. A few customers lazed about on couches. A lone tuxedoed attendant hovered behind the bar. Sally dismissed him with a glance. Then she took down three glasses and poured—Jack Daniel's for herself and Flip, Gordon's for the magician. Tark downed his quickly, and immediately wandered off.

Flip placed the photograph of Durkin on the bar.

"Seen this man before?"

Sally lifted an eyebrow.

"Maybe," she said.

"Maybe?" Flip asked. His tone said this was not the time to be coy.

"That's right," Sally said. "Maybe. He feels familiar. Looks like he's been here before, but. . ."

"But what?" Flip pressed.

"But I don't know," Sally said, averting her gaze.

"What does that mean? You've seen him or you haven't."

"He hasn't been here as a customer," Sally explained. "I'd remember that detail. But he seems like he might have come around with one of my clients. Like he worked for them. Who is he? A driver? A hired gun?"

"Yes," Flip answered. "The last one."

He gave Sally a quick report on what he had learned on the top floor of the library. Sally listened intently.

"Then I've seen him," she confirmed. "I can't recall anything he said or did. So many like him pass through."

"That's all right. I don't expect you to remember every detail. But there's something more. Something I've learned since we talked last. Back in 1910, there *was* another twin murder. Two brothers were killed in their own home. Bodies mutilated. No motive. No arrest."

Flip told Sally all he'd read in the *Defender* clipping, and then of his unsuccessful sting with Tark.

"I'm sorry I couldn't be there," Sally said.

"You have a business to run," Flip answered. "Besides. . . You're welcome to help if you want to, but you don't have to. I'll say it one more time; your being involved in this is all your own idea."

Sally took a sip of her Jack. She glanced around for Tark and found him in a corner of the bar, admiring a painting of a reclining nude in a gilded frame.

"The reason I had to come back last night. . . is a count," she said.

"A count of your money?" Flip asked. "People can do that for you."

Sally shook her head.

"A count from Europe. Comes to see me whenever he crosses the Atlantic. Says he wants to marry me one day, if you can believe it. When all this silliness—that's what he calls the war—when this silliness is over and the fighting stops, he says he wants to take me away to his castle. Make me a countess."

"That's more of an offer than I've had lately," Flip told her.

"I couldn't do it, Flip," she confided.

"No?" he asked. "Live with a rich man in a more enlightened country? *In a castle*? Never have to work again a day in your life?"

"But I would be so dreadfully *bored*," Sally said, shaking her head. "I would miss my old ways. I would miss my girls. I would be so listless and unhappy. And that would break the poor man's heart. I can see that a mile away. So it's out of love, ultimately, that I tell him no. Out of care for him, you see? Yet . . . he will not relent."

Sally glanced down at her own hand as it rested against the bar. Flip followed her gaze and saw that a new bracelet of shining emeralds encircled her wrist.

"Well," Flip said with a shrug, "least you always got options."

Sally laughed.

She lifted her glass to toast the policeman. There was a sadness to it, it seemed to Flip. A genuine mournfulness to the toast. Nonetheless, he lifted his own glass and touched it to hers. They downed their drinks.

Flush from the previous evening, Sally ordered a late lunch to be delivered from a steakhouse in the Loop. They ate outside, on a back balcony of the Palmerton that Flip had never before visited. It had a fine floor of Italian tile, and Sally had a proper dining table brought out.

Tark ate as though he had not had food in several days.

"This is the best steak I ever tasted," he told Sally. "And I ate at St. Elmo down in Indy."

"We get 'em fresher here," she reminded him. "It was probably mooing this morning."

Tark liked that.

Flip only picked at his meat.

A thought occurred to Tark: "So then, we spent that day at the *Defender* for nothing?"

"You might have found something," Flip answered. "It was worth a try before I went to use up a favor with Bob Abbott. It'll take a lot to keep him from printing a story. That concerns me. His nature won't let him do otherwise. He's like a dog who needs a bone."

Tark finished his steak and turned on his potatoes.

"It's nice to see this boy eat," Sally said. "Tark, the way you drink, and then not eating?"

She shook her head, perishing the thought.

"We have to consider trying again at the circus grounds," Flip told them.

He placed his steak knife and fork back onto the table.

"What?" said Tark. "Didn't everything just change? Because of what those rich men told you?"

"Did it?" Flip asked.

As though it involved great effort, Flip took up his fork and began stabbing at a slice of tomato.

"Yeah," Tark said. "Doesn't it mean we're looking for a white man named Durkin instead of a Negro man with a hole in his head? I mean, what proof do we even have that it's the man with the divot? A desk clerk says a man with hole in his head once asked after twins, and suddenly that's all we can see? What if that desk clerk was having us on? It was early in the morning. Maybe he didn't have nothing else to do. Maybe he read that word 'divot' in the dictionary and was wanting to use it, and so he made up a story. And maybe the man with the homburg coming to the circus was part of a misunderstanding, yeah? Maybe he's just a fan who wants my autograph."

Flip nodded distractedly, looking down at his tomato piece.

"Why ain't you talking more about Durkin?" Tark pressed. "He's the one the mayor wants you to follow."

"Mostly, because I think he is dead," Flip said, wiping his mouth with his napkin. "The photo they showed me. Not the one in my pocket, but the other one. That was real, and he was dead. I know a dead man when I see one. Another reason I'm not talking about Durkin is that I didn't get the whole story back there. I can also tell when I'm being told half a tale, Tark. And that was half a tale. And finally, I don't see the connection between Durkin and the twins. How do they know it was him? *Why* would he kill them? Does he think it will embarrass them—embarrass the rich and powerful men—to kill Negro twins? Does he think it will besmirch the character of this city, where they have all made their fortunes? No. There are better, more direct ways of doing that."

There was a knock and one of Sally's men—a liveried butler of advanced years—stepped onto the balcony.

"Ma'am, a gentleman to see you . . . and also to see the officer," the butler informed them. "He says he is from the *Defender*."

Flip spat a piece of tomato onto his plate.

"Dog got to have his bone," Tark observed. "Like you say."

Sally turned to Flip. The policeman gave a gesture that said she might as well let it happen, because now it was bound to.

"Please send him up, Conroy," Sally told her man.

The butler left. A short minute later, he returned with Bob Abbott right behind him, clutching his bowler hat tight by the brim. Abbott looked up in a strange way, like a tourist taking in the tall buildings downtown. Flip wondered if Abbott were trying to physically prevent himself from spotting anything prurient while inside the Palmerton.

Flip was seated closest to the door, and received Abbott first. The men shook hands. Flip smiled, but also gave Abbott a look that asked what the fuck he was doing there.

"May I join you?" Abbott began, ignoring Flip's expression and nodding warmly across the table to Sally.

"Conroy, another chair," Sally ordered before Flip could object, and so it was brought.

Abbott sat and fished himself a roll from the basket, as if the luncheon were his own.

"Don't I recognize you two?" Abbott said, winking at Sally and Tark as he buttered up his bread.

"What is this, Bob?" Flip pressed. "You know you'll endanger this investigation if you print anything. Letting the killer know he is being hunted is the worst thing to-"

"Calm you down," Abbott said like a preacher. "I'm not here for a story, Flip. You said I should be in touch if I remembered anything else. Well, this morning, something struck me. I ought to have thought of it before, frankly. I directed all my recollections to stories of twins in our newspaper, and so overlooked a thing that was right under my nose. A woman who works for me—name of Janice Collins—once mentioned that a neighbor of hers was an identical twin. Back when she first came to Chicago, this was. Would have been 1905 or '06. She rented the upper floor of a house from him. During this time, Janice told me the man was assaulted. Beaten up. This is a secondhand story, now. But I if I recall, Janice said this neighbor. . . he got him a look at the man who attacked him. He was a Negro man, and—again, this is me recollecting from some years ago—but she said there was a way in which this man was . . . *deformed* in the head."

Flip could not contain his smile.

Abbott smiled right back and reached for another roll.

"I don't think Janice knew why the attack happened," Abbott continued. "Could have been random street violence. No meaning to it. And I only have on secondhand that he—her landlord, the victim— was an identical twin. But it sure did make me think. Made me think I ought to share this with my friend Joe Flippity."

"And does Janice Collins still work for you?" Flip asked with growing excitement.

"Yes," Abbott said. "She's a full reporter now. A very good one."

"Does she still live-?" Flip asked.

"Above the identical twin?" said Abbott. "No. Janice got married a few years back. Seems like that happens to good looking women when they move up to Chicago. I don't even know if the twin lives in that house anymore. And alas, now I've told you all I can."

Flip began to ask something, but Abbott cut him off.

"Let me guess; you want to speak to Janice."

"Of course," Flip said. "Very much."

"And here's where things become uncomfortable," Abbott replied, setting down a half-eaten roll. "I can vouch for my *own* ability to keep a secret temporarily. To play ball wit'cha generally, Flip. But Janice is another matter. Another game entirely. Janice is here, on this earth, to tell the truth. To get at the truth, and then get it out to as many people as possible. That's what a reporter's supposed to do, and it's why I hired her."

Flip's expression said he might have tasted something sour.

"Anything she finds, she'll want to run with," Abbott warned.

"You could stop that," Flip suggested. "Refuse to print it. You operate the damn presses, Bob."

"But I'm not the only game in town, am I?" Abbott reminded the policeman. "Story that big—with that kind of grisly detail?—she could take it to the *Daily Journal* or the *Tribune* or five other papers who'd pay her for it. She'd publish it under a false name and get a nice big check. Officially, we'd never know it was her."

Flip tasted something sour again. He knew that Abbott was correct.

"But here," Abbott said, sensing Flip's frustration. "Maybe *you* could do it. . ."

"Do what?" said Flip.

"Convince her to wait," Abbott said. "You're good at convincing folks. You can be persuasive. I think back over the years—think about the things you've convinced *me* to do—and I think 'How did that man do that?' And I still don't know . . . but you did."

The sour taste seemed to fall away from Flip's mouth. There was hope again.

"Is Mrs. Collins in the office at the moment?" Flip asked.

Abbott shook his head no.

"She's on assignment writing up the real estate scandal in the Fox River Valley," Abbott explained. "But I expect a story from her first thing tomorrow morning. You could stop by when she comes to drop it off."

"We might just do that," Flip said.

"We?" said Abbott. "The three of you working as a team?"

"Something like that," Flip told him.

The newspaperman finished his roll and pushed back his chair.

"Thank you, Bob," Flip said, also rising. "I appreciate you coming here. All this way I mean."

Abbott smiled. He took up his bowler hat, made sure his gaze was fixed in an upwardly—possibly celestial—direction, and departed.

TWELVE

That evening they tried again at the Singling Brothers Circus grounds. Tark dressed as his brother and Flip once more donned the costume of a carnival hand. Sally, who insisted upon coming along, proved—for a woman who made her living at least partly on her looks—surprisingly game to gussy herself down until she could pass for the kind of person who might hang around a smelly circus encampment.

"Are there any other women here?" Sally asked as they crept into the field.

"Yes," said the magician. "We have some female acrobats and a lady who does contortion tricks. And a couple of the roughnecks too—if you checked under the hood, you'd find they were of the female variety."

"Try to stay in character, you two," Flip advised. "He could be watching us right now."

Tark chuffed like a horse to say he thought it unlikely.

As he had before, Tark took a lion-taming podium and marched it to the edge of the field near where the stranger had left his hat. Tark sat, took out a glass bottle, and began to drink and to dream. Sally joined Flip. They sat half underneath a caravan with a clear line of sight to Tark. Cloud cover had gradually formed over that afternoon, and a light rain began to fall. Most of the circus workers stayed out of sight; they'd either left the grounds or were huddling in tents alongside the animals. Sally let her legs—fitted in ratty white stockings—stick out from underneath the caravan. Flip worried this might attract the wrong kind of attention. He decided he would say something if it did, but only if it did.

"This is how you did it last time?" Sally asked as they watched Tark put his bottle down and close his eye.

"Most essentially," Flip replied.

"Can I ask you a question?" Sally said.

"You just did."

"About the case?"

Flip nodded.

"Tark brought it up before . . . but you didn't really answer him. Why are we doing *this* tonight, instead of out looking for Durkin?"

"Maybe we are," Flip said. "Maybe he's gonna come through those trees in just a few moments, with two big bullet holes in his belly, just like in the picture I saw."

Sally crossed her long legs.

"How is it all those rich men want you to find him if he's already dead?" she asked. "How can he be the one doing the killing?"

Flip took a sip from a tin flask on his hip, but did not speak.

"I tell you. . . I have seen some *shit* over the years, Joe Flippity," Sally continued. "I have seen things—just inside the Palmerton— would make a grown man faint dead away. I've seen a man's ear torn off, slowly. I've seen murder for no reason at all. All manner of perversion. But a dead man coming back to kill? Come on now."

"What's the oldest customer ever come to the Palmerton?" Flip asked, almost as though he had not been listening.

Sally tilted her head to the side.

"Does this have to do with the case . . . or are you askin' for your granddad?" she wondered.

Flip silently took another swig.

"We've had men close to ninety, I believe," she told him. "Is that what you want me to tell you? Men who seemed very close to the end of their lives. I suppose it was like having a last meal. A last drink.

Men that age, wasn't much happening downstairs. It was all about the ritual."

"How about the oldest person you've ever seen?"

"Oldest person I. . ."

"Last time we talked, you told me you thought Ursula Green was 105 now," Flip said to her.

"That sounds about right," Sally replied. "Of course, I haven't actually *seen* her in years."

Flip turned to Sally and cocked his head to ask 'Oh really?'.

"She rented out the basement. . . I don't know," Sally recollected. "It was before I took over at the Palmerton. I was just a working girl then. Had to be ten years ago."

"She *could* be 105," Flip said. "But you know, I think she could be older, too."

Sally's expression said that she found this doubtful.

"My mother," Flip continued, "she used to talk about old men up in the hills who drank ramp juice. Do you know what that is? A plant. They would ferment it. She said it made them hibernate like bears. They would drink the ramp juice—jars and jars of it—and then sleep all winter. Wake up again in the spring. By doing this, she said they would live to 150 or 160."

"I never heard of such a thing," said Sally. "But people in the South tell tales. Your momma from down South?"

"Of course," Flip said.

"Where from?"

He did not answer.

"Ramps are like leeks, yes?" Sally asked after a moment. "I don't know if I ever tasted one."

"They grow around here," Flip said with a nod. "Cross between garlic and onions. Lore holds that the Indians named the city after the smell of wild onions. That could be true. I've seen ramps growing along the lake, plenty of places."

"You ever taste one?" Sally asked.

Flip shook his head.

"No," he said. "I tried smelling one once. That was enough."

Sally put her hand to her chin and drummed her fingers.

"I wonder about Du Sable, the first man who lived here," Sally said. "Back in history, you know? Maybe he ate them. Or drank them."

"Everything about that man is a mystery," Flip said of the founder of Chicago. "Nobody knows what happened to him when he left. Some say he moved to St. Louis or just drifted away downriver. I don't think they even know where his body is buried. *Where* he died. *When* he died. *If. . .*"

"He's dead, Flip," Sally said. "That was 100 years ago."

Flip smiled.

"I get to thinking about Ursula, and I don't properly know anymore," he told her. "I think about how Ursula could have known him; known Du Sable. And then I know Ursula. So. . . So I don't know what that means. Maybe she knows if he ate or drank the ramps that grew here back then. Maybe I should ask her next time. What you think?"

Sally put her hand to her hip. Though she was in a seated position, the desired effect was achieved.

"Flip, all respect to your momma, but that is crazy. This whole line of thought. Drinking ramp juice wouldn't do nothing but make a man sick. Or a woman."

Flip grinned.

"You got another explanation for how Ursula is 105?" Flip asked, if only to pass the time.

(There was no compelling reason to let the conversation die. Tark was now motionless at the end of the grounds, probably unconscious. There was nothing to do but watch.)

As if this answer were obvious, Sally said: "Sheer dumb luck. Chance. The nonsense of the world."

Flip put his hands behind his head and relaxed against the ground.

Sally said nothing else for a long time.

"This is how it was before, watching him?"

Flip nodded.

"And you expect the killer to come through the trees just beyond?"

Flip nodded again.

"Then I still got to ask. . . Are you expecting a white man named Durkin, or a Negro man with a hole in his head?"

"At this point, I'm liable to take whoever I can get," Flip said wearily.

They looked out across the field. Though his visible eye was closed, a strange expression had crossed Tark's face. Then he began to moan. His foot kicked once, twice, three times. His mouth began to hang open.

"Like a dog having a nightmare," Sally observed.

"First time we did this, he dreamed that an insect with a triangle head was watching him," Flip said. "A giant one. That's what he told me. Maybe it came back."

"Hell of a thing to dream about," Sally said.

"I don't know," Flip replied. "I've had plenty of dreams that were stranger than a big bug."

Flip surveyed the treeline. There was no movement except for rain on leaves. The sun went down completely and the wind started to blow, cool and wet. Usually, Chicago winds blew west to east, so the weather went out over the lake. But on this evening, it seemed to Flip that the weather came *in* from the lake, unnaturally. The breeze smelled like sea spray and sewage and dead fish, like after a rain. The clouds parted only once, and Flip glimpsed the indifferent pale moon, just beginning to rise.

Out on his animal pedestal, Tark stretched himself, massaged his neck, and adjusted his groin. If he had gone into a trance to summon someone—or something—he was coming out of it now. And, plainly, it had not worked.

"We're not going to catch anybody tonight," Flip whispered to Sally.

"Well, it *is* Sunday," Sally said absently.

"What does *that* mean?" asked Flip.

"Sunday is special," Sally insisted.

Her tone said that this fact was so plain that no further explanation should be required.

"I'll admit I thought it was unlikely he'd show, but this was still the best use of our time," Flip told her.

"That *who* would show?" Sally pressed.

Flip did not answer the question.

"Tomorrow I want to go to that reporter, Janice Collins," he said. "And I'd like you to come along."

"Oh?" Sally said. "Why? Because I'm a woman?"

"Partly," said Flip. "I don't know if she'll want to help us, especially if she's not going to get a story out of it. Maybe we'll have to convince her to cooperate out of the goodness of her heart. I ain't met her, so I don't know what kind of heart she has. But hearing about your own twins—from you—seems like it might get us a good result."

Sally worked her jaw back and forth, considering. Tark walked up.

"We done," Tark stated. "He ain't coming tonight."

"I don't think so either," Flip said.

"Naw, the giant insect told me he ain't coming," Tark said, rubbing his eyes. "It was pissed off about it. I think it wanted a show."

"What does a giant insect sound like when it talks?" Flip asked.

Tark pointed to his temple.

"It talks into the side of my mind," he said. "It's like a buzz. I think you gotta be a magician to understand."

"Or just drunk enough?" Sally wondered.

"Maybe that too," Tark said, removing the eye patch that made him look so much like his brother. "Maybe that too."

The next morning Flip stood outside the apartment building that housed the *Defender* and thought to himself that if he never saw or heard about a twin again for the rest of his whole goddamn life that would be just fine.

Tark and Sally stood with him, a few paces off. The pair whispered to one another. It seemed to Flip that the two were perhaps becoming chummy. He had not yet decided if this was a positive development.

Some of the *Defender* staff recognized Flip and said hello as they headed in to start their workdays. Flip had already asked two women he did not know if they were Janice Collins. They had not been. But then a third appeared. She wore a white blouse and a long blue skirt, and she carried a brown purse. Her hair was covered against the summer heat by a blue and white scarf.

For whatever reason, Flip liked his chances.

"Janice Collins?" he asked.

The reporter widened her eyes and smiled to show he had her attention.

Flip introduced himself, and said it was police business. Then he said he had a few questions that would only take a moment.

"I'm on my way to turn in a story," Janice Collins explained.

"About the real estate in the Fox River Valley," Flip said. "Bob told me about it. He's the one who said I should talk to you."

"Oh. . ." the reporter said. "Well, all right then. How can I help you?"

Flip conducted her to the side of the apartment building, away from the entrance. The magician and the madam also headed over. While more *Defender* employees filed past, Flip introduced Janice Collins to Sally and Tark. The reporter's face showed she was already familiar with both, by reputation if not personally. Introductions out of the way, Flip got right to the point.

"Bob says when you first moved to town, you rented a room from a man who was an identical twin."

"That's right," Collins said. "Ed Nash. He sold insurance. It was in a little house by the yards. Nasty neighborhood. Rats as big as cats at night. And the smell! I got away as fast as I could—soon as my lease was up."

Flip took out his notebook and wrote down Ed Nash.

"And Ed was once attacked by a man with a deformity in his head?" Flip asked.

Collins looked around, searching for what to say.

"I *do* recall him telling me that," she replied after a moment. "Said he'd been assaulted quite seriously one night. But officer, don't tell me you're here trying to solve a mugging from nineteen hundred and six?"

"We think the man who attacked your neighbor might still be at it," Flip told her. "Any information you can give us—whatever you remember—might help us catch the criminal."

"What else do you want to know?" Collins said, shifting her purse to her other shoulder.

"Street address be a good place to start," Flip said.

Collins gave it, but quickly followed with: "I've no idea if Ed still lives there. I've no idea if the *house* is still here. Hmm. I can't think of what else to tell you. Ed and I, we didn't talk much. He tried to flirt a couple of times. I shot that down."

"Did you ever meet his twin?" Flip asked. "And do you know the twin's name?"

"Rotney," she said. "Not 'Rodney,' but with an R-O-T, like something gone bad. He came by a time or two. He flirted with me also. Looked a lot like Ed, but more disheveled. More dirty. Always wore blue overalls, I seem to recall."

"But he *was* an identical twin, yes?" Flip pressed.

Janice Collins' stare became suspicious.

"Why does that part matter?" she asked, her reporter's brain working now. "Why are you interested in the twin part? I suppose if one twin did something, he could blame the other? Or if a witness saw one, the other might get blamed. But if Ed Nash is the victim . . . then what does his brother have to do with it?"

Flip continued to believe the less he told any *Defender* reporter, the better.

"We just want to ensure we have the right man," Flip said as though it were all routine. "There could be more than one Negro man called Ed Nash in a city this size. Being a twin narrows it. We got to check we're accurate."

Janice Collins' eyes again went back and forth very fast, like someone watching a tennis match.

"No, no," Collins said, almost to herself—almost in a trance, now, with the figuring of it. "That doesn't make sense. You would not come here and ask me this—not in this way—if that were your goal. . ."

To Flip's surprise, Collins reached into her purse and took out a notepad of her own. She took out a pencil too, and prepared to write.

Flip stood opposite her, sizing her up as though they were set to duel—with notepads and pencils instead of swords and bucklers.

"Officer, why is the Chicago Police Department interested in Edwin R. Nash who once resided at-"

"I've told you what this is about," Flip said testily, talking over her. "We're trying to apprehend someone involved in an assault. That is a function of the police department, you will remember. To catch criminals who commit ass-"

"What, *specifically*, does Mr. Nash's being an identical twin have to do with this case?" said Collins, nearly shouting. "How does that figure into the Chicago Police Department's investigation?"

A hand came forward—a lithe, long woman's hand—and fell across the front of the reporter's notebook.

"Miss," Sally Battle said softly, "do you have any children of your own?"

Janice Collins tugged her notebook away, frowned. . . but then considered the question.

"I do," she said. "But I don't see what that has to do with anything. My status as a mother does not negatively impact my ability to do this job. Or *any* job. If anything, my work is *enhanced* by the perspective motherhood brings."

Sally Battle smiled a strange, sympathetic smile.

"Oh honey," she said. "We need to talk."

Flip stood beside Tark in front of the *Defender* building while Sally Battle and Janice Collins took a long walk to the end of the block. Flip looked on intently, as though the two women were deciding his fate. It seemed that Sally was doing the balance of the speaking. Flip could not hear what was being said. Janice had put away her pencil and notepad, however, and Flip counted that a small sign of progress.

"What're they talking about?" Tark whispered.

Flip did not respond. Not because he could not guess, but because he did not want to cast a hex by saying anything aloud.

Sally and Janice hovered at the corner of the block. The morning wind picked up and blew at their backs, making audible for Flip the tiniest scrap of their conversation. He heard no distinct word or words; only a single syllable came on the wind. But in the syllable, Flip detected powerful emotion in Sally's voice. The sound of someone close to tears, if not quite there yet. The noise of someone bearing her soul.

Flip was pleased with himself. He had had this feeling about Sally Battle—that she could get the job done. That she would know, innately, what to say.

Something told Flip his feeling was about to be proved correct.

A few moments later, the pair returned. Sally dabbed at her eyes with a handkerchief, but her makeup was not disarranged. Before anyone could speak, she flashed Flip the smallest, most secret smile. It was a challenge for him not to smile back.

Janice Collins kept her notebook in her purse. Flip had put his away also. With weapons sheathed, the pair resumed a palaver.

"All right then," Janice said to Flip. "I'll let you do your thing."

"Thank you," Flip said, as much to Sally as to her. "That's all we ask."

Ed Nash lived in a house with a yard full of maple trees, not far from the Chicago stockyards. The smell of ten thousand hogs waiting to die hung omnipresent in the air. Flip wondered how Janice Collins had stood it, even for a little while. What had to be your life that you lived *here*, day after day, year after year? Maybe, Flip reasoned, it would be a good place to live—a bargain—if you couldn't smell. Had only four senses.

"You think he's going to be home?" Tark asked. "What time do insurance salesmen go to work?"

Flip did not respond. He looked over at Sally, who was holding a handkerchief to her face.

"Sally, can you put that away?" Flip said. "We don't want to offend the man."

"I may have to burn these clothes," Sally said, placing the handkerchief back inside her purse with great effort. "The air here. Something's not right about it. It's literally brown."

"That's dust from the hog lots," Flip informed her.

"Maybe," Sally said, now holding only her gloved hand to her nose. "But it feels like something else too. Something worse."

They started up the paved walkway that led to the small, clapboard house. A man immediately came out and stood on the porch. To Flip, who carried no insurance of any kind, he seemed as likely a candidate as any. The man had milky brown skin, thick eyebrows, and powerful looking shoulders. His short hair had been treated with lye and combed to the side. He wore fine, shined shoes, and straight trousers. The sleeves of his dress shirt were rolled up to his elbows against the summer heat, but his armpits were already heavy with sweat.

"Can I help you folks?" he asked brightly. "Y'all friends of Melissa; she lives upstairs. Take the fire escape entrance around the back of the house."

"We're here to see you, Mr. Nash," Flip said.

The man straightened up as though a drill sergeant had just said 'Ten-SHUN.' It was clear he anticipated a sale. Perhaps he worked out of his home.

Flip prepared to dash some hopes.

Flip opened his coat. In the late-morning sun, his badge positively gleamed. The insurance salesman squinted as the reflected light from the star hit him in the face. Then Flip's coat closed again. Nash warily reopened his eyes.

"What is it?" Nash asked grimly. "You here about an adjustment gone bad? You take that up with corporate, not me. You call the home office. That's how it works."

Flip reached the foot of the porch, but did not climb it.

"We heard that you had a man attack you. *That's* why we're here."

Nash made an expression as though—for the first time, amid the offal stench that hummed in the air as if alive—he smelled something strange.

"Attack me?" he said. "What are you talking about? When was I attacked?"

"Some years ago, as we heard it," Flip clarified. "Back in oh-five or oh-six, maybe?"

Nash nodded slowly, but only to show that he was listening. It was clear to Flip the man recalled nothing.

"We heard that an assailant with a deformity—maybe like a divot in his head?— attacked you in a serious way," Flip continued.

Nash's eyes searched the hazy stockyard horizon, then seemed to hit upon something. He visibly relaxed. His shoulders fell as though the drill sergeant had left the room.

"You been talkin' to old Janice Collins, I do declare!" Nash said brightly. "How is she, after all this time?"

Flip shrugged evasively.

"*Whoever* I heard this from. . ." Flip continued, "we think you might have been targeted because you're an identical twin. We have reason to think someone in the city is doing that now—focusing on identical twins for violence. If we can step inside and talk to you—and you could tell us what you remember—it might help us stop that person."

"Am I in any danger?" Nash asked.

"I don't think so," Flip told him. "But may we come in?"

Nash nodded, turned, and opened up his front door.

As it happened, Nash did work out of his home. A Continental Illinois Insurance sign hung above the desk in his living room, alongside several framed certifications and corporate awards that almost looked like diplomas. Chairs were arranged for visitors, and they sat around the desk.

"What can I tell you?" Nash asked, easing with familiarity into his seat.

"First, describe the attack," Flip said.

"Well. . . how much do you know already? I don't wanna repeat things. Waste your time. What did *Janice* tell you?"

Nash leaned back in his chair and put his hands behind his head. He scanned the doorway behind Flip.

Flip wondered if Nash would tell the quickest possible version of the tale, just to get rid of them before paying customers could arrive. Probably, that was exactly what he would do.

"Assume that I don't know much, and we'll go from there," Flip said sternly. "I'll let you know when we've heard enough. Don't leave out any details."

Nash smirked to say that if that was what Flip wanted, it was what he would get.

"This is a while back, so I don't recall every part of the night. Thing about someone trying to kill you—you forget most of the encounter, except for a few seconds of it. But those few seconds? They stay in front of your brain the whole rest of your life."

Flip nodded and said: "People try to kill me all the time. I know just what you mean."

Nash nodded back cautiously.

"So I worked door-to-door then," the insurance man said. "I came home one evening. It's winter. Not six yet o'clock, but already dark. Cold, too. So cold. I'm climbing up my front porch, and I suppose that was when he came at me—when I was opening up the door. I figure he planned to bust me in the face right when I undid the lock, then get inside and rob me. But he swung too soon! My keys fell from my hand and the door was still locked tight. I think he used a length of pipe or a bat. I never saw. Anyhow, I fought him back, and I don't think he expected me to. I spun and tackled him. I used to carry melons on the farm down south, you know? Built up my arms real good. This man was strong, but I was stronger. He ran around the back of the house, right by Janice's window, then headed off into the trees. I think I must have pulled myself inside my apartment and closed the door. I don't remember. The next day—yes, that's when I saw Janice again—I told her what happened and she made me take myself to the hospital. She was concerned for me, Janice was. Insisted I go. A very kind young lady."

Flip shifted in his chair.

"Tell me about the man," Flip said. "Describe what you saw."

"Negro. About my size. I don't remember much of his face, but I saw the feature you were talking about. I told Janice about that too.

He had a spot on his head about the size of a golf ball that was plumb gone."

"You said it was cold that evening," Flip observed. "The assailant wasn't wearing a hat?"

Nash shook his head.

"Not that I remember."

"How old was he?" Flip asked. "Did he move like an old man or a young man?"

"I really can't tell you," said Nash. "Anything would be a guess. Younger man, I suppose."

Flip shifted once more.

"This isn't much. Any chance you could draw me a picture of him?"

Nash frowned regretfully.

"Naw, I . . . I can't draw much more than stick men. Never had the talent for it."

"Anything else you can tell me?" Flip said sternly. "Did you hear his voice? Did he look like he worked over in the stockyards? Was there blood on his clothes?"

"Nothing. . . I . . . No, I'm sorry."

Flip sighed in frustration and rose from his chair.

For a moment, Nash seemed to believe the interview might be concluding. He smiled, hopeful he'd be able to receive paying customers soon.

But instead of departing, Flip began to pace. He strode to the wall where Nash's certificates hung. He slowed his gait and leaned in close to inspect them, one by one.

"Do you make it known that you are an identical twin, Mr. Nash?" Flip asked, squinting to examine the small type on a property and casualty licensing document.

"I don't keep it a secret," Nash said. "I'm honest if somebody asks me. But let's just say I don't bring it up first."

"Why don't you bring it up?" Flip said, turning suddenly. "No shame in being a twin, is there?"

Nash winced uneasily.

"It is if you got a twin like I do," Nash replied, letting his chin fall to his hands. "It is if you got a twin like my brother Rotney. He. . . He's a good man, deep down. He tries to be. But when our daddy lost his land and our momma got sick, he didn't come back from it the way I did. Never recovered. He drinks too much now. Carries on. Spends too much time in the Levee District. Finds all the places you just shouldn't go. They know him by name at the Bucket of Blood. That alone ought to tell you something."

Across the room, Sally Battle clucked disapprovingly.

The Bucket of Blood was Chicago's most notorious brothel—a place for derelicts, criminals, and those whose sexual tastes ran to the extreme. (Some said the Bucket took its name from the sadistic, gory acts practiced by the sporting girls within. Other said it merely referred to the soap and water pail used to clean the human blood from the floors each night after fistfights. Near as Flip could tell, both origin stories held a kernel of truth.)

"What does Rotney do for work?" Flip asked.

"He was a janitor, last time I heard," Nash answered. "Works in the basement of a building up in the Loop."

"And where does he live?" Flip asked.

Nash rubbed his chin and thought for a moment.

"Not far from here," he said. "Closer to the yards than my place. Deeper inside. I can give you the street address, but it's not much more than a garage. I don't like it that he lives that way, but it's what he seems to choose. He'd rather spend all his money at the Bucket than try to better his lot. Some folks is like that."

Nash took a Continental Illinois Insurance envelope from a stack on his desk, turned it over, and wrote an address on the back. He held it out to Flip. The policeman put it in his coat pocket without a second glance.

"Sounds like your brother runs rough," Flip said. "Way I heard it, Bucket of Blood is a good place to get into a fight or two. Maybe you don't walk out of there everybody's favorite person?"

"I. . . I see where you're going with that," Nash said. "And yes, my brother's the kind of man who probably has some people who'd like to give him a licking. *And yes,* could have been that the man with the chunk out of his head was someone Rotney had rubbed the wrong way—and thought I was him. Hell, maybe Rotney's the guy who gave him the chunk! Who can know? Yes. All right then? Is that what you want me to say? The answer is yes. It might be that's why that man came after me."

Flip looked as though he had finally got what he wanted. He moved away from Nash's wall of certifications and awards, eventually ambling over to the front door. Sally and Tark realized the policeman really did mean to depart this time, and stood as well.

"Mr. Nash, you think your brother would be home this time of day, if we wanted to pay him a visit?" Flip asked.

"If he still has a job, he'll be at work now," Nash said. "Quite a bit rests on that 'if.' You never know with Rotney."

"Thank you," Flip said. "You've been very helpful."

"You think this man's gonna come back for me, after all these years?" Nash asked.

"Actually, I think you're quite safe," Flip told him.

Nash nodded in relief. He scurried to the door and held it open for his departing guests. Flip, Tark, and Sally walked back into the stinking, dusty morning.

Outside, Sally asked if they were going to the brother's house.

Flip said they were.

I t was unbelievable. More than once, Flip stopped to check the address on the back of the envelope in his pocket, just to be sure. That any human could or would choose to live so close to these stinking, fetid rivulets of offal and pigshit was difficult to credit. Was literally astounding. They had thought—from the stench and the brown air—that Ed Nash's house had been practically within the stockyards. Only now did they realize that, compared to their new destination, it had practically been a suburb.

Flip wondered if the address might be a penitence. A self-flagellation. One would have to hate oneself, truly, to keep such an address as Rotney Nash.

"This can't be right," Tark said, whispering aloud what they were all thinking. "No person lives here."

They walked down the center of a dusty street where the concrete underfoot was permanently covered in a thin powder of pigshit. Fences of barbed wire rose beside other fences of wood. It looked like something out of a war. The fences were stained with mud and blood. The cries of the beasts were now distinct. No longer a great hum from a background chorus, Flip heard specific bleats and oinks and human-like screams. The workingmen visible between the fence slats wore grey and brown colors only, and were covered in pig dust. They stared at the trio of interlopers suspiciously. Observation platforms rose into the air above the individual hog lots. Security lights like the spotlights at the back of theaters stood atop them. At the far end of the street was an endless sea of animal pens. Train tracks crisscrossed this broken maze of fences and shit every hundred yards or so. The permanent structures that stuck up here and there—the few remaining teeth in the mouth of an indigent corpse—looked abandoned and burnt out like after a riot.

A final time, Flip took the envelope from his pocket and stared hard at the address that had been written.

Sally Battle carried her handkerchief back at her nose.

Tark swore and said: "That insurance man was having a laugh at our expense. We ought to go back and box his ears."

Flip shook his head no, and made for one of the burnt-out husks.

It was a squat stone building with a segmented vertical door—the kind of a place a maintenance crew might use to store equipment. It was crumbling and half-destroyed, with holes in the roof. There was a lone workman standing near this grim structure. He was holding a long awl that could be knocked into the brain of a pig to kill it.

Flip showed his badge and gun. The man smiled to reveal black gums and yellow teeth. Though startling and unpleasant, the smile was real, and the man seemed glad for visitors to break up his workday.

"We're looking for Rotney Nash," Flip said. "He around here?"

The workman's shit-and-piss smile grew wider.

"Rotney. . ." the man croaked. "What he gone and done now? Not dead, issy?"

"No, he's not dead," Flip said. "This is where he lives, correct?"

"Sometimes Rotney comes around. Pert never during the day though. He comes at night. Sometimes he has a woman with him. She'll be—they both are—very drunk. No sober woman wants to come to Rotney's place."

The workman nodded to the broken garage beside them.

"Can we get inside?" Flip asked.

The man shrugged to say it was something of an open question.

Flip felt around the front of the garage and tried to lift the segmented metal door. It rose easily. Flip noticed a lock on the ground next to it—intact but unused. Perhaps no one would find such a place worth burgling.

Inside were truly pitiful environs. A single room with a mattress and a wood stove. Clothing kept in metal bins or piled in corners. Spoiled food everywhere. An old couch with broken legs occupied the center of the room. Behind it had been piled pieces of mechanical equipment—parts and conveyors that might have come off a killing-line. Beside the mattress was a pile of pornographic prints on very cheap paper. There was also a massive collection of liquor bottles. The place seemed to have its own smell, even above the pig stench.

Flip looked at it all doubtfully.

"When was the last time you saw Rotney?" he asked the man with the awl.

"I just work here," the man said. "Sometimes Rotney is around, and sometimes he ain't. Not a bad man at heart. One time, a killer hog got loose, and he helped us ketch it."

"What?" Flip said.

"Hog from the line went crazy. Knocked a man off a walkway and he died. The hog broke out and we had to chase it down. It was in the paper and everything. We gave Rotney a copy. I can see it over there, on the stack by his lady-pitchers."

Flip approached the dingy mattress and saw there was indeed an issue of *The Broad Axe* crumpled beside it. Flip held his breath to avoid the odor of the bed, stooped, and picked it up. The issue had been turned to a page with a story headlined:

KILLER SOW APPREHENDED BY STOCKYARD MEN

There was a photo adjacent to the article. It showed several workers posing proudly with the pig in question, by then deceased. One of the men was Rotney Nash. He was, indeed, a dead ringer for his brother Ed. He manifested a harried, hunted look—his overalls, hat, shoes, and face were filthy and speckled with shit—but otherwise, it could have been the same man. The other workers in the photo smiled proudly beside the dead pig. Rotney Nash's grin was halfhearted at best.

Flip handed the paper to Sally.

Tark was grimly inspecting the empty liquor bottles with the toe of his shoe.

"I know Sally thinks I drink the cheap stuff," he said. "But this here? Woo. This the *real* cheap stuff."

"He looks just like his brother," Sally said, handing *The Broad Axe* back to Flip. Flip placed the newspaper back atop the pile.

"You have any idea when Rotney might return?" Flip asked the worker.

"Rotney's like a cat," the worker said with a shrug. "He'll come around regular for a couple, three evenings. You think you got a new friend. Then you won't see him again for a month. It is what it is."

"You ever hear of anybody wanting to hurt Rotney?" asked Flip.

The worker looked back and forth.

"He seems to be getting on with *that* just fine himself. Don't b'lieve he needs help from anybody."

"Can you tell me anything else about him?" Flip asked, his frustration mounting.

The man scratched his own head with the tip of the bloody awl. Not hard.

"Naw, I ain't got much else. . ." he trailed off.

Tark finished inspecting the empty rotgut bottles and sauntered over.

"How did you meet Rotney?" Tark asked the man. "You personally?"

The man smiled coyly, flattered to find himself at the center of the questioning.

"I *personally* came to work here eight years ago," he said, as though 'personally' were a fifty-dollar word. "Rotney was already around. One day he was let go for being drunk on the job. He didn't leave though. Kept lingering here in his garage. Became like a fixture. We'd see him time to time, just as we still do. I heard now maybe he works maintenance somewhere downtown."

Flip asked: "Do you know where he is now? That's to say, at this moment?"

"At work?" the man replied. "Same as I ought to be before I get a talking-to. We should close up this garage now. Someone liable to notice we in here."

"I'm the police," Flip reminded him.

"*I'm* not," the man said. "And my foreman don't care who you are. It's my hide that matters."

The worker prepared to shutter the garage. Flip, Tark, and Sally stepped out. After a mighty pull, the segmented door rattled shut. The worker put his killing-awl over his shoulder, gave them a friendly nod, and disappeared around one of the pigshit fences. Then there was only the pig dust and the cries of the hogs—soloists shrieking in front of a cacophony of background players.

"Fuck me running," Tark said. "Who could live like that? I wouldn't believe it if I hadn't just seen it."

"I have to go home and bathe now," Sally said, making clear the matter was not up for debate.

"Fine," Flip said, as they turned around and began to head out from the stockyards. "But we meet up this evening at your place, Sally. Six o'clock sharp. And have something on your stomach by then."

"The way this place smells, I don't know if I'll be eating for a week," Sally told him.

"That's your business, I suppose," Flip replied. "But we got a long night ahead."

THIRTEEN

Tark went with Sally to the Palmerton, and both enjoyed long baths—at different times—in the same large, claw-footed tub. Tark applied unguents and perfumed soaps usually reserved for women, vigorously and without hesitation. Anything to scrub the lingering awfulness of the stockyards from himself.

Sally had a meal brought, but—true to her own forecasting—touched almost none of it. Tark managed an appetite, but avoided pork. (He stared angrily, wordlessly at a plate of chops when they were proffered.)

Flip caught up with them at six on the dot. He had also bathed and changed clothes. He still wore his leather jacket, but his trousers and shoes were different and shabby. His shirt had a frayed collar and a large nonspecific stain extended down the left side. Several buttons were missing. He stood in the lobby of the Palmerton and waited until Sally and Tark came downstairs.

When Sally saw him, she froze.

"We're *not*."

Sally looked Flip up and down in horror.

"I was thinking we might be, from what that man said, but *please* tell me we're not. . ."

Flip's face told her that, indeed, they were.

"What?" Tark asked, looking back and forth between Sally and Flip like a confused child. "What's happening?"

"We're going to the Bucket of Blood, is what's happening," Sally said, placing a very annoyed hand on her hip. "And if we are, I'm *not* ruining another of my better dresses. You two can wait ten minutes for me to change into something I don't damn care about. Stay here."

She stalked up to her rooms with great commotion. Flip and Tark seated themselves beside the golden piano. Girls milled past and smiled politely. The front door to the brothel was open, and the air that evening had an energy to it. The house would do good business, Flip felt sure. It was that kind of energy.

"You been to the Bucket before, Tark?" Flip asked without looking over at the magician.

Tark shook his head no.

"That's good," Flip said matter-of-factly. "I've been trying—all afternoon—to think of a way that we don't have to go there. But I can't. Tomorrow my week is up. I'm due to report to the mayor. Tell him what I have. And I got to be able to look that man in the eye and say I checked under every rock."

"What *do* you have?" Tark asked.

"I'll know more about what I have—and what I don't have—if I can talk to Rotney Nash tonight," Flip told him. "No use trying to do a full accounting of what you know until you've followed all the leads. As far as I can tell, there's still one left."

"What're you gonna ask him?" Tark wondered. "Sounds like he's the sort of man liable to be too drunk to talk."

"There's an art to questioning a drunkard," Flip told him.

"And you know it?" asked Tark.

"I got you interested in this bullshit, didn't I?"

Tark waved a hand, dismissing any similarity.

"I got myself interested," Tark insisted.

"Rotney Nash surely has enemies, and it's likely he's been attacked at various points," Flip continued. "Stumblebums, drunks—they often are, sometimes for no reason. Part of me is surprised Rotney has survived this long without a fatal beating."

Sally reappeared. Half of her makeup was gone, and she wore a long dress with a high collar that had been in fashion about fifteen years prior. It was as old and as frayed as Flip's shirt.

"Oh my," the policeman said.

Sally took out a handkerchief and dipped it in a golden spittoon in the lobby corner. Two of her girls passed, and did their best not to gawk as Sally blotted at the front of her dress until there were heavy, deep stains that looked as though they would never come out.

Then Sally dropped the handkerchief into the spittoon.

"Let's do this," she said.

They did.

The Bucket of Blood was a short walk north along State Street and then a little bit west, to the corner of Nineteenth and Federal. A small distance from the Palmerton, but worlds away in terms of character and feel. The Levee District. Or what remained of it after the reformers had got done. That great shuttered wonderland of vice. It held the air of a boardwalk carnival closed for the season, though everyone knew it was likely gone for good.

Nearly all the bars, brothels, and gambling dens in the district had been put out of business during the anti-vice sweep a few years prior. The Bucket, however, survived, albeit in diminished form. (The campaigners had seemed to accept this. Perhaps, Flip thought, they realized the Bucket was a particularly stubborn carbuncle—one that would require multiple treatments to eradicate entirely).

Amidst a string of boarded-up bordellos and casinos, the Bucket operated as the lone remaining outpost of sin. The chaos and mayhem and nudity that might have spilled from its doors onto the street in prior years—even on a Monday night—were now safely contained inside. But Flip knew that most of this change was cosmetic only. The Bucket might have dimmed its lights, but they still burned just as hot.

"I heard they used to call this Bedbug Row," Tark said, examining the shuttered flophouses. "Maybe this is what happens when the bedbugs are finally through with you. When you're all et up."

"So help me, if either of you bring actual bedbugs inside the Palmerton. . ." Sally said, trailing off into a fury. "Well, I was going to burn this dress anyway. Just see that the both of you burn your clothes as well."

"But I *like* my clothes," Tark said.

"I'll buy you some new ones," Sally snapped.

"But these are special, magician's clothes," Tark objected, glancing down at his seemingly unremarkable duds. "There's a hole for a cord to run from my wrist, down my trousers, all the way to my big toe. You wouldn't understand, but it can put something in my hand that's not in my hand, even when my sleeves are rolled up."

"New ones can be had," Sally said. "I will purchase them for you. I presume there is some sort of specialized catalog for such clothing, yes?"

Tark shrugged sheepishly.

Apparently, there was.

Sally nodded in satisfaction.

The Bucket glowed in the darkness ahead of them, red light spilling out from under its shuttered windows. They approached the front door. A kind of a doorman—bald and enormous and mightily crazed from the heat—tottered outside, shifting back and forth. He seemed to be concentrating on a spot on the wall just a few inches above his head. He thrummed in the heat. For the life of him, Flip could not figure out what the doorman was looking at. There was no longer a sign above the Bucket's entrance. It had been taken down during the raids.

"Tark, we never talked about this, but you don't like to do more than have a drink, do you?" Flip whispered as they neared.

Tark seemed genuinely puzzled by the question.

"More than?" the magician said. "What more would you do? Drinkin's plenty."

Flip nodded to say this was meet.

"People in here will offer you morphine, opium, cocaine," Flip said.

"I stick to a liquid diet," Tark said.

"Well if anyone hands you a drink—especially a woman—make sure you watched the bartender pour it," Flip continued.

"I'll take care of him," Sally said, putting her arm around the magician like an affectionate auntie. "Show him how to handle himself in a big-boy place."

"What?" said Tark, attempting, unsuccessfully, to shrug her off. "Damn. I know how to handle myself. Who do you think you're talking to?"

"That's what a lot of men say before they go inside here," Flip told him sternly. "Then they end up poisoned, robbed and froze to death in an alley out back."

Sally released Tark from her embrace, and patted him encouragingly on the back.

'Big-boy,' she mouthed, as they walked past the strange, vibrating doorman and inside the Bucket.

The interior was most immediately defined by its low, wooden ceiling. A very tall man could reach up and touch it. It was like an inn from Colonial times. There were doors and hallways leading away from a large central barroom. Filthy red curtains had been hung here and there, creating nooks and aediculae into which one might duck to perform small, intimate rites. Because it was still so early in the evening, there were not many customers. Against the far wall stood a long, low bar. It was, for most visitors, merely the staging area where they would queue before being whisked off to wonders and horrors in other rooms. In a wicker chair near the entryway sat an elderly prostitute— entirely naked except for her shoes. If a visitor had come to get straight to the point—without a lot of froufrou—she was, presumably, there to accommodate. The naked woman looked Flip up and down, but soon switched her gaze over to Tark, sensing a keener vulnerability in him. Tark glanced at her from the side of his eyes. She made a smooching kiss into the air like a French woman.

Flip laughed.

They walked up to the bar. Seated at it was a very drunk man in late middle-age. He was unshaven, and had a red, ruddy face. He was dressed like a sailor who worked on Lake Michigan. Seated beside him was a woman in a flouncy, ruffled skirt like a can-can dancer. She wore too much makeup and had had her nose broken to one side. The sailor—loudly, with much basso—was telling a story about a fishing accident that had left seven men dead. One of the sailor's meaty hands clutched a mug of cold beer. The other was buried inside the woman's skirt. Every few moments—when he needed to make an especially enthusiastic point—he would remove his fingers from the woman and hold them up to gesture. Then, the desired emphasis achieved, would return them. (Flip thought the courtesan did a fine job of showing herself equally stimulated by the raconteur's tale as by his efforts underneath her garments.)

"You!" a voice suddenly cried.

It was the barman, half-Chinese and thinly bearded. His body was covered by a sheen of sweat and not-bathing. He wore a blue shirt with the sleeves rolled up, and had a great round belly.

"I remember you!" the barman called to Flip, as though this successful recollection both astounded and pleased him. "We only allow high-class Negroes in this place. I forget, are you high-class?"

"Any higher and I'd be hittin' the ceiling," Flip said. He reached up and touched the wooden boards above to make his point. The barman laughed and squinted and clapped his hands like a baby.

"You been here before?" Tark asked quietly.

"Course I have," Flip whispered back. "Workin'."

The enthusiastic barman laughed again, seemingly at nothing. Underneath the bar was a smoking pipe. The barman stooped and took a long draw from it. Then he nodded vigorously, as though the pipe had helped him make up his mind about an important matter.

"Here," he said. "I know just what high class persons like yourselves need."

The bartender took three tall glasses down from a battered shelf behind him. Into one, he poured dark bourbon. Into the next, a sweet amber liqueur. Into the final glass went something thick and mysterious and green, which Flip hoped was Chartreuse. As the barman poured, the wailing cry of a prostitute being fucked behind a curtain rose and fell like the whistle of a fast-moving train. Tark stayed more or less motionless, but his eyes circled in wild alarm. Flip put a hand on the magician's shoulder to steady him.

The bartender nodded in satisfaction, as though the drinks had been satisfactorily consecrated by the artificial cries of lust.

"Here you go," he said, pushing the glasses forward. Flip got the whisky, Sally the sickeningly-sweet liqueur, and Tark the mysterious green concoction.

"It'll give you all the seeming of a demon that is dreaming," the barman said to the magician. "That's what I tell people, anyway."

He laughed.

"Thank you," Flip said, placing a few coins on the bar.

The bartender immediately pocketed them.

Flip said: "I've never seen a man tending bar who could smoke an opium pipe and keep himself awake. Much less serve drinks. Must take some talent."

"Thank you for noticing," the barman said proudly. "The pipe helps to keep me even. I eat so many snow-balls, you see. Last year, before I found the pipe, I stayed awake for fifteen days on those things. By the end, I was serving drinks to people who weren't even there. The pipe makes it one beautiful balancing act."

"I'm sure it does," Flip said.

"Would you like a snow-ball?" the bartender asked, in a where-are-my-manners sort of way. He brought up a small sachet from under the bar.

"Not quite yet," Flip told the bartender.

Tark picked up his green drink. He sniffed at it carefully, and took the smallest sip.

Flip put his back to the bar, surveying the room. His eyes lit on a darkened doorway. A sign reading "Torture Chamber This Way" was affixed to the wall above it. As Flip watched, a man and a woman—convivial, drunk, and happy as jaybirds—passed, arm in arm, into that darkness.

The barman had another puff of his pipe.

Flip turned back and said: "My old friend Rotney Nash. . . Has he been in tonight? He owes me twenty dollars, and I intend to collect."

The barman searched what was left of his memory.

"Rotney. . ." he said. "Has he been around recently? Let me see?"

Flip wondered if the barman was angling for a bribe.

The barman glanced over and saw that Tark had already drained his glass. Flip glanced over too. The barman brought down the green bottle and refilled it.

"So wait. . ." Tark said. "I thought you only let high-class Negroes in this place."

"That's right," the barman said, replacing the bottle.

Flip looked at Tark hard, asking what he thought he was doing.

"And you telling me someone like Rotney Nash qualifies?" Tark continued.

"I see that you all truly know him," the bartender said, giggling.

Tark shrugged.

"But Rotney Nash is the highest-class customer of all!" the barman declared. "He's one who spends his entire paycheck within these four humble walls. That's as high as you can get."

Abruptly, Sally began tapping Flip on the thigh. He looked over. She indicated with a nod that he should follow her glance across the room. There, a lone woman lingered, very strange.

The woman was tall and pale and thin almost to the point of boniness. At first glance and at a distance, she seemed possessed of beauty far too great to be working at a place with "Bucket" in its name. Yet, as Flip trained his eyes more carefully, other aspects became clear. The deep scarring across the cheeks and neck. The subtle but unmistakable positioning of one eye higher than the other. The hairline that went jagged on one side of her scalp. These could only have been the result of terrible injuries—of being burned, and having one's face broken and healed and broken again.

The woman was looking at the trio of newcomers with a curious expression. After a long moment, she made her way over. While she walked, she screwed up her face, as though the effort it took to move in a straight line was very great indeed. Flip had seen this kind of walk in those who had suffered an injury to the inner ear.

"You are looking for Rotney?" she said in an accent that was impossible to place, but definitely not Chicago.

"That's right," Flip replied. "He owes me twenty dollars."

"That's funny," the woman said. "He owes me twenty dollars, too."

Flip looked the woman over and inclined his head to the side.

"Seems like maybe we have something in common," she continued. "Perhaps you'd care to discuss our mutual interests somewhere a bit more private?"

She took Flip's four fingertips in her hand and eyed one of the many dark passageways leading away. It was framed by red velvet curtains—smokestained, ripped, and rubbed filthy. (No sign above it promised torture, but that counted for almost nothing.)

"You misunderstand me," Flip said. "I actually *am* looking for Rotney Nash. That's the long and short of my agenda."

The mutilated courtesan made a point to glance down at the crotch of Flip's pants after he said 'long and short.'

"I think *you* misunderstand *me*," she whispered.

The courtesan leaned in close.

"Do you know what your man there just drank?" she asked, nodding ever-so-slightly at Tark.

Flip did not know. He looked back to the bartender for guidance. The bartender had taken another puff of his pipe and was lost in a world of his own.

"Chartreuse," Flip said. "Or absinthe."

The courtesan smiled and shook her head no.

"That was fermented ramp juice," she whispered. "That's why it smells so awful. And why it's so green. Most men get nothing from it. But some men are, let's say, *receptive*. The drink is one of Rotney's favorites. The barman here . . . He only serves it to Rotney . . . and to Rotney's friends. I wonder how he knew you were friends with Rotney."

"Like I said," Flip replied—even as he began to grow uncomfortable, "the man owes me twenty dollars."

"Yeah," the woman said. "And like I told you, he owes me the same amount."

She looked at Flip—one eye a half-inch above the other—hard and fierce.

"You know, I believe we *should* go and compare notes. My friends here will be safe at the bar, yes?"

Without glancing, the courtesan said: "The madam of the Palmerton House knows how to handle herself anywhere in the city—even if she doesn't want to let it show."

Sally did not respond.

"The other one. . . Buy him another ramp juice and he'll be fine, I expect."

Flip tossed a coin down and nodded to the barman. Then the strange woman took him by the fingertips, and pulled him deeper into the Bucket of Blood.

They walked down a dark passage framed by red curtains, then through a second hallway that led to a side room. Outside the room was a spent-looking man lying across a small settee. His clothes were fine but rumpled. Pinned to his chest was a six-pointed metal star. He was in a deep narcotic haze. Unnatural amber drool depended from the corner of his mouth. Flip let his fingers drop from the woman's and stooped down to take a look.

The star had been issued by the City of Chicago, but was not a policeman's. It was engraved to read: "FOR VALUABLE SERVICES RENDERED TO THE CORONER."

"Don't mind him," the woman said. "He's always like that."

"A deputy coroner," Flip said. "Work for the damned to do. Eastland Disaster? Nine-hundred bodies all at once like that—all bloated and burned by the sun? Make any man need to forget himself, I s'pose."

"A normal man, yes," the courtesan said. "But not this one. This one *misses it.* The days after the Eastland were the finest of his life.

Nothing he ever does will capture that feeling again, and he knows it. So he numbs himself here. . . waiting, hoping for another catastrophe. Come on."

They went into a bedroom and the strange woman shut the door.

Here, she was like an actress stepping off stage. She relaxed. Her face fell. When it did, it became even more crooked. Her eyes appeared even less aligned. She was like two faces sewn together.

"So. . ." the woman said. "What *do* you want with Rotney Nash?"

"He owes-" Flip tried.

"What *really*?" she growled. "Come on. You didn't come to a place like this to play games."

Flip was unflappable and stern.

"It's something serious, I'll tell you that much," Flip said loudly. "Whether you're a friend of Rotney's, or whether he really does owe you money—and you want him to live long enough to pay you—you ought to help me out. I'm interested his safety. The safety of some other people too. You're right, I didn't come here to play games. I'm here on a matter that is deadly dire. If you know where he is—whether it's here or somewhere else—you better tell me."

The room had a bed and a small chest of drawers. The broken courtesan walked to the chest and took out a cigarette. She lit it and held it between her lips, considering.

"You're not like the others," she said, looking Flip up and down. "And that's just a matter of fact, not my opinion."

"What 'others?'" he said.

"The others who come here and ask after Rotney," she replied, taking a long drag. "His friends. His enemies. Whoever they are. I don't know. But the others are odd. Very odd. Odder than you, even. And you *are* odd. Anybody ever tell you that?"

"I don't understand," Flip said. "People come looking for Rotney? Wait. . . One of them wouldn't be a white man—thin and balding? Kinda mean-looking? Goes by Durkin?"

He pulled out the photograph of the hitman smiling in his pin-stripe suit.

The courtesan shrugged.

"Maybe," she said. "Some people who come in—their faces get obscured by the shadows. It's so dark that maybe I don't see."

Another angle for a bribe. Everybody was the same. But Flip was not about to start doling out cash. Not until he had a better sense of whether this woman could truly be of help.

"I'm not with vice and I've no interest in shutting this place down, but I'll tell you plainly that this is a police matter," Flip said.

"What in here *ain't* a police matter, potentially?" the woman said with a shrug.

Despite himself, Flip smiled.

"I tell you one thing," she continued. "You flash a star and a gun out there, your chances of finding Rotney go to nil."

"I know that," Flip told her.

The courtesan sat down on the bed.

"Now then . . ." she said. "What *can* I tell you about Rotney Nash? He comes in here, drinks himself insensible, and winds up on the floor most of the time. They have to carry him out. He usually starts with the fermented ramp juice, but he'll switch to whiskey or beer after a pace. Drinks like there's no tomorrow, that one does."

"How often does he come in?" Flip asked.

"Maybe once a week," answered the courtesan. "And I hate to tell you honey, but Monday is not his night. He likes Fridays and Saturdays, when the joint is really hopping."

Flip sighed. So he would not have his man this evening after all.

"What else?" Flip pressed. "Anything you can tell me while I'm here?"

"He . . ." the courtesan began, hesitating between puffs. "He . . . always wears the same clothes. They're not nice clothes, and they're always the same. Dirty trousers that smell like shit. Rumpled shirt. Muddy shoes. Bowler hat pulled low . . ."

"Does he-"

And then Flip stopped speaking because he realized he had spoken over her. The courtesan had said something more.

"What was that?" Flip demanded. "*What did you just say?*"

"Huh?" the woman replied, confused by his insistence.

"Tell me what you just said under your breath?" Flip pressed. "When I cut you off. It sounded like-"

"He keeps his bowler hat pulled low. . . to hide his deformity," she clarified. "Rotney Nash is like me, all right? He looks different. He has a hole in his head, like a scoop taken out. That's one reason I protect him—one reason I look out for him when people like *you* come around. I can relate to him. He and I are alike. Rotney wears that hat all the time because a piece from his head is missing."

Tark was still on his third glass of fermented ramp.

Halfway finished with the drink, he let his tongue linger on the lip of the glass, savoring the strange salty taste. Sally, despite her tobacco-stained clothes and general *deshabille* had had to turn three men away already. (A lack of eye-contact and a stern "Keep walking" had done the trick so far, but she knew they would be less likely to take no for an answer as the night progressed.) Sally thought that Tark's green drink smelled horrible. Now and then she got a whiff of it, and turned up her nose.

Flip barged out of the back, trailed by a courtesan who appeared both alarmed and confused. He looked around wildly for his friends. The brothel had become busier, with new patrons filing inside every few moments. All the seats at the bar were taken.

Flip found Sally and Tark, and moved in close between them. He spoke in low, intense tones.

"Rotney Nash is our man," he said.

"What?" said Sally. "We know that. We're here looking for him here, aren't we?"

"No," Flip said, putting his hands on their shoulders to urge them off their barstools. "I mean that Rotney is our suspect."

"For the. . ." Tark said, setting down his drink.

Flip nodded.

"We need to go," Flip said. "I don't believe there's a good chance of catching Rotney here tonight."

Tark and Sally gathered themselves and headed for the door.

As he turned, Flip felt something hard and stiff hit him in the side of the chest. He glanced up and saw the broken courtesan, her fingers square against his ribs. Her face was drawn into a sneer.

"You see that man there in the corner?" she hissed. "And the one standing behind the couch? All I have to do is say a word, and they can keep you from walking out of here. Or from walking ever again. You follow me?"

Flip reached out.

Slowly, deliberately, he moved her hand down from his chest.

But the woman put it right back on him.

Flip saw the shadows nearby begin to shift. The confrontation had been noticed. Flip kept his hands at his sides.

"What do you intend to do with Rotney?" the woman asked.

"What I intend to do . . . is save lives," Flip replied. "Look into my eyes if you doubt me. See if you think I'm not telling you the truth. Go on."

For a moment, nobody said anything. Nobody moved.

The broken courtesan lowered her hand. And she did look into Flip's eyes. She looked longer and harder than Flip could remember anyone ever looking into his eyes. Not a lover. Not his own mother. He allowed it to happen. He tilted his head slightly, so his own eyes might line up more directly with her crooked sightline.

Other patrons of the Bucket stopped to watch, or to watch patrons watching. (Stranger things took place within the Bucket, to be sure, but this wasn't bad for early on an off night.)

Eventually, the broken courtesan said: "I believe you."

Flip brushed past her and marched outside.

Back on Nineteenth Street, a man had been stabbed. He did not seem badly hurt and was limping away from his attacker (another drunk who seemed as astounded as the victim that the altercation had occurred). The hypnotized lummox of a man guarding the Bucket's door had not noticed the fight. He stayed watching the space on the wall. Watching something invisible and irresistible. Flip began to wonder if he was even employed by the brothel. A handful of men had gathered to see if there would be more violence between the two drunks. When it was clear there would not, the onlookers shuffled off.

Flip, Tark, and Sally stood alone on the sidewalk, not far from the patch of fighting men's blood.

"What's happening, Flip?" Tark asked.

"That woman," Flip explained. "She said that Rotney Nash was missing a piece of his head. Said he conceals it under a hat."

"So . . ." Tark began, gears turning.

"So, like I said, Rotney is our man," Flip continued. "That woman told me Monday isn't his night to come to the Bucket, and I believe her. Men are creatures of habit. They stick to certain calendar days, or only come out when a girl they like is dancing, or a drink they like is pouring. Rotney's days are Friday and Saturday, but I don't want to wait that long. I think we go back to his garage in the pigyards and try to pick him up. I have a lot of questions right now. Foremost, I'm wondering why Ed Nash lied to us. Why he didn't say it was his own brother who attacked him. But experience has taught me you can't wait to act until you have all the answers. You've got to move when you have the scent. And right now, I have it."

Before Tark or Sally could object, Flip turned east down Nineteenth Street at a brisk pace.

"Welp," said Sally. "At least I'm wearing the right clothes this time. Though, two baths in a day isn't a wonder for anybody's skin."

Flip did not respond. The smells they might accumulate over the course of the night were the least of his worries.

He thought of telling Tark and Sally that they didn't have to come along; not for this part. That they were not *needed*-needed, not really. He had always had his greatest successes apprehending criminals when working alone. But Tark spoke before Flip could articulate any of these things.

"Do you think he was born with it?"

"Hmm?" Flip called back distractedly.

"The thing in his head," Tark clarified as he jogged to keep up with the striding policeman.

"I don't know, kid," Flip said. "You could get something like that in an accident, or from being shot in the head just right. More people are shot in the head and live than you'd imagine. Though they are always changed after. It might explain Rotney's need to drink fermented ramp juice at the direst brothel in Chicago every weekend. To live like he does."

"I dunno," Tark said thoughtfully.

"You don't know what?"

"The fermented ramp didn't taste half bad. It was different—don't get me wrong—but I wouldn't say it was awful. You sure can taste the living plant in it, just like you can taste the berries in gin. I can, anyway."

Flip wondered if he should send the magician and the madam home.

"Well I think he *could* have been born with it," Tark continued. "Rotney, I mean. Hey. . . What if they both have it!?"

"Both?" Flip said, not seeing the idea.

"Yeah," said Tark. "And then that would explain why Ed Nash had that hairpiece."

Flip.

Stopped.

Walking.

Sally, following close, ran into his back.

"Ow," she said. "What are you. . . Flip?"

The policeman acted as though she were not there at all. He turned his entire attention back to the magician.

"*What did you just say?*"

Tark looked around the empty, filthy streets for anything, anyone to account for why his words had left Flip so astounded.

"I . . . said that it would explain the hairpiece, is all," Tark replied. "I was just thinking—'cause they're identical twins, right?—what if they were both born with a piece missing from their heads."

Flip leaned in so close to Tark that he could smell the horrid fermented ramp on his breath.

"What do you mean, *hairpiece*?"

"Oh, it was a fine one," the magician said. "No doubt there. But it *was* a hairpiece. My line of work, you get good at spotting fakes. You spot fake eyelashes on women. Fake bosoms or fake figures entirely. And on men? There you spot all manner of fakes. Some men wear girdles. Some men dye their hair. Some wear fake hair altogether. And Ed Nash does, sure as I'm alive. At the time, I only thought he had it 'cause he was bald. I thought it was a regular wig. But if you had the money—and he probably does, if he runs his own insurance agency— it would be nothing to commission something special. A toupee that has a ball of felt, say, that goes down into your head-hole. Plugs it up so you look normal again. It would probably help the toupee to stay on, too."

Lightning and thunder struck Joe Flippity. He saw no flash and heard no report, but the effect was nearly the same. He looked up into the night sky, crowded with the reflected glow of the streetlights, to see if there were indeed thunderclouds above. All that came back out of the ether were Ursula Green's words. *One is two. Two is one.*

The thought inside his brain seemed so terrible that he feared if he spoke it loudly the universe might simply strike him dead—with real lightning, this time. Something in Flip's soul told him to keep it clamped shut in an iron-tight lockbox.

Tark and Sally looked on in concern.

"Flip, what is it?" whispered Sally. "Do you think it's Ed Nash instead of Rotney Nash?"

"Yes," Flip said slowly. "Yes and no."

"I don't follow," said Tark.

The policeman took his eyes back down from the skies above Chicago. He spoke carefully and soberly, like a physician explaining a complicated condition to a patient.

"In your act, Tark, you and your brother pretend to be one man. That's how you appear across the circus tent. You let on like there's just one Tark brother, but in actuality there are *two*. The trick works because no one in the audience is even thinking you might be a twin."

The magician nodded.

"If I'm right, we have the reverse," Flip continued in deadly serious tones. "Everyone acts like there are two Nash brothers—Ed and Rotney—but what if, really, there's just one?"

Now Tark looked confused.

"Just which one?" Tark asked. "Cause we've met Ed, and we've seen a newspaper picture of Rotney."

"I don't know the details yet," Flip said. "But I can imagine a man who runs a respectable insurance brokerage during the week, but on the weekends likes to do things that would keep anybody from wanting to trust him with a policy on their life. So he decides to become two people. He's Rotney Nash when he's carousing at the Bucket, and he's Ed Nash the rest of the time."

Tark looked halfway convinced. Sally, less so.

"Wait. . ." Sally said. "That still doesn't explain what Janice Collins saw. Or thought she saw."

"I'm thinking about that right this moment," Flip told Sally, inclining his head like a man listening for a sound in the far distance. "In my experience, people with something to hide will spin a lie so that it can work both ways. So that it can work 'just in case.' I can imagine a night ten or so years ago. . . Ed Nash came home drunk as a skunk, after being out as Rotney. Maybe he was careless. Maybe he stumbled around the back of his house where that pretty young newspaper girl worked—tried to look into her window, even. And maybe the next morning he thought she might have seen him without his hairpiece on, so he made up a story. When he saw her again, he told her that a man with a divot in his head had attacked him. That it was a mugger. I'm still not sure, but it's got to be something *like* that."

"This is all very strange," Sally said.

"Maybe so," said Flip. "But I get the feeling it means we need to find Nash, and we need to find him right away. Mr. Hyde only comes out on the weekends, so I think we got to go arrest Dr. Jekyll."

When they reached the south end of the Levee District where you could still catch a cab, Flip used his policeman's star to hail one and they piled inside. Flip pushed money into the cabbie's hands and gave the address of Ed Nash's neighborhood in the stinking shadow of the stock-yards. The neighborhood only. Flip told the diver to stop at its edge.

Flip said nothing more. He was distant, lost in thought. He was still turning over the strangeness in his head.

"Why we ain't go directly to his house?" the magician whispered after they had gone a few blocks.

"Because that's not how I choose to handle it," Flip said, looking up at the stars above the city—smelling the lake and the hogs on the summer breeze. "Ed Nash is already under arrest. He was under arrest the moment I thought to arrest him. The only question is what makes him more liable to talk. More liable to tell us the truth about what he did. I could go to the station right now, come back with enough police-men to surround his house. Then we'd take him downtown and put the screws on."

Flip inhaled a bug or piece of pig mummified pigshit floating in the air. He paused to spit it out the side of the cab.

"But that doesn't always work," he continued. "I'm thinking it might not work at all on a man like him. He'd just clam up. And I feel like what the mayor wants, really, is answers. That's what I'd want, if I were mayor. If we're not bringing in Durkin—which I don't think we are—I got to be able to say why. So I want to make Mr. Nash explain himself to me."

The cab paused at the edge of the neighborhood. Flip directed the cabbie to press just a little further inside. The pig smell was strong now. The scent did not ease up overnight. Perhaps it never eased up. Maybe in winter, Flip mused. Maybe then.

The surrounding homes were dark and quiet. Nobody was out on the street. Flip told the cabbie to stop at the end of Nash's block, and then to turn around and leave the way he had come.

On foot, Flip led the trio into a row of trees that grew parallel with the street and wound through different yards and properties.

Flip seemed uncannily able to pass into shadow and become one with it. Despite being a tall man, he concealed himself so completely that Tark and Sally Battle found this ability to disappear positively disturbing. Tark was on the point of commenting upon it when Sally hissed: "Someone is liable to think we're burglars and shoot us, creeping around like this."

"Then I'll shoot back," Flip said. "Now stay quiet. We're almost there."

They were.

The trees led to the edge of Nash's yard. His house was visible only by the light of the moon; there were no streetlights close by. Flip remembered that a young woman rented the upstairs flat. He hoped she would not become involved tonight. With luck, she would prove a very sound sleeper.

"There's a back door to his place," Flip whispered. "I mean on the first floor. I saw it when we were inside. If he's going to run, that's how he'll do it. I think he's too wide to fit through any of the windows. None of you saw other exits, did you?"

Tark and Sally shook their heads.

"Me either," said Flip. "I'm going to knock on his front door and get in under a pretense. Sally, I'll ask you to come with me. I think he's liable to believe I have softer intentions if he sees a woman along."

It was too dark to view Sally's reaction to this idea.

"Tark, I want you to go around back and hold the rear door shut. It opens out. Place your foot against it. If he tries to run, you only need to buy me enough time to get back there. Understand?"

Tark said that he did.

They stepped out of the trees and into the darkened yard. Flip and Sally headed up toward the front door. Tark split off and picked his way around to the back of the house. Flip thought again of the young woman sleeping up on the second floor. His eyes traced the dark window panes above them. He looked hard but saw nothing, only blackness and reflected glass.

Because his eyes were adjusted up, he and Sally were fairly close to the house before Flip chanced to peer into the darkened first floor windows. And he saw it immediately. A visage so close and clear that it seemed for an instant to be his own reflection. Ed Nash. Or Rotney Nash. Wearing trousers and a sleeveless white undershirt. Staring back out at him from the other side. Stone bald headed, and with a piece of his forehead missing.

And he had been watching them, maybe the entire time.

Flip opened his mouth to say something, but Nash was too fast. He disappeared like a ghost into the darkness. Flip heard his footsteps padding fast to the back of the house. Flip changed his course and broke into a run.

"Tark, he's coming your way!" Flip shouted.

Flip raced around the side of the house. Sally trailed after him. They heard a crash and the sound of glass shattering. Flip reached inside his coat and produced his 1911. They turned the corner, and Flip swung his gun left and right, looking for a target. He saw nothing, not even Tark. Then he noticed the crumpled pile on the flagstones behind Nash's back door. Glass was all around, and the door was ajar.

Flip ran over.

Tark sat up out of the pile. He was the pile. One hand still held the neck of the broken gin bottle. The other held his head.

"You all right?" Flip asked, training his gun into the trees.

A neighbor had heard the commotion and was turning on lights.

"He came before I could get my foot on the door," Tark said apologetically. "I was just having a nip for courage. Then the door slammed into my head and knocked me over."

"Where!" Flip cried, squinting into the darkened yard. "Where did he go?"

Tark pointed into the trees, due east.

"There, I think."

Sally approached. She placed her hands on her hips and clucked disapprovingly, then bent to help Tark right himself.

Flip went immediately after his prey. He lunged into a sprint and disappeared in the darkness. His footfalls fell away and soon Tark and Sally heard and saw nothing more. Flip was like an eagle launching himself into the night sky. It chose not to silhouette itself against the moon. It chose not to show itself, period.

Sally inspected Tark's wounds. He had a small gash on brow where the door had connected with his face, but it was not deep. Other than that, he might only have some bruises.

"Come on," Sally whispered. "Stand up. You just got the wind knocked out a little."

Tark dropped the jagged neck of the gin bottle and rose.

Moments later, they heard Flip's quick, sharp breath and he came padding back out of the trees. He held his 1911 low, with two hands. There was nobody with him.

Flip shook his head, answering no, he had not found Nash. He stared at Sally intently.

"He didn't come back here either," she whispered.

Flip suddenly became interested in the back door, creaking on its hinges.

"Tark, you're *sure* he brushed past you?" Flip said urgently, taking the magician by the shoulder. "He didn't just bump you and run back into the house?"

"No," Tark insisted. "I saw him run that way."

Flip sighed in frustration and put his gun back into his coat. He opened the door with his foot and looked doubtfully into the dark house. There was no movement or sound. Flip saw no trace of Nash.

"What do we do?" Sally asked.

"Is Tark all right?" Flip asked, leaning in to have his own cursory look at the magician's brow.

"He's fine," Sally said. "Cut like that can be stitched right up."

"Come on then," Flip told them, heading back into the yard.

"To where?" asked Sally.

"There's a thousand places he might go," Flip said. "But I know men like this. Men with double lives. In this situation? There's one place I *know* he'll go."

Flip took off into the night.

Tark and Sally Battle looked at one another, then followed after.

F lip walked quickly but did not quite run. He knew that Sally's shoes and skirt were making it difficult for her. He also knew that nothing could be done. The woman would have to soak her feet after this, surely, but she could afford the Epsom salts.

The stockyards were near now. The trio could hear low bayings in the distance. A night ocean of animals awaited.

"Why don't we find another cab to take?" asked Tark.

"I don't want to beat him there," Flip said. "He sees that, he goes someplace else. We *never* catch him. I want to chase him into his hole. I want to be right on his heels. And I think that's where we are."

They made their way deeper into the yards. The horrid smell increased.

Flip had not made up his mind as to whether or not a cornered Nash would be dangerous. Many predators could be positively meek when you first met them, but then the claws would come out when things got underway. Many predators, but not all. . . Flip had not seen any real claws from Ed Nash. That he had fled was a good sign. His knocking over Tark had probably been an accident.

They turned a corner and the walls of the stockyards rose before them. And there, in the distance ahead, at the center of it all, amongst bunkers and outbuildings just like it, was the garage of Rotney Nash.

The air around them seemed to crackle. Not with electricity, but not with airborne pigshit either. The wind blew in hard off the lake, the way it should not. The strangeness might have come directly from the great body of water itself, or from another place entirely. Flip had the sudden sense that something *else* was present in the atmosphere above.

Flip slowed his pace enough for Tark to ask, "Hey, what're we gonna do when we get there?"

"When we get there, I want you to look *in*," Flip said. "And Sally, I want you to look *out*. That is to say, Sally, you keep an eye on the pens and the walls around us. You see guards, you go up to one of them. They'll be less alarmed to see a woman. You go up to them and tell them to fetch the police. Tark, you watch the garage. You see Nash come out of there—out through a place where I'm not—you shout to me. You raise an alarm loud as you can."

Sally and Tark both nodded.

"Otherwise, you both stay away," Flip told them. "The rest of this is up to me."

"But what if he's *not* in there?" said Tark. "He could be in any one of these buildings; there are hiding places all around us."

Flip said nothing. He lowered his stare. For a moment Tark believed the policeman was angry with him for having brought up the possibility. Then Tark realized why Flip was looking down.

Just visible in the pig dust was a single set of footprints, hard to see in the moonlight, but not impossible. And they headed straight to the garage of Rotney Nash.

Once again, Flip produced his 1911.

"Just keep an eye on that garage," Flip said. "You see him come out—and I ain't directly on his heels—you start shouting."

Tark nodded and Flip moved off, stalking deeper into the pigyards.

FOURTEEN

Who was Nash?

Who was he really, and where had he come from?

Flip had to remind himself that most cities in America weren't like this. Weren't like Chicago. People in most towns—or in the Negro parts of those towns—weren't all from elsewhere. You knew people's mommas. Families went back generations and had reputations. Folks had roots.

But Chicago was different. Migrating to Chicago was something anyone could do, and nobody questioned why you would do it. In many quarters, the only question was why you *wouldn't*. What would have to be wrong with you to keep you planted where you were?

Flip considered for the thousandth time that he might as well have been a sheriff in a frontier settlement out west, or a constable in a gold rush camp in Alaska. These men and women in Chicago . . . you had only their word on who they were and where they had come from. If you were lucky, you also had the word of a friend who had come up with them. But that was *all* you had. Chicago was a place where people began again. Where you could make or remake yourself as you saw fit. Anyone could.

Including killers.

Flip knew that if he shot Nash dead tonight he would never know who the man really was. That or anything else about him. If he killed him, then there would be no bargaining. No true reckoning of the facts in exchange for a lighter sentence.

Flip's goal was not simply to swat the bug. No. He wanted to capture this strange insect, put it under glass and study it. That, and *only* that, would kill the horrible mystery of why this thing was happening. To catch something like Nash and simply grind it into the pig dust underfoot? That would ensure only that the mystery lived forever. And Flip knew the wondering of it would probably give him nightmares for the rest of his days.

Flip reached the door of the filthy garage and pressed himself flush against the edge. There were no windows into which he might peer, and no sure way to scale the side of it. The only thing to be done was open the door—either all at once or gradually. If Nash were indeed within, Flip could imagine no way that he could easily escape.

Flip kicked the door hard and shouted.

"Mister Nash, you need to come on out! Chicago Police! Come out, and no harm will come to you! When the other officers arrive, I can't promise you'll get the same deal."

At first, there was no response. Flip heard only the nearby hogs in their pens. Then a very singular sound arose. It started as a kind of mechanical 'pop,' then built into an omnipresent hum. Soon it became lower and quieter, until it almost could not be heard at all.

Something inside the garage had just been turned on, Flip realized. Some kind of machine.

Flip's initial concern was that the metal door to the garage had been electrified. Yet that did not feel right. A standoff hardly seemed like Nash's plan.

Flip kicked the door again, and no electric shock coursed through him. He risked a pound with his fist and got the same result.

The deep, quiet hum continued.

Concealing himself partly at the side of the garage, Flip gripped the base of the metal door tightly with his free hand. He lifted it slowly at first. Then, as the door gained momentum, he threw it upwards all in a rush.

In Flip's experience, there were good cops who went in fast, and bad cops who went in fast, but *no* good cops who went in slow. Either you knew what you were doing (or acted like you did) and you went and did it . . . or else you lingered and the bad guy got away.

Accordingly, Flip would allow himself only the quickest glance around the corner of the garage before bounding inside. In that glance, he saw the darkened, filthy garage interior, looking much as it had earlier in the day. He saw an empty couch, an empty mattress on the floor, a pile of papers, and a mound of empty glass bottles. Yet he saw no person or persons; no telltale glint of eyes in the darkness.

Flip sucked a series of three quick breaths, then charged around the corner and into the garage, 1911 raised.

Immediately, there was a mechanical click and Flip was rendered totally blind—not by a darkness, but by light. The brightest light he could remember seeing hit him squarely in the face. And from a source so close he could feel the heat.

Flip's reaction occurred too quickly for it to have been based on any series of proper, conscious deductions. Something told him that the pile of mechanical equipment stacked haphazardly behind the couch must contain one of the security lights from the stockyard guard towers. And, further, that Nash had blinded him with it . . . either to escape, or to. . .

Shielding his eyes with his free hand, Flip dove to the side of the garage and landed hard on his stomach. An instant later, gunfire began to pour from behind the light source. A handgun, fired repeatedly.

Rising to his knees as quickly as he could, Flip leveled his 1911 and shot back.

The noise of the reports inside such a small space was thunderous. Flip pulled his trigger with maniacal intensity. One of his bullets must have struck the spotlight, for the garage was suddenly plunged back into darkness. As his eyes adjusted, Flip momentarily saw the outline of Nash, ducking in and out of cover behind the couch. Then there was another loud report, and Flip felt something like a brick thrown impossibly hard slam into his shoulder. He rocked backwards and his head connected with a wall. Then he fell forward into a darker, deeper blackness.

In that place, he saw and heard nothing more.

FIFTEEN

A horror of a smell. A caustic, chemical stench that seemed to crawl up through his nose and mouth and enter his very brain.

Flip's head jerked violently away.

Smelling salts, he realized. These were smelling salts.

He opened his eyes.

Flip was on his back. Time had passed. He was still inside Nash's garage, but now the place was full of people. People wearing blue.

A police surgeon hovered over him, holding the salts in one hand and a lantern in the other. Nearby on the ground was a black medical bag with a fine rattan handle. Flip tested his eyes and took a wide scan of the garage. He saw several other police milling about. He also saw Tark and Sally—waiting in a corner, looking on intently.

Flip found that his shoulder had been bound.

And also that it hurt like the dickens.

"He's coming 'round," the police surgeon announced to the room.

Heads turned. Faces smiled. Flip felt too weak to sit up properly, but he managed to grin back at this new audience.

Sally stayed silent, but nodded like she was trying to tell Flip something good. Tark flashed a thumbs up.

"The man you shot . . ." the surgeon explained slowly and loudly, as though Flip were a bit deaf. "During the gun battle, his bullet passed through part of your shoulder muscle. You fell back and hit your head twice—once against the wall, and then again on the floor. I've treated your shoulder with carbolic acid and sewn it shut. Later in the week, you must go to the hospital to have it further examined. I'll write you a note to take to a Walgreen. They will give you something for the pain. Do you understand me? Can you nod if you do?"

Though the act of moving his head seemed a supreme effort, Flip managed to bob it up and down. And then to wheeze: "Man I shot . . . ?"

A friendly, familiar voice came from somewhere above.

"Stone dead," Salvatore Crespo announced with great satisfaction. "You got him, Flip."

The surgeon's face seemed to narrow, as though he were fighting against a bad memory. Flip leaned further back and looked up. Crespo was there, and he exchanged a glance with the surgeon. More than a glance. Crespo positively stared the man down. The surgeon relented, looking away as he placed his smelling salts and thread back into his bag.

"Need to see. . ." Flip wheezed.

"What you need is bed rest," the surgeon said as he packed his equipment. "A man who hits his head hard enough can fall down dead an hour later if he doesn't rest. But those are only my medical opinions. Which, clearly, you men can take or leave. . ."

Crespo gave the surgeon another stern look. Flip understood immediately that the two had had words. The physician gathered up his bag and stormed out. Flip wanted to ask what was the matter, but knew he would have to gather the strength first. His head rang like a bell.

Tark began to approach Flip. A policeman stopped the magician with a forceful hand to the shoulder. Tark whispered something into the policeman's ear. The officer smiled, nodded, and allowed the magician to proceed.

While a beaming Crespo stood over them, Tark took a knee beside Flip and produced a small flask from his coat.

"Here," he said, unscrewing the top and tilting it up to Flip's mouth. "Trust me. This'll do you good. It's quality stuff. I swiped it from Sally's place before."

Flip hesitated; then—figuring nothing could make him feel worse than he already did—opened his parched lips and took a sip. Swallowing was more difficult than he had anticipated. He coughed a couple of times, and spat up as much of the gin as he downed.

"There's a good man," Crespo pronounced from above.

Flip leaned in toward the magician.

"Tark," he said with great strain. "What happened?"

The magician looked up to Crespo, as if for permission. When the Italian nodded, Tark began to speak.

"I was watching the garage from down the street, like you said to do. I watched you creep up and open the door. I watched you jump inside. As soon as you did, he hit you in the face with that spotlight. 'Fore I knew what was happening, you two had a shootout. I saw you go down and I thought you were dead. Sally and I ran on over and we found you, but you were still breathing. Then we looked behind the spotlight, and we saw that you'd shot him, Flip. You shot and killed that man from your photo. The white man, Durkin."

Flip widened his eyes and blinked them rapidly.

"That's right," Crespo clarified. "You got him. There was a basement room underneath that old couch. Trap door. We think Durkin had been living down there."

This was too much to take anybody's word on. Flip had to see for himself.

Despite the strain, he attempted to right his body. It was wobbly going, but he made it as far as sitting up.

"Tark, Crespo . . . can you help me to my feet?"

"Easy now," Tark said. "You heard the doc."

"Eh, what do croakers know?" Crespo responded, gripping Flip hard by the armpit and pulling. "Help me out, magician."

They pulled him up. Flip felt as though he had been kicked by a horse (which he actually had been once, so he knew the sensation). Nonetheless, he managed to pick his way across the room to the broken spotlight. The policemen inventorying the grim contents of the garage gave him a wide berth.

The spotlight had been completely shattered by rounds from his 1911. Several of his bullets had also made holes in the cinderblock wall. Flip saw a dark shadow of a man on the ground behind the couch. He crept to it. Crespo, following behind, shone a dim lantern upon the body.

There was Durkin. No question about it. He wore the same suit from the photograph. He had indeed been shot twice in the chest, just as in the photograph. Beside him on the ground was an ancient Colt SAA revolver.

And it looked wrong. All wrong.

Flip did not know how long he had been unconscious—it had likely been an hour or more—but he had seen men recently shot. He knew how their bodies looked in the hours passing after. This was different. Durkin already looked like a medical cadaver. Something dead for days or weeks, kept on ice. He looked drowned and suffocated. His hair was the hair of a body washed ashore from Lake Michigan, all soaked to nothing.

Crespo moved his light away quickly, as if he did not wish Flip's gaze to linger.

"The person I followed here. . ." Flip began, leaning against the couch for support. "Negro man named Nash. . ."

"Yes, this garage is rented to a person by that name," Crespo said loudly. "The yard foreman confirmed it. We think Durkin had paid Nash to use the place."

"I never saw. . ." Flip began, but trailed off.

"Relax; we've put out a call on Nash as well," Crespo said. "We'll get him. If he was involved in this, we'll find out how. But I hope you understand what you did here, Flip. You got him. Do you realize that? You got the man we wanted."

Flip stepped to the side and looked down into the trapdoor in the floor beside the couch. It was open, and there were steep, rung-like steps leading down.

Then the pain swelled and Flip felt as though he might pass out or lose his lunch. He steadied himself against the couch.

"Can I see down there?" Flip asked when the sensation passed.

Crespo exchanged a glance with two of the nearby officers.

"In your condition, I wouldn't try those stairs," Crespo said.

"Yeah," one of the policemen added. "Almost slipped going down there myself . . . and I *didn't* just get shot."

"We'll search it thoroughly," Crespo said to Flip, leaning close. "Do a full inventory. If we discover anything interesting, I promise to let you know."

"All right," Flip said.

Wooziness overtook him. Involuntarily, he sat down on the filthy couch.

"Whoa now," Crespo said. "This looks like a man who needs a good night's sleep. And he's earned it if ever a Chicago policeman has."

Some of the other police seconded this with jocular calls of "Hear, hear!" A couple gave applause with their leather-gloved hands.

"Jimmy, can you give Flip a ride home in the wagon?" Crespo asked an officer.

Jimmy confirmed that he could.

"And my friends. . ." Flip said softly, gesturing to Sally and Tark.

"Of course," Crespo said. "We'll get them home as well."

In such pain and stupor, Flip found it difficult to further contemplate what had happened.

He knew the man at whom he had been shooting had been Nash. He felt certain of this beyond any room to doubt. It *had* been Nash. Yet there was Durkin—the man from the photo, plain as day—in Nash's place. Was there a connection Flip did not see? Perhaps it was an obvious one, and he would be embarrassed, later, to have not discerned it immediately.

But thinking along these lines felt perilously close to resisting. And Flip was now too weak to resist anything. He wanted only to collapse and to vomit. His body commanded him to rest. It felt as though a full month of sleeping—give or take—was probably called for.

Flip slumped forward and moaned. His head fell between his legs.

"That's it," he heard Crespo say. "Give me a hand with him, boys."

Amid additional calls of congratulation, Flip was helped outside toward a waiting police wagon. Flip found enough strength to lift his head and turn it one last time toward Sally and Tark. Sally made a kind of praying motion with her hands. Flip realized it was a 'Thank you.' Tark extended a wrist and seemed to toast Flip with an invisible gin. Then Flip's head fell once more to his chest, and he was loaded into the wagon.

He did not remember the ride home.

When the wagon stopped, Flip was able to look up enough to see that they had reached the building where he lived. He could smell dawn in the air, though the sky was still pitch dark. A pair of indistinct policemen, like strong animated shadows, helped Flip to the doorway of his home. One asked if he was well enough to go the rest of the way on his own. Flip said he was.

Flip crept up his stairs on all fours like a dog, and managed to let himself into his apartment. He had felt this weak only once before, when a bout of pneumonia had leveled him completely for the better part of a winter.

Flip removed his clothes and found them sticky with sweat.

Before he headed for his bed, he took a long look out his front window. The police wagon had not moved. The pair of shadowy officers stood to either side of the flagstone walk leading up to his building. They were already joking and funning with one another the way policemen do when they are settling into an easy, safe assignment. Flip was under watch tonight, like a visiting dignitary.

With the wonder of this rushing through his head, Flip crashed into his pillow.

He did not fall immediately to sleep.

It was not the wound in his shoulder or the exhilaration of the shootout that kept him awake. Rather, it was the vision of the corpse of Durkin. That man had been dead for longer than an hour. Flip had seen every kind of dead man there was to see, and he knew what kind

Durkin was. As the sun began to rise, Flip felt surer and surer that something was amiss.

When he did fall asleep—wondering if the intense pains in his shoulder were the first encroachments of death—Flip dreamed of walking dead men.

He had heard tales of zombies from those who had come up to Chicago from the Caribbean. (Zombies were as old as the city. Du Sable himself had probably known of them.) Zombies were men who could be commanded to walk after death. But they came from a place stepped in so much murder and horror that this likely seemed unremarkable. It was a place where Caribs had murdered Indians, and British and French and had murdered Caribs, Negroes had been enslaved and brought in, and then the British, French, and Negroes had taken turns murdering one another for the next hundred years. Straight through, no stopping.

A place like that. . . What export would it develop? What would it cultivate to give to the world?

Walking dead men sounded about right to Flip.

Flip dreamed that he was standing in the Loop among the tall buildings, surrounded by men in fine clothes who walked the streets and sidewalks. Yet when he looked closely at these men, he saw that each man was dead. That each man had a face like Durkin's—expired for days, and half-frozen in lake water. Each man looked with eyes that did not see. And each man was a copy of the one beside him.

A twin.

Identical.

There was a knock on Flip's door late the next morning.

He had not locked it. Someone turned the handle and walked right inside. By the time Flip had maneuvered his torso upright enough to reach for his gun, Crespo was already striding into the room. The Italian had a jolly look on his face.

"You survived the night," he said.

Flip nodded and set his gun back down.

"How do you feel?"

Flip made an expression indicating the answer should be obvious.

"It happens," Crespo said. "We had our fair share in the Black Hand Squad."

"You said they never touched you," Flip hissed with a voice like sandpaper.

With a supreme effort of will, he brought his feet around to the floor.

"They never *killed* us," Crespo happily clarified. "But plenty of us got 'touched' the way you did last night. That includes me. Can you walk?"

"Let's see," Flip said, rising shakily to his feet.

He took one step, then another. The pain was manageable. It appeared walking, at least, would be no trouble. He inspected his bandage. The wound was still tender. The wrapping was covered with dried blood, but the wound was not bleeding more. The surgeon's stitches had held.

Flip walked to his kitchen sink, carefully poured a glass of water, and drank it down.

"I don't see any leaks," Crespo said. "They must've sewed you up good."

Flip set down the glass.

"That surgeon last night was mad at you," Flip observed.

"We had different opinions. . ." Crespo began, then started over. "Let's say, he thought we weren't taking in to account that that body. . . maybe, in a way. . . looked like it had been dead for a while before you shot it."

At least the Italian would be honest.

"Then what do you think I shot?" Flip asked, his voice gradually returning to normal. "You think that was a dead man walking around?"

"All I know is what you did last night seems an awful lot like what the mayor asked you to do. And that's our job. To do what the mayor says."

Flip stared hard at the Italian, unmoving, until the pain in his shoulder forced him to wince.

"Where is Nash? You at least have some men on his house . . . like you do on mine?"

Crespo nodded.

"No sign of him yet."

"And what did you find in that basement room, beneath the couch?" Flip asked.

"Enough to know we got our man," Crespo answered. "It was like a little smuggler's den, filled with horrors. There were weapons. Boning knives. Blades. And then metal tanks filled with blood. Others filled with ice water. And body parts too. Things so mutilated they're never gonna be identified."

"Jesus," said Flip.

"It's our own H. H. Holmes," Crespo told him. "Holmes of the Stockyards. That's what the papers would call him if they knew about this. But they're never gonna know, are they Flip? *Are they. . .*"

"You find out I talked to some people at the *Defender*?"

Crespo did not answer.

"Don't worry about that. Abbott will have to run something, but I'll make sure it's not too. . . spectacular."

"Good," Crespo said. "Do you feel well enough to go downtown?"

"Today? Now?"

The Italian nodded.

"I ain't sure," Flip answered honestly.

"Come on; this is the fun part," Crespo cajoled. "You've run the race. Now you've only got to stand on the platform while they do the medal ceremony."

Flip cocked an eye.

"You make it sound so nice. Why do I get the feeling that the mayor told you to drag me out of bed no matter how I felt?"

"You can put it in those terms if you like, I suppose," Crespo allowed. "C'mon."

Flip sighed and hung his head.

"Just give me a moment to dress."

An hour later, Crespo and Flip walked—slowly—into the massive new city hall on the corner of Washington and La Salle in the heart of the Loop.

Flip had been quiet for most of the ride in the motorized police wagon. Only after they had ventured within the great stone hall of government did he remember to ask Crespo if his friends had made it home safely.

"The madam and the carnival magician?" Crespo said. "We had 'em dropped off. Say, I sort of want to ask you what they were doing there . . . but also, I sort of *don't*. So maybe we don't mention that part to the man, eh? I'll trust they know enough keep their mouths shut."

"They do," Flip said. "They were in this for themselves. To keep people they loved safe. Talkin' doesn't further that goal, does it?"

Crespo agreed.

They traversed the ground floor of the crowded municipal building—filled with lawyers, clerks, low-level politicians, and those who aspired to be low-level politicians—and made their way up a stone staircase to the mayor's office. It had a high wooden door that reached nearly to the ceiling. Its entrance was flanked by a row of American flags. Several on each side, mirroring one another. It was meant to appear grand, but the flags hung flaccid and grim. Flip wondered how frequently they had to be dusted.

The entire floor was quiet, as if the regular functionaries had been warned off.

Flip and Crespo approached the row of flags, and the door to the mayor's office was opened from inside by a pair of men from the security detail at the GAR room. Plumes of cigar smoke wafted from the office out into the hall, and so did the sound of conversation.

Inside, the mayor was laughing and smoking. Ten other men were gathered with him. Some were the men Flip had met previously; he recognized Wrigley, Marshall Field, and Oscar Meyer. They lounged across the mayor's couches as though the office were their own.

The mayor looked up from his high-backed chair. He noticed Flip and Crespo, and sprang to life. He was nimble for such a large

man, and on his feet in a trice. (Flip remembered that the "Big" in Big
Bill Thompson predated the man's descent into girth. The champion
footballer's physique was still there, concealed somewhere beneath all
those extra calories.) The mayor drew close and eyed Flip's shoulder
sympathetically. He helped the policeman into a chair as though helping an injured sportsman off the field.

"Now! Now comes the conquering hero! For the vanquisher!" the
mayor cried.

The rich and powerful men burst into applause. One, who was still
wearing a hat, doffed it.

Flip was bewildered. He smiled and said nothing. Before he knew
what was happening, a cigar and a scotch were thrust into his hands.
Something told him to simply hold both, but the pain in his shoulder
barked for relief. He threw back the scotch in a single gulp. The rich
men cheered, and someone poured him another.

"I had asked you for a progress update by today. . . but you have
beaten my expectations and resolved the case completely!" the mayor
announced.

He sat on the edge of his desk now, fat legs adangle.

The rich men raised their glasses and cigars.

"You got him; you really did!" cried Oscar Meyer. "That was
Durkin. I went and viewed the body myself!"

"We owe you a great debt," said young Marshall Field. "It was done
so quickly and so quietly. You are a credit to your race, my friend."

Flip took a drink of his second scotch—only a sip this time. His
eyes flitted over to Crespo who stood silently by the door. The Italian
smiled from underneath his wide mustache.

"Just doing my job," Flip managed.

"And so modest too!" offered Wrigley.

The mayor looked over the rich men and a strange smile crossed
his face. The rich men quieted down until all were silent and grinning.
It made Flip uneasy.

The mayor tented his fingers conspiratorially, as though he had a
secret to tell.

"Officer Flippity . . . New York City does not. . . to *my* knowledge. . . yet have a Negro Police Sergeant within its ranks," he began in a tone of abstract, almost academic consideration. "But we are going to move ahead of them in that respect very shortly, I think. When you return to duty, it will not be as a mere patrolman. Do you understand?"

Flip swallowed hard. His throat was scratchy and peaty from the scotch, and he tried not to cough.

"Yessir," he said.

"And the funds we provided you with which to operate . . ." the mayor continued.

"Less than half spent," Flip reported. "I can give you a proper accounting if you give me a pencil and paper. Write it all down for your bookkeeper."

The mayor shook his head.

"As far as the city is concerned, those funds were *entirely expended* in the course of this investigation," the mayor announced.

Flip realized they were allowing him to keep the balance that remained. He looked down to hide his amazement.

"How was it?" one of the men asked—Flip did not see which. "How was it to kill a walking dead man?"

The room grew silent again. Flip opened his mouth but struggled to find any words that might make sense.

"I expect it's like killing any other kind of man," Flip eventually said. "I shot him and then he died. Again."

The rich and powerful men applauded this. The mayor smiled. Flip's head swam.

The men asked flip to recount the shootout in greater detail. Though he felt woozy and as though his head were stuck inside a fishbowl, he did his best to tell the tale of storming the garage. His audience listened, rapt. They applauded once more when he had finished.

By this time, they had emptied the mayor's crystal decanter and significantly diminished the cigar collection in his desk humidor. As if this were a signal, they gradually began to depart—each one shaking

Flip's hand and slapping him on the back as they did so. Though slow and casual, once this parade started, it did not stop. In a few short minutes, they had all left the mayor's office.

All but one.

It was one of the men who had not yet been introduced to Flip. Flip recognized him from no newspaper photograph or prior encounter. He was in early middle age, had a pronounced mustache, and sat with a top hat on his lap. He had wide spaces between his front teeth, but appeared quite handsome when his mouth was shut. As the other tycoons made their way down the granite corridor leading away from the mayor's office, this gentleman stayed put.

Big Bill Thompson shut the door. Then—quite soused—he sloppily poured himself another drink from a fresh bottle in his desk drawer. He refilled Flip's glass too. Then he motioned that Flip should join him and the mystery man over on the couch. The private security had departed with their employers, leaving only Crespo behind. The Italian stood stock still, blending into the granite.

Confused but also curious, Flip reseated himself. The mayor sat too, on the opposite end of the same couch. The cushions wheezed under Thompson's weight, but ultimately held fast.

"Mister Flippity," the mayor said, "This gentleman is Adolf Graf."

The man holding the hat smiled awkwardly, and met Flip's eyes for only an instant.

The beer baron from Milwaukee. The one who visited the Palmerton House whenever he was in Chicago.

"Yes," said Flip. "I b'lieve I've drank some of your beer in my time, sir. Off duty, of course."

The baron nodded silently.

"Mr. Graf has asked to give you his personal, private thanks for your job well done," said the mayor. "To speak with you alone. Is that all right, officer?"

Flip nodded.

"Very well," the mayor said, lifting his great heft from the couch. "Then I will leave you to it."

The mayor pointed to Crespo, snapped his fat fingers, and gestured to the door. The Italian went outside to wait beside the flags. To Flip's surprise, the mayor—scotch in hand—left also.

Flip was alone with Graf.

The beer baron looked up.

The expression set into the baron's face was something Flip had seen before. Priests and physicians might see it more frequently than policemen, but policemen still saw it an awful lot. Confession. Contrition. The look of a man who was being eaten up inside by a secret that gnaws at his soul. By something he has done. In such a man's mind, the only thing that can make the pain stop is to bring the secret out into the open. To speak its name.

"They told us you were probably the best policeman in Chicago," Graf began, speaking numbly, like a man who had seen into great, horrible distances. "They told us you employ a kind of a magic witch to help you in special cases. Is that really true?"

"It seems word has gotten out," Flip told Graf candidly.

"Secrets are hard to keep, eh?" Graf said, for the first time smiling a little.

"Looks that way," Flip replied cautiously, still wondering what was going on.

"See, I know that you are a good policeman, because they tell me you involved the madam of the Palmerton House in your investigation," Graf said. "Your instincts are correct."

Flip did not know what this meant, but nodded.

"I can tell you are the kind of man who learns everything eventually, anyway," Graf continued. "Were I to try to conceal the truth of what has happened here, you would soon discover it. And then you would think even less of me."

Graf hung his head.

"I don't understand," Flip said. "I don't think any less-"

"I *never* told him to kill them!" Graf cried suddenly.

Flip shrank back. His scotch jostled. A few drops splashed onto the mayor's fine couch.

"I *never* said to kill," Graf insisted. "I *certainly* never said that he should do . . . any of the things that he did to those children. That was his own devising. And then we could not stop him."

"I don't-" Flip began.

Graf put up a hand to stifle him.

"I must tell it to you plainly," the baron said. "From the start. Then you will see how I am not. . . at least not *entirely*. . . to blame."

Flip leaned back on the couch and fell silent.

"As Miss Battle has doubtless informed you, I am in the habit— when visiting Chicago—of retaining a large portion of the Palmerton House for myself," Graf said, tenting his fingers. "This fact must be kept secret. It must be kept secret for so, *so* many reasons. If my share-holders learned of my predilections, they would not take it kindly. My competitors would use it to generate popular sentiment against my beer. My wife and my children, not to mention my father-in-law, the senator . . . well, I do not like even to think of it."

"You have to keep your visits to the Palmerton quiet," Flip said, in a tone that tried to assure the man this did not make him quite so unusual. "You, and half the men on the South Side of Chicago."

"Yes," Graf agreed. "And for many years I was successful in doing so. But then came that fateful night at the start of this summer. I was in the western suite at the Palmerton. Do you know the one? No mat-ter. It is a large first-floor room with a high ceiling, tall bookshelves, many couches, and. . . and a single tall window. And that window was my downfall. It faces an empty alley. I had cavorted within that room perhaps twenty times before, and never seen a face through it. I thought the narrow passageway beyond was inaccessible, truly! But that night. . . Let us say, plainly, I learned otherwise."

Graf shifted uncomfortably in his seat.

"It was a warm evening, and so the window had been opened by the girls. The breeze did us good. There were perhaps five sporting girls inside the room with me. It was because the room was so crowded—five at one time is a bit excessive, even for me—that I did not initially believe anything amiss when I heard my own name being called by a strange voice. I thought one of the young women had called for me from across the room. It was a high-pitched voice, you see, in an accent from the Deepest South. But in the course of our revels, I was thrust onto my back, and there I found myself staring up into the open window. And that was when I saw them! Two Negro children. I think boys, but I am not certain. Perfect identical twins. Exactly the same. They had sneaked into the alley and were looking at us! And something more. My valise sat on a nearby table. I liked to have my cologne and a fresh set of clothes along, you see. But the problem is that my valise is monogrammed, very clearly, in all capital letters, with my full name. The two urchins in the alley were reading my name. Even pronouncing it correctly! This was most alarming. If word began to circulate that a white man named Adolf Graf spent time in the Palmerton—even as an unsubstantiated rumor among Negroes—then it could spell disaster. And so. . .

"And so I did what any reasonable man would do. I shouted at the twins. At which point, they promptly fled back down the alley. I disengaged from my revels, dressed to a degree, and went to find the only man I knew who could solve such problems. You must understand this about Durkin. He really was remarkable. Friends and associates had told me of situations in which—when I imagined myself in them—I would have planned to leave the country entirely, or to end it all. Predicaments so unsolvable and impossible. . . And yet Durkin found ways to solve them. If he did not completely make them go away, then he always made them into things that could be handled. Managed.

"I do not need to tell you where I found him. Only that I did. I informed him of the details—and gravity—of the situation. Identical twin Negro children with southern accents had seen something they should not have seen. Had read my name and knew it. It must be ensured that they did not speak it. I only meant—God help me!—I only meant for Durkin to scare them a little. And I meant for him to use an olive branch, in addition to a stick. I gave him money to bribe the parents. Scare the kids into silence, sure, but then throw a little cash their parents' way. Not such a complicated idea, is it? Not so strange? I told Durkin I did not know who the twins were, or where to find them, but he took my money and assured me it would be solved. The twins would be silent, he swore. My secret doings in the Palmerton would remain forever unknown."

Graf nervously reached for a glass on the table and had a drink.

"Of course, Durkin was always a man of his word," Graf continued. "But killing children and mutilating them? When I learned what was happening, I went straight to our group—to the men in this room today—and let them know he had finally gone too far. Whatever his prior usefulness, Durkin had become. . . excessive. Perhaps he enjoyed killing children. Enjoyed mutilation. But now he worked for *us*. We could not afford to be connected in any way to such depravity. That was when we enlisted the outfit from New York to come and finish him off. And we thought we had. . . until the killings resumed. You can imagine what a low point it was for us when we were forced to turn to the mayor and the *municipal* police."

Flip was in too much physical pain to take this personally.

"You need to understand. . . I never intended to harm those children. Scare them?—surely—but harm them? Absolutely not! I was horrified by what Durkin did. And I hope you will agree that I did everything within my power to stop him."

The beer baron seemed to be finished with the confession. Flip let a few seconds pass before responding.

"Did Durkin ever say things about hating twins?" Flip asked.

"No," Graf replied. "Such an idea is ridiculous, is it not? Why hate twins? Of all the things to hate a person for, it would be most arbitrary."

"He was found. . ." Flip began, then started over. "When I shot him, Durkin was in the home of a man who everybody thought was a twin."

"Maybe he had gone there to kill him too?" Graf said, leaning back in his chair, relaxing now, as if the hard part were over. "Really, I don't know. He had always been discreet before. When he did jobs for us, he made it look like a robbery gone bad, or even an accident. Once, he crushed a man with a piano, if you can believe it! But mutilation was entirely out of his character. By sending him after twins, did I awaken within him a sleeping twin-mania? Hmm. Who can say? It's as if I told

him I needed him to silence a red haired man, and he began butcher-
ing every red headed person in Chicago."

Flip nodded. Graf smiled and set down his glass. Then he rose, as
if they were finished.

"I see that you have been wounded in the line of duty," Graf said, as
Flip also stood. "If you need further attention, my personal doctor will
be glad to treat your injury without a fee. Is it very serious?"

Flip could tell that—after the fever passed—it was the kind of
wound that would take a year or two to stop hurting completely.

"Nothing I can't handle," the Flip told him.

"Well, anyhow," said Graf, "come up to Milwaukee any time you
like, and you can see my specialist. You would be a personal guest
inside my mansion. I receive many Negro visitors, you know. In the
meantime, I'll see that a barrel of beer is delivered to your home within
the week. Goodbye then."

The guilt seemed to have been washed clean from Graf's face. The
man genuinely felt better, Flip realized, just as he had hoped to.

Graf extended his hand. Absently, Flip shook it.

Back outside, the mayor, still very drunk, was leaning against the
passageway, pressing his face against the cool stone wall. The mayor
started and opened his eyes as Graf reemerged. Big Bill Thompson
walked over to the beer baron and gave him a full-on embrace. His
chest lightened by the unburdening of his horrible secret—washed and
absolved—the beer baron hugged him back, then walked cheerfully
down the stone steps to the first floor of city hall.

The mayor motioned for Flip and Crespo to wait. Flip thought the
mayor might have final words to say to them, but after a moment he
simply indicated that Flip and Crespo could now depart as well. There
was enough space between the baron and the policemen.

All was, once again, as it should be.

On his journey home to resume convalescence, the only coherent
thought holding steady in Flip's mind was that he must never—ever—
tell Sally of the connection between the killings and her establishment.

Doing so, he feared, might literally break her heart.

SIXTEEN

Two weeks later, Flip's fever broke and the pain in his arm retreated some. At the mayor's urging, his lieutenant had given him a further month off. There was no urgency about anything. For the first time since he had come to Chicago, Flip had money in his pockets and time on his hands. It was still summer, but, in the evenings especially, Flip started to think he could smell fall on the breeze.

On this first morning of feeling unfevered, Flip tested his legs with a walk down to Miss Heloise's home. His plan had been to leave the fireplace poker on her porch, but Miss Heloise was standing in front of the house when he approached, picking up toys. She watched the policeman come down the street.

"Here," Flip said brightly. "I come to bring you this back."

Miss Heloise looked at the poker doubtfully.

"Oh yeah?" she said.

"Yeah," Flip answered.

"You catch the man who killed my girls?" she said, taking the metal rod from him.

"I can't talk about it," he told her. "But yes."

Miss Heloise leaned on the poker like it was a cane. She was short, and the implement came up nearly to her waist.

"I ain't hear about it," Miss Heloise said.

Flip nodded.

"You won't," he told her. "Least not directly. Except from me, here, today. *Defender* might run something, but it won't be the whole story. You'll have to read between the lines."

Miss Heloise seemed to consider this.

"You get any answers?" she said. "The man. . . He tell you why he did these awful things to my babies?"

"Those answers will come next," Flip said. "I'm getting to that presently."

"What does that mean?" Miss Heloise asked, turning her head to the side. "How you don't know the answers, but you already caught him?"

But Flip was already walking away.

Later that morning, Flip stood in the stockyards, in the ruins of the garage formerly inhabited by Ed or Rotney Nash.

The structure had been demolished by sledgehammers. Its parts stood in a great pile, waiting to be hauled away. There were bricks and twists of bent metal from the garage door and assorted machine parts. Flip knew there was almost no chance he would find anything useful in this pile, and that access to the underground den beneath the garage was probably also impossible. Even so, for a while he toed the bricks with his foot, investigating.

After a few minutes, two stockyard workers approached. One was the man he had met before, who hefted the pig-killing awl. The other was less decrepit looking, and might have been junior management.

Flip expected them to ask him his business—or at least to greet him—but for several moments they merely looked on.

Then the man who used the awl said: "We done it right. We done it just like the police said. I seen to it."

Flip looked up at the men.

"What police told you to demolish this place?" Flip asked.

"Hell, I don't know," the awl man said. "Italian fella. Mustache."

Flip rubbed his chin.

"Did they take things out of the garage before you demolished it?" he asked.

The two men looked at one another.

"Could have," said the awl man. "I didn't watch the whole time. Nobody could've. They were here for days. Don't you cops talk to each other?"

Flip did not answer.

The junior manager said: "Is it true you're the one who shot somebody in here?"

Again, Flip did not answer.

"That means yes," the junior manager said proudly, like a child teasing a prickly truth from an adult.

"You haven't seen Rotney Nash around have you?" asked Flip.

"Naw," said the awl man. "I get the feeling he's finally gone for good."

"Yes," Flip said. "So do I."

Flip toed the rubble for several minutes more, looking for something, anything. In the end he picked up a scrap of cinderblock and placed it into his pocket.

He thanked the men and went on his way. Unmoving, like a pair of dusty statues, they watched him leave.

Further out from the source of the pig-stench, Flip found the two-level house containing the insurance office of Ed Nash. The front door had been boarded across, the windows too. It appeared the Chicago Police had been here as well. Anything useful had already been taken away and burned. Someone had decided to make it hard for Flip to follow the very trail he now intended to pursue. The footprints in the sand were being covered over.

A signboard had been placed against the front of the house advising policyholders that they could follow up with another Continental Illinois agent with offices in Hyde Park.

Flip strolled around to the side of the house and took a look up at the entrance to the apartment where Janice Collins had once lived. It was boarded too. The CPD sought to take no chances.

Flip crept to a rear window, picked up a fat chip of white paint from a sill, and placed it into his pocket.

He spent the rest of the day back in bed, recovering strength and looking at the blue sky outside. Some time after darkness fell, he rose again, dressed himself, and headed out to South State. The night was warm and inviting, but a hint of autumn crept into the air. The nights would soon grow long, and the monstrous chill that could be killing would come with it. Yet tonight, South State was still alive and vibrant. Folks having a final summer hurrah before it was time to put on layers. Men walked about with jaunty steps and mischief in their gaits. Women relaxed in windows and doorways, and wore scandalously few clothes.

As Flip paced north toward the Palmerton, he got more than one "Hey Flip, where you been?"

One bold soul—whom he did not even recognize—addressed him playfully as "Killer" and made finger guns in his direction. Flip trusted Sally and Tark to have kept their mouths shut, but the lampposts had eyes and ears in this town. Word of what had happened would come out. It already had.

When the Palmerton came into sight, Flip was disappointed to find Sally absent from her perch. Three sporting girls in robes chatted and smoked to one side of the porch, but that was all. The entrance was otherwise empty.

And then she appeared

Sally was radiant in a blue Edwardian gown and pearls. She stood and watched the street, her hands on her hips. Flip cleared his throat and began to climb the Palmerton's front steps. When Sally turned to him, the light from her smile burned more brightly than any fixture along the avenue.

For a while, the two just stared at one another.

"You get the food I sent over?" she asked. "Cause I know you don't eat right as it is."

"Yes," Flip said awkwardly. "Thank you for that. And thank you also for not doing more. I wasn't right 'till near about today. Fever was bad."

"I'm sure it was," Sally said. "Did you get some opium for the pain? Use that surgeon's note?"

Flip sucked in his lips and looked away. She knew that he had not.

"Well, even so, it does me good to see you walking around," Sally told him.

Flip nodded. Kept looking away.

"What is it?" she asked. "You need to sit?"

"Maybe." he told her.

"Maybe?" said Sally.

"Maybe . . . if she's not in yet."

Sally searched Flip's face.

"You come around to see *Ursula*?"

Flip nodded.

"Don't tell me they got you working on something new already?"

"No," Flip said. "Same case."

"But. . . But. . .the bad man's dead," Sally said. "You shot him yourself."

Sally's eyes flit down to a locket on her wrist where she kept a photograph of her children.

"Yes, he's dead," Flip told her. "You saw the body, same as me. But I ain't heard they caught Nash yet. Crespo's supposed to come and tell me if that happens. He hasn't. Have *you* heard anything about them catching up to him?"

Sally shook her head.

"See. . . I want to know what happened to *that* man," Flip said.

"But why?" asked Sally.

Flip looked around frantically, as though his eyes chased the haphazard path of a bee.

"I don't know," he told her. "This is for me. I ain't on the clock right now. I just got to know for myself."

"Well then. . ." Sally said. "You're welcome to come and wait in the lounge, of course, if you need to."

Flip smiled.

Sally approached and kissed him on the forehead.

"Thank you for everything you've done," she said.

"I ain't done yet," Flip replied, and headed for the back of the building.

U rsula was home.

A single pound on the metal door was enough to rouse her. Flip heard her say something indistinct. He did not take the time, really, to listen to what the horrible voice called in reply. Whatever she had said, the sound of it suddenly made him feel hot. Angry. He was done with pretense. Done with mystery. He forced the door open and barged inside.

The path of lanterns cut its swath through the abject darkness. At its termination, there was the familiar thin figure propped at a table. There was the ball with a shroud over it. And all around, broken furniture and machinery covered with blankets and sackcloth until it looked like a sea of deformed terra cotta soldiers, awaiting the snap of Ursula's fingers to come alive and start marching.

Flip ducked his head and hurried forward along the illuminated trail. He had to fight the urge to kick the odd lantern as he went. With no ceremony, he sat on the empty stool beside Ursula. He reached into his pocket, producing the scrap of paint from Ed Nash's house and the bit of cinderblock from Rotney's garage. He placed them on the table. Then, with an exaggerated motion like a man pushing poker chips to a winner he despises, Flip slid them deliberately across to her. The cinderblock made a long, low scraping sound.

Then he took a thousand dollars out of his pocket, and placed the ten crisp bills underneath the cinderblock.

"This ought to get you going," Flip said.

Ursula seemed to move ever-so-slightly, but also not to. Flip glanced down and saw that the irregular, head-sized glass ball had been revealed.

He said: "I need to know where to find the man with the divot in his head. Rotney Nash. Ed Nash. I don't know which is his real name, but let's just call him Nash. These are the bits from the houses where he used to live. He was one man, but pretended to be twins."

"One man. . ." Ursula said.

Then the marine laughter.

It was all Flip could do to fight the urge to physically plug his ears. In the end he failed, and put his fingers in until it passed.

"You still don't understand what is happening!" Ursula said with great amusement. "After all this, you are still no closer to grasping it. But I see now that you are possessed, and there is truly no hope left for you. What a pity. It uses him, just as the mayor used you. It wants what was taken, just as the mayor wants to please his wealthy friends."

"I don't need to understand what is happening," Flip said carefully. "I *need* the location of the man called Nash."

Ursula hesitated for a moment.

"*You* don't want to find him," Ursula affirmed. "*It* wants you to find him. That's what you don't see. It works through you now. You are a rodent with an insect crawled into its brain. The insect commands, and you do its bidding."

Flip hesitated. He had found such hybrid creatures before as a child. Raccoons that had gone insane—rotting and with botflies and spindly worms crawling out from their ears.

"Do you know where Nash is or not?" Flip asked.

Ursula laughed again. This time, a mercifully brief cackle.

"Oh, I know that man, Joe Flippity," she said, not directly answering. "But why must you find him? The mayor is happy. The city is happy. You have protected the vulnerable just as you sought to. If he now vanishes into the darkness forever—like a green flash on the edge of the sunset—what is lost to you? Nothing, Joe Flippity. Nothing is lost."

"I want to know where he is," Flip insisted to the witch. "I want to know why he did these-"

And suddenly Flip was directly adjacent to a whale that had just heard the funniest joke of its life. The laughter was nautical, phlegmy, and made him want to vomit to hear (and to feel—for the reverberations seemed to echo through him). This time, Flip did not hesitate to immediately stick his fingers deep into his ears. He stuck them in hard and held them fast, until the auditory horror subsided.

"You want to know *why*?" Ursula asked, cackling. "Why is the sky blue? Why do the stars come out at night? *Why*? What on earth makes you think *you* can know the why of it, Joe Flippity?"

He opened his mouth to say something, but she continued.

"I'll tell you why! Because it is no longer the mayor whom you serve. You serve *it*. You serve the thing. Only you don't know. You don't yet see that you do."

"What?" said Flip. "I don't understand."

"It is the old story," the witch replied. "The tale that has been told before, and will be told again—right here, and in other places too—a thousand-thousand times. It is the tale of eld. Listen! Someone took it from the other place. From *it*! And now it wants the thing back. Only madness will follow. There is no reason for you to dive into that madness—like a man diving into a pool of water—but you are adamant and will not be stopped. You have no idea, Joe Flippity. You simply jump on in."

"What other place?" asked Flip. "What are you talking about?"

"It is from beyond the land and above the sea and nowhere at all," she said. "It is the same place a rabbit goes when it vanishes in a magician's hat."

"So. . . a pocket in the bottom of the hat?" said Flip.

He had seen Tark operate a rabbit trick before.

Ursula did not respond.

"Who took *what* from *where*, and why does it have anything to do with Nash?" Flip tried again.

He was becoming angrier now. Ursula often spoke abstractly—or in digressions that were almost riddles—but, as Flip thought on it, it seemed that never before had she introduced new information in this particular way. Never before had she added-on while remaining so obscure and obtuse. And never so late in the game.

"I need you to tell me plainly what is happening," Flip said loudly and slowly. "Where can I find Nash?"

"I have told you everything that can be said," she croaked. "You're askin' me why a brook flows, or why moss grows on a boulder."

"No," Flip shouted. "I don't accept this. You need to say more. Because you *know* more."

There was a long pause as the mummified-seeming woman considered.

"I know there is no mystery," Ursula finally whispered. "I know this has happened before. And that it will happen again."

The pain in Flip's shoulder seemed to grow exponentially. He could feel his blood running hot, and it was not merely from fever. He felt like a person forced to bite his tongue a thousand times, and who is powerfully sick of doing so. Like one who has gladly suffered abuse for such a duration that it has almost become a second nature. But who, now, will suffer it no more. Flip felt a tangible heat course through his neck and head. The feeling told him this time was different. That this time, it *had* to be different.

Flip took something long and heavy and metallic out of his coat and slammed it hard on the table. Then he leaned forward aggressively.

"Enough," Flip said. "Why have you always got to hide the meaning of your words? And why have you got to hide your body in shadows? Always hiding. . . Do you know what this is? It's not a length of pipe. We got them fresh from New York City last year. It's a tube that can shine a very bright light from the end. It works without an electrical connection, and I can take it anywhere. Even into a dirty basement where lives a hoary witch who won't be straight with me!"

For the first time in his life, Flip saw something akin to alarm on Ursula's cracked moonscape face.

"Joe Flippity, do not do that."

"Why?" he said. "Why this darkness, Ursula?"

"To examine something in the light is to change it. Some things can only be seen in the darkness. A great fish lies underneath the lake. Look at the lake in the noonday sun, and the fish's scales reflect the

sunlight back at you. The creature shines just like the water. You will
see nothing! But come again on a moonless midnight. Train your eyes
on the shadows at the water's edge. Then and only then, you may begin
to discern, in the layers of murk, the dimmest outline of the leviathan."

"Nuts to you," Flip said. "I think you hide in the shadows for the
same reason you hide your words. You want to conjure something *that*
isn't there. Give the impression you know more than you do—probably, so you can charge more money. You want these shadows to hide
your flim-flam. Maybe bringing you out of the shadows will bring your
words out. Maybe you'll finally be clear with me."

"Don't you do it!" threatened Ursula.

"Why not?" Flip said, rising to his feet.

"Because *you can't take it!*" Ursula shrieked. "Because inside, deep
down in the pit of your belly, you're a weak man, Joe Flippity, and you
know it. I don't think you could bear-"

And that was all she had time to say.

Flip depressed the button on the side of the heavy tube.

A blinding, unnatural beam leapt forth instantaneously. At first,
the beam was directed upwards. Flip saw now that the pitch-black ceiling of the basement did not extend up into infinity. It was just a row
of planks and boards terminating a few inches above his head. And if
something up there had ever twinkled at him like a midnight star, it
could only have been the heads of nails gleaming momentarily in the
lanternlight.

Flip brought the beam of light down on Ursula Green.

Already—through witchcraft, perhaps—she had vanished and
been replaced. The rocking chair was still rocking, but now it was filled
with old logs wrapped in canvass. A quilt was draped across them.
What had been Ursula's face was now an old, rotting gourd with the
crudest semblance of a mouth. Small, black insects crawled across it.
What had been Ursula's feet were two stones. Her arms, two wooden
sticks. Her hands, rotting mushrooms.

"Ursula!" Flip cried, staggering backward and turning in a slow
circle. "Ursula!?"

There was nothing.

Flip shone the light frantically at the broken furniture around him. He looked for any place where the witch might hide. He pulled and shook sheets until dust billowed up. (It was so dusty, he thought. So dusty. She could not have moved in so dusty a place without leaving a trail, surely. Yet the furniture and machine parts around him appeared unmolested.)

Then Flip looked back at the table. The seer's crystal ball had suddenly changed into a grimy fishbowl. Several dead fish floated at the top the murky water.

Yet his thousand dollars remained.

Flip looked down at the money for a long time. He shined the flashlight at the greenbacks, waiting for them to transform also. When they did not, he picked them up and put them back inside his coat.

Then Flip saw the fine paper lanterns flanking the rug had changed to crooked, hand-dipped candles. Half of them had burned out, and the other half were about to. All were slightly asymmetrical. The imported rug they framed had been replaced by a painter's stained dropcloth.

Flip followed the candles back to the door and let himself out.

He extinguished the flashlight and breathed in the warm night air. He half expected the city beyond to have changed as well. For the Palmerton, South State Street, and the city of Chicago itself to have transmogrified into some other, lesser versions of themselves. Yet the summer night seemed real as ever. The back of the Palmerton rose high and firm and elegant as it always had. The buildings in the distance looked hale and strong and real.

Flip walked back around to the front.

Two gentlemen in ten-gallon hats were hitching up horses and laughing. A parked motorcar stood a few spaces off. Sally was nowhere to be seen, but Flip noticed the one-eyed courtesan relaxing on the balcony. The emerald set into her eye patch gleamed brightly in the streetlight, as her good eye watched the cowboys.

SEVENTEEN

T he night was cool. It smelled, properly now, like autumn—even beyond the strong scents of the perfumed people, the fragrant salty food, and the pungent circus animals. The evening wind carried some hint of hoarfrost down from Canada that threatened to spread across the city. It was the first raiding party of chill and cold. Most men would not adjust themselves more than to cross their arms absent-mindedly. Women, however, seemed to have less compunction, and readily reached for shawls or blankets.

Flip waited stock-still in the darkness beside the circus tent. He had positioned himself so as to be utterly invisible to any casual pass-erby. Only paces away, circus-goers filed in, hoping the late show was not yet sold out; Singer-cum-Singling was running two each night during this particular homestand. And no one in the flowing throng noticed the tall, dark man waiting in the tangle of wagons beside the entrance. Even the circus employees—who often stepped within five feet of him—did not sense Flip's presence.

Flip was not looking at the circus patrons. His eyes were watching the darkness at the edge of the brownfield, carefully searching the treeline. Having performed this task over the past ten evenings, Flip had already developed some acumen for knowing how best to squint and shade his eyes in order to plumb the variations in the darkened strip of land that was his focus. Yet there were many other factors at play which he could not control. Flickers of light from the raw torches behind him often blurred his vision for frustrating instants. Then there was the interplay of the very atmosphere itself. The twinkle of stars and light of the moon. It played games with his eyes as he attempted to probe the subtle nuances of grey and black along the trees. To study the leafy folds where a man might hide.

On this night, the moon rose full and wild and awesome above the city. The metropolis's electrified grid could do nothing to diminish it. The moon's cratered face looked upon the circus and cast its magic. Spells rained down. Flip sucked them in the way he sucked in the Canadian air and the miasma of human and animal and food and shit smells all around him. He was thankful for the moonlight. He was counting on it.

And it was then, on that bright night in September, that he saw the man once more.

The figure hesitating at the edge of the field—near to the where the caravans were kept, and where roustabouts like Ike would be sleeping soon—wore nothing on his head. It was easy to see then, when he turned to the side, that something was missing from just above his temple.

Nash kept nearly motionless as he spied upon the circus. It made Flip think of a mannequin being slowly rotated at its base. The figure stayed stiff, with only small rotations. It did not appear hurried or concerned. It would pause for a minute or more, then shift ever so slightly for a better view. Nash's eyes reflected in the torchlight like an animal's.

Flip's only concern was that Nash would—like an animal—bolt into the trees before he could close in.

The policeman slunk sideways through the tangle of wagons and equipment, knowing that to do so he must break his clear line of sight to Nash. He left the wagons entirely. In a mad, silent dash, he circled around and connected with the edge of the treeline farther up, moving to ambush Nash from the side. Flip could not see Nash at all as he began this approach, picking his way hurriedly through the trees and high grass and circus detritus. As he did this, Flip did not notice that he was holding his breath. Yet neither did he bother to listen for Nash, for he knew he'd hear nothing until it was too late.

This was a game for other senses.

Flip heard only his own footsteps and the indistinct murmuration of patrons entering the circus tent—occasionally punctuated by the "Step right up! This way folks!" of a distant barker. None of it registered in his mind.

But Flip smelled. He smelled the new autumn air. He smelled the funk of animals. And, then—when he had crept fifty yards down along the treeline—he smelled the musk of a man who had lived among stockyards.

Flip stopped. The smell crashed in fast. Strong, and growing stronger.

Then, before he could decide if the lumpy shadow in the lee of a tree looked a little off, it came alive and punched him in the stomach.

The great fist sped out of the darkness and caught Flip in the center of his leather coat. The breath was immediately knocked out of him, and his thin frame careened backwards. He fell against a tree, doubled over at the waist, yet somehow still remained on his feet. One hand held his stomach. The other went frantically for his gun.

Flip was quick to draw, yet too stunned to aim the 1911 properly. The weapon gleamed in the moonlight, searching erratically for a target.

Flip had time to wonder if Nash would hit him again, or pause to draw a weapon of his own. But in the moment it took to think this, he heard the heavy thud-thud-thud of Nash's retreating footfalls.

The third option, then.

The man had chosen to flee.

Flip gritted his teeth and pulled his torso upright. He craned his neck just in time to glimpse Nash hightailing between the trees, speeding away from the circus field and into the neighborhoods beyond. For a large man, Nash ran quickly, navigating the foliage as though this was a favorite spot of his.

Which, Flip realized, it was.

Flip forced himself to take a step in the direction of the fleeing man. His chest and stomach did not feel good, but he could manage it.

He took another step. Then another.

Nash was heading east. Flip would follow. He must.

If he lost Nash now, he would never see the man again. Flip felt certain of that fact.

Flip believed Nash was driven by something so strong and primal that he would, indeed, return again to these same hunting-grounds, despite the danger, and despite the fact that he knew Flip had seen him here. But he would assuredly bide his time. And in that time, Flip would have to go back to work. Resume his normal duties. Nash would begin to notice that the tall, thin policeman didn't come around anymore. He would grow bolder. And then, one dark night, when the stars aligned, he would come and murder Ike and Drextel Tark.

Flip hobbled forward. He considered trying to shoot Nash in the back. Yet over so much distance and in the dark, it would be an unlikely thing. Plus, worse than missing him entirely would be shooting him stone dead. In that scenario, nothing would ever be explained.

Flip put his 1911 away and began to stagger after Nash. Then, though it pained him grievously, he broke into a run.

Nash sped east, toward Lake Michigan, and Flip followed. Within minutes, Flip could smell the water and hear the night cries of the seabirds. For whatever reason, Nash never turned. He could have slipped down any number of alleys or ducked into a hundred different doorways, but he didn't. Nash ran straight east along 55th Street, almost as if the water were calling his name. Like he had a need to get there directly. The path took him through residential neighborhoods. They started Negro, but turned white and Jewish as the lake drew closer.

There was no honorable reason for a man to be running in these neighborhoods at this hour, and Flip entertained the distant hope that some good Samaritan would stop Nash and ask what he was doing, or even stick a leg out to trip him. Yet foot traffic was light on most blocks, and nonexistent on others. What pedestrians there were generally let Nash pass unmolested. (As the second-place runner, Flip received more attention. Several passersby opened their mouths to give him a

"Now see here!" as he barreled past. In these cases, Flip summoned just enough breath to shout: "Chicago Police! Move!")

They raced through the city this way. The high-end apartment complexes that dotted the edges of the lake glowed on the horizon ahead. The houses grew newer, finer. Some were still in the process of being built. They ran past a large horse stable being converted into a parking garage for cars. Iron wrought fences demarcated property lines. Rooftop spires and widow's walks rose into the night sky. As they neared the university, Flip prayed he would see someone—a likely student, a campus cop on patrol, anyone—who might be game to help tackle a fleeing man. Yet the avenues and alleyways stayed empty. Flip's stomach cramped. His legs ached. His throat burned. Where the pain of the gutpunch ended and the agony of a relentless footrace began was no longer possible for him to tell.

Nash ran evermore east, to where the white dinosaur bones of the Columbian Exposition lay in a massive skeletal heap. These structures had been the pride of the nation a generation ago. Now they hunched like broken carnival attractions, stark and pale in the moonlight.

As pain coursed through Flip's body, he took some solace from the knowledge that it must course through Nash's as well. And soon they would arrive at the edge of the lake. Unless the fiend could walk on water—or finally made up his mind to turn north or south—then he must surely stop.

At last, the water came, properly, into view. They ran almost comically now, like marathoners at the end of a race—slowly, with exaggerated lopes, lost in worlds of their own. That their actions constituted a chase would seem absurd to any passerby, as it would be easy for a rested man to catch either one. (This was doubly frustrating to Flip, who still longed for help to appear. Anyone—a child!—might have come to his aid with only a modicum of effort. But there was no one. The midnight lakefront was bare.)

Flip could hear the seabirds and smell the fresh lake water. And there was something else beneath it. Something he was only certain of because he had recently smelled it in concentrated *and distilled* form.

There was wild ramp, growing somewhere ahead in the darkness. Perhaps on the rocks that lined the coast. Perhaps down in the water itself. But it was here, Flip realized. The thing for which Chicago had been named. Wild onion was all around this place.

Flip followed Nash to where a manmade outcropping extended from the shoreline into the lake. This small peninsula had been formed by construction detritus left over from the exposition. It had taken decades to assemble itself, but now this mighty promontory jutted a hundred yards into the water. It had not been properly reinforced, and it seemed to Flip that a few days of rough water might cause the whole thing to crumble away. Yet trees as tall as a man grew upon it. Its surface was grassy and mossy and—he suddenly realized—covered with ramp. It was also strangely pliable. In most places, the ground sank underfoot when he stepped on it. Sank down a good half-inch.

Above the ramp, Flip could smell the lake and the fish and the night wind. He could smell, it seemed, the very stars overhead.

Where was Nash running? Where? There was no Chicago left. He had run across all the natural city. Now, only this small, manmade extension remained. And soon that would be gone too, and there would be only the lake, stretching forever, it seemed, into the dark horizon.

Flip made his way onto the promontory. Nash—just ahead of him—was silhouetted starkly against the sky. What made Flip uneasy was that even in this desperate moment, Nash still ran like a man with a destination in mind, when, plainly, that could not be the case. There was nothing here, only muck and weeds. Flip had been on his share of foot chases. He knew how men ran when they had no goal; when they were making it up as they went along.

And this was not that.

Flip prepared to go for his 1911 on the off chance Nash had a compatriot waiting in ambush at the end of the peninsula.

Then Nash reached the water's edge and stopped. To Flip's surprise, he did not dive off into the chilly lake, and no confederate rose from the shadows. Instead, Nash fell to his knees—his back to Flip—and leaned forward like a man praying.

Out-of-breath, covered in sweat, and tingling from exertion, Flip crept up from behind.

Nash bowed his head before the lake and began to mumble. His hands were clasped tightly. Flip carefully leveled the 1911. He waited for Nash to pull out a gun and turn to face him—to risk it all in one last, desperate shootout. Flip had seen men do it before, and he knew he would see them do it again many times before his career was through. The things that occurred to a man in the moments before he was captured—when he could already feel the jail doors closing behind him—Flip knew that anything, *everything* felt like an option in those dire final seconds.

The ground of the promontory squished and sank underfoot. The onion-smell was sharp. Flip risked a glance down and saw that all the green underfoot—all of it!—was now *not grass*, but wild ramp. It swayed as if possessed by something beyond the gentle breeze. The broad green stalks seemed to stretch up toward the moon with a horrible *intentionality*.

Flip crept close. There was no approaching silently in the squishy ooze. It was like trudging through an inch of cold onion soup.

Flip took up a position behind Nash, and gently placed the cold metal barrel of the 1911 against the back of the cowering man's head. Nash did not react. He not seem to register what was happening.

Flip leaned in close and whispered one word into Nash's ear.

"Why?"

EIGHTEEN

"They come here to steal it. To steal the magic of the ramp. Every one of them. Du Sable. The Fort Dearborn soldiers. The traders shipping grain across the great lake. There's magic here, and they come to take it for themselves. But He doesn't like that. You shouldn't take things that don't belong to you. Everybody knows not to steal. Everybody knows there are consequences if you do. That's what I finally figured out. *I* am the consequences."

Flip took a series of deep breaths, still recovering from his run.

"You killed those twins for Durkin, didn't you?" the policeman said hoarsely. "For a fella named Durkin who worked for very rich and powerful men. Yes?"

Nash turned his irregular head to the side, just enough for Flip to see his smile.

"I killed those twins . . . but not for Durkin," Nash said with a terrible grin. "Not *only* for Durkin."

"What do you mean?" Flip asked.

"I killed twins before him," Nash said, turning back to the lake.

He lowered and raised himself, like a man praying. It seemed that the ritual occupied the bulk of his attention, and conversing with Flip was some sort of afterthought. Nash's speech was distracted. Ramp water soaked Nash's knees and the legs of his pants and the tops of his shoes. He was sinking down into the muck, already a couple of inches deep, as if he were gradually becoming a part of it.

"The Haymore brothers," Flip said confidently. "You're referring to the Haymore brothers, who you killed in 1910."

Nash began to vibrate as he prayed.

"The Haymores," Nash said. "Mmm hmm. And about five other pairs as well. I had a reputation on the streets as a twin-killer. I always had the feeling I should kill twins, you see, and so I did. Durkin knew that much of me. My taste for it. Maybe from the Bucket or maybe from other places; I don't know. I always did it clean. Never spilled no blood. That was my rep. Durkin took me aside one night and said he had a deal to propose. He would pay me richly for every pair of young Negro twins I killed—and reward me with a great boon if I killed the *right* pair. They would have southern accents he said. Be new to the city. Older than five but less than fifteen. I did not say yes right away. No, sir. Some part of me felt like it would be a distraction from my project. From my true calling. I was called like a man in the Bible. It was holy, this thing. But then I thought about it, and I realized Durkin's task *was part* of my calling."

"And what was your calling?" asked Flip.

"The one who lives in the lake," Nash said, as though it were obvious. "They have stolen from him. He lives down there, on the other side . . . but He cannot come all the way through. And so He uses me."

"In the water?" Flip asked, glancing into the murky lake. "Somebody lives down in the water?"

Nash turned back and flashed a coy grin, but gave no answer.

"I don't understand," Flip said. "And *this* is why you kill twins?"

Nash hesitated.

Rocked back and forth.

Prayed.

For a moment, Flip was afraid the man might have stopped speaking for good. But then Nash coughed—as if clearing dust from his lungs—and spoke again.

"It has been a crooked, muddled path. I did not always understand why He needed me to do these things. See, I didn't know that twins had stolen something. I just knew He made me hate them. But then. . . one day he showed me. Whispered it to me on the wind. He said I had proven trustworthy, so now he could tell me about the secret of the ramps. The ramps don't know better, you see. They're free and easy. They give their power away to anyone. But He. . . He was the first to discover them. Long before the Indians, or even the wanderers who muttered and fished here before the Indians. *He* was first. He haunts this place because He wants the power all for himself. He lives forever and can never die, but still, He *wants*. He wants to hoard the magic like a dragon wants to sit on gold. The ramps are such a powerful magic. You could use it to become mayor, or governor, or even President of the United States. To become a millionaire, sure, or the most famous man in the world. But it's all *stolen* power. You don't know it at the time, but it's not yours to take. A man comes here—a *receptive* man—and he has some sense of what the power can do. But he doesn't really know. Not *really*. The Indians, bless them, had a better understanding than most. Why else would they even name this place—this little nothing river inlet? I'll tell you. It wasn't an invitation. It was a warning. The Indians understood to stay away. But then the white settlers came anyway. The Frenchmen and Englishmen passed through, and they didn't know better. Some of them got blessed—blessed by something, even if they ain't know what it was. Du Sable for sure felt it. Thought he would use the blessing to get rich here. And for a while he started to. But then the thing in the lake drove Du Sable off. Ask me, Du Sable got off easy. The thing in the lake. . . it let him live. I think it was kinder then. It thought interlopers would be rare. But people never stopped coming, did they? The builders who made this city? They felt the magic. They stole blessings from the ramps. Then, fifty years ago, the whole damn city burns to the ground. They act like they ain't understand why, but it was him, of course. Jealous. Angry because they took it. Angry because the blessings of the ramps are his and his alone. He didn't come out and set the fires himself—because He can't do that—but He molded the minds of the ones who did. Yessir, he got his revenge."

"Why does he want you to kill twins?" Flip asked. "I don't understand what twins did. You killed identical triplets in one case, too. Why?"

"It all came together for me this summer, while I was doing the jobs for Durkin," Nash said. "The one in the lake. He spoke to me—this time, in a dream—and showed me the second part of the mystery. He told me why I always wanted to kill twins, ever since fifteen years ago. He showed me a scene in my mind, like out of a photo play. Two twin Negro boys, one dumb in the head, and one smart as a tack. Playing together along the lakefront, right near here, where the ramp is thickest. The sharp one pretended to transport a pebble from one hand to the other by magic, without the dumb one seeing how it was done. It delighted the dumb one—made him so happy—which gave the smart one great pleasure. The ramp immediately understood what the boy wanted. He wanted the power to bring this delight to others, just like he'd done for his brother. And so the ramp gave it to him. The ramp acts on its own, y'see. The one in the lake is like a jealous man whose woman gives her favors away. That's how He sees it. Yes, the ramp might have given . . . but the ramp don't know better. And it wasn't that boy's place to take."

Flip's eyes searched the ground. He lingered on a spot where he imagined two youngsters might have frolicked innocently.

"The Tark boys?" Flip said. "Drextel and Ike Tark? *That's* why you hate twins?"

Nash nodded, still looking away.

"But Drextel Tark is just a carnival trickster!" Flip objected. "Nothing in a lake gave him any special power! I know his tricks and how they work. I've got them back for him when they've been stolen by other magicians. They're simple props. Flim-flam. He's not. . . magic."

"No matter," Nash replied. "The thing in the lake is still jealous. Still angry. That's why I had to switch the heads. I didn't understand that part either at first—why He was always telling me to do that. But then it hit me, that day when he showed me the Tarks in my dream. Drextel Tark had used the gift of being a twin for success on the stage.

But it was the ramps that had given him the idea, shown him the way. It was them, not him. The thing in the lake wanted me to send a message. Switching the heads. It shows that you don't get away with nothing when you steal from *him*. You like your twinning? You like being interchangeable. Then be *truly* interchangeable, young man! Be truly one with the other who is you and not-you at the same time! Be that way *forever*. Be that way in death."

"My God," Flip said, shaking his head.

"And that's why I always done it so clean," Nash said. "Not like a butcher. It couldn't look like body parts thrown together. Like a jumble. It had to look like what it really was. It had to be a particular message. A message to anybody who would think of stealing from *him*."

Flip opened his mouth. He hesitated for a moment, but a moment only. He knew if he did not speak now, he would forever lose his chance.

"You killed these children two at a time, or even three in a go. They didn't escape. They didn't bleed everywhere. How? How on earth was that possible? In all my years in law enforcement, I never saw anything like it."

Nash smiled a dumb smile like a grinning animal. Like a pleased horse. It was one of the most disturbing things Flip had ever seen.

"The smaller ones were easy," Nash said. "I only had to be a little bigger and faster. For the others, well. . . Twins have a bond closer than any other sort of kin. You use that against them. Grab one and start beating on him, but make it a tussle. Give the other the feeling he can jump in and save the day—fight you off, yeah? So he always does come back and try. *That's* when you grab the other. Then, when you got your arms around each of their necks, you squeeze real hard and end it. Triplets were a challenge, yes, but I still found a way to make it work. I'm no magician, but. . . I do have a trick or two up my sleeve. I learned how to strangle a boy with my legs."

Nash continued to vibrate and sway.

Initially, it had seemed to Flip that Nash might be imitating a rocking way of prayer that he had seen Jews perform. But now he realized this was something else entirely. That Nash was imitating *the leaves of wild ramp* as they swayed and shivered in the breeze off Lake Michigan. And it was a skilled impersonation. Nash seemed to literally blow about in the wind, as though his body were no more solid than a wiry green leaf. Nash had done this—moved his body like this—a thousand times before, Flip was sure. He must have. He was practiced. Expert.

"I wondered what it meant, of course, when I found Durkin dead among the shoals," Nash said, as if in afterthought. "The water washed his body up right here; it come to rest against this very promontory. I took the body home and thought on it some. And I realized He had another message for me. That Durkin might be gone, but that didn't mean my project was over. It meant I should continue."

Flip swallowed hard and did a quick mental review. He asked himself if he had everything he'd come for. All the answers.

Nash's mania was wild and beyond explaining—beyond anything Flip had ever encountered. Any further justification the man might give seemed liable to raise twice as many new questions as it would answer. Flip decided to close the book while he had the chance.

Then Nash spoke up once more.

"He's telling me to kill you now."

Flip raised his 1911.

"He's telling me to kill you now. . . but only so that you will kill me."

Flip lowered the gun back down.

"The world can't know about him," Nash said. "He's telling me I tried my best, but it's over now. He'll send another to finish what I started. Then another again, if that don't work. He'll send even more until all who take from him see final justice."

Nash stopped swaying and rose to his feet.

Flip reluctantly lifted his 1911 once more. It suddenly seemed that one of Nash's hands had grown spiky and deformed, like the paw of some undersea monster. Nash raised it up high.

Against the moon, Flip saw Nash held a trench knife—a small sword with a knuckle duster extending around his hand and over his fingers. Needle-sharp protrusions jutted out at each finger joint.

"Put that down or I'll shoot you," Flip said.

"Can you see him?" Nash asked.

Flip hesitated, then risked a whip-fast glance along the waterline. There was nothing there.

"Drop it to the ground," Flip commanded.

"Can you see him up there in the sky?" Nash continued. "He's standing out there in the water and he's about a thousand feet high. Big head like a triangle. I only seen him before in my dreams."

Nash turned to face Flip, a stark mania in his eyes.

"*Before tonight*," he cried ecstatically, "*I only seen him in my dreams!*"

Nash charged.

There was no one to hear the report of Flip's 1911. Three shots. Each connecting. Each opening a hole in Nash's chest. Flip delivered them near to instantaneously, through a reflex he could not properly control.

Nash went limp and the spiky weapon dropped from his hand. The killer fell face-first into the muck, beginning, almost immediately, to sink down into it.

Flip breathed-in the sharp stink of gunpowder. Cautiously, he put his 1911 back into his coat.

He looked down at the body, already half-consumed by the oozing bed of ramp. Thinking on it, Flip realized that, actually, he had about a thousand more questions he still wished to ask. Maybe a thousand thousand. But he had all the answers that he would ever get, and he knew it.

In the sky above the lake, a seagull cried. Then another. Then several more began to shriek together. Twenty or thirty birds—not known by Flip to be active nocturnally—circled the promontory in a strange display, bleating out their jagged calls. The ramp around the body seemed to shudder in response.

Flip looked up, then, into the night sky. He tried to gaze a thousand feet high, to the place that Nash had described.

The seagulls distracted and confused Flip's eyes as they sped back and forth across his line of sight. They flew out over the vast lake, and also inward toward the promontory. One nearly brushed against his face. They zigged; they zagged. They created a practical wall of motion. Flip realized it was the kind of thing that might distract you from seeing a thing that was very large, very tall, and very far out into the water.

Then—one by one—the gulls began to dissipate. They flew inland, or else off down the coast.

And Flip realized, very gradually, that there was nothing left to see.

EPILOGUE

The uniform was dark, royal blue. The brass buttons down the front
gleamed if you kept them polished, which he did. So did the star.
The fabric, though, was almost too heavy for the humid summer
nights. It made him sweat in the armpits and also down his back. Even
so, Flip liked the uniform because it made him look wide and substantial in the shoulders. It was not quite a leather jacket, but it would do.

A Friday night in summer. Still early. Glorious weather, and the
sun not yet set. Flip walked alone. Despite the clear sky and pleasant breeze, the street felt more than a little off. Wrong. Subdued. Like
when they hold the parade even though the president or the Pope has
just died. You still go through the motions, yeah, but nobody's really
feeling it.

The other men—and a few women—who walked past Flip seemed
furtive. Hunted. They kept their eyes low and their hat brims lower.
They looked straight ahead, giving no indication they intended to duck
into a storefront or head down a dark alley, until the very last moment
when they did.

South State Street felt like a one-industry town where the mill
has just closed. Only just. People want to pretend that it's going to be
fine. Just a small setback. But you can see it in their faces. They know.
Inside? They know.

The Palmerton came into view, and here, Flip saw a welcome sight. A familiar figure, furtively taking in the air on the front porch.

He made a beeline.

When he got close enough to be noticed, Sally turned her head and ducked back through the doorway. There she paused, examining the approaching policeman more carefully. After a moment's hesitation, she crept back outside.

"Shit," she said as Flip walked up. "I'm still getting used to you in that thing."

"So am I," Flip said, running a finger around his collar.

It had been weeks since he had seen her last, but ages since they had really talked.

"How the twins?" he asked, keeping his voice low.

"About to turn four," Sally said. "Can you believe it?"

"*Four* already?" Flip said politely. "How the time does fly."

The look in Sally's eyes told him her mind was far away. It hardly taxed Flip's skills of deduction to know she was thinking about what the future might hold for her young ones.

Flip glanced through the front window of the Palmerton. There were customers, but not as many as there should have been. And those there were seemed cautious and reserved. The funereal mood held here too. Visitors had the sense it would be gauche to celebrate anything too heartily.

"There's ways around it," Sally said glumly. "That's what we're all finding. You can't sell booze on the open anymore, but it's not illegal to drink what you already had in your house. So we're thinking: What if my place was a private club, which is practically a house in the eyes of the law? And lord knows we got a stockpile in the basement. I ain't a fool. I knew this was coming."

Flip nodded. If anyone had sensed the shifting winds, it had surely been Sally.

"And I've partnered up with some people," she said, brightening a bit. "There are organizations that specialize in operating under this kind of situation. Did you know that? I aim to work with the best of them."

Flip leaned against the railing of the Palmerton's front porch.

"I've heard about those organizations," he told her. "We known each other too long for me ever to tell you to be careful. But, Sally? Do me a favor and be careful just the same. These folks moving in. They give me a feeling."

Sally smiled.

"You mean a feeling like making hooch illegal ain't gonna get rid of all crime forever? That feeling you used to talk about?"

"That . . .and some others too," Flip said.

"Anyhow," Sally continued, "they're not so bad. They know how to handle things. And that one over there's even kind of sweet."

Sally gestured to the entryway of the Palmerton. Her new partners had installed a pair of their own as doormen. They were meaty Italians who bulged in their suits. Sally waved to one—indicating he should join her and the police sergeant.

The man could not have been much more than twenty, but his face already seemed to hold a lifetime of experience. He had an unpleasant nose, ugly fish lips, and deep scars that ran all across one cheek. Flip immediately recognized these as what happened when somebody tried to slit your throat, but you lowered your chin just in time.

"Alphonse is one of their best," Sally said. "Helps with hospitality and security both. Does top notch work."

The young man turned to Flip and shook his hand vigorously.

"If there's ever anything I can do for you, officer—*anything*—you just let me know," he said.

Flip assured the young man that he would. Then Flip and Sally returned their attention to the street, and Alphonse hustled back to his post.

"Ursula used to say it would happen again," Flip observed, looking down at South State Street. "A war in Europe again. Big Bill mayor again. A killer in the city again. Maybe she's right. But the other day I was thinking . . ., maybe that also means the good times will come back, yeah? We'll have Mardi Gras once more here along this stretch. Maybe your arrangement with these people is temporary. Maybe it just gets you through . . . until those good times come back."

"It's not all that bad," Sally said, shaking her head. "Like I told you, they're nice people."

"For now," Flip said.

Sally's face curled into a tight, forced smile. Flip realized she was thinking of something deeply troubling. Or painful. The policeman wondered if perhaps he had been too unserious regarding her predicament.

"Forgive me, Sally," he said. "You're your own woman, and you make your own decisions just fine. I don't mean to come across as though I've forgot that. You got—what?—about a thousand times what I do in the bank? *Counting* that money the city let me keep. If anybody has proven they can handle themselves—whatever the times—it's you."

"No, it's not that," Sally said. "You're sweet, Flip. But it's not that. It's just . . . I seem to remember that there *was* a woman named Ursula Green . . . Right? Like you just said. And she lived in the back of this building, down in the basement? And told fortunes?"

Flip nodded slowly and encouragingly.

"There are times I start to think she wasn't here at all," Sally continued. "She doesn't feel real, you know? Some days, I wake up and I just forget about her. Not like I forget that the capital of France is Paris. But like I forget France exists altogether. It's like I can remember another past in which she wasn't there. Or where there was just a pile of rags and wood in the basement that maybe we called 'Ursula Green' as a joke, but it wasn't a real woman. But then, other times, I'm sure she was there. That I spoke with her and knew her. Isn't that strange, Flip?"

"It's strange," Flip agreed. "But I've seen stranger."

Sally took a deep breath and steadied herself on the porch railing. Behind them, Alphonse gripped a misbehaving patron by the collar of his jacket. The Italian pulled him close and whispered something into his ear, nearly biting it. Flip watched the exchange, and understood for certain that those hands knew murder.

Back down on the street, a drunken man howled at the sky and flapped his arms like a bird.

"You never did tell me about those things," Sally said. "Those strange things that you took care of."

Flip looked over at Sally to say she ought to know better.

"My babies really going to be safe?" Sally pressed, watching the flapping man.

"Yes," Flip said quietly. "They are. At least from-"

"How do you know *for sure*?" Sally pushed.

"Because they're not what he was after," Flip said. "*Who* he was after."

Sally looked down at her shoes.

"Why won't you ever talk about it?" she whispered. "Why won't you just tell me straight what happened? Just tell me you found him and killed him? I know you've done it, Flip. Can't you just *say* it? I'd feel a whole lot better if you did."

Flip said nothing. Stared at the flapping drunk.

"I mean . . . I can *guess*," Sally said. "I'm not stupid. I can guess just from what they printed in the *Defender*, scant though it was."

Flip stayed silent.

"How long have we known each other?" she entreated, cooing almost sensually. "Do an old friend this single kindness? Why, Joe Flippity?"

"Because the story doesn't end with him," Flip replied. "Because it's bigger than one man. I won't lie to you, Sally."

"Then just tell me you done him," Sally pressed coyly. "That's all I want. Nod once if it's yes."

She smiled. Flip looked at her for a very long time.

"You *really* want to know what happened?" Flip asked.

Sally did not have to speak.

"Fine," Flip said. "Then I'm going to tell you something I never told nobody. Are you ready? Are you listening carefully? Nash was after Tark. All that time, he wanted Tark and his brother. To kill them both at the same time. He thought Tark had stolen magic power from some beast that lives out in the lake—an invisible giant with triangle eyes. Its power came up through magic ramp. I don't fully understand that part."

Sally opened her mouth to ask about ten questions, but Flip kept going.

"The night after I did it—yes Sally, after I put three bullets into Nash—I went directly to see Tark. I planned to catch him after hours in his caravan, but they were doing a double midnight show and it ran into the early morning. I found Singer outside the tent and talked to him while I waited. Singer said Tark had a new trick that was knocking 'em dead. Said I really ought to see it. He let me in for free, and I sat in the back. Pretty soon, Tark came on. He began with tricks I'd seen before. Manipulations with cards. Pulling a rabbit from a hat. All that bit."

Flip swallowed hard. He slowly brought his gaze up from the drunk flapping in the street to the sky above the buildings. There, he let his eyes linger.

"But . . . the act was building to something, Sally. It had this *feeling* about it, that it was leading someplace. At first, I thought I could guess to what."

"Yeah, sure," Sally said. "To that trick where he transports himself across the tent. Like always."

Flip nodded, still looking up at the sky.

"That's what I thought too. But when it came time, he did something new. He brought a long mirror out onto the stage. Big as a chalkboard in a schoolhouse. First, he held it to the side where the audience couldn't see. Then he tilts it and we can see his reflection. And already, I know where this is going. I watch him do a pantomime dance with the reflection of himself. He touches his toes. Tips his hat. Does a flexing routine with his fingers. The reflection matches it all perfectly. Then he turns to the audience and smiles. But the reflection doesn't turn. It keeps looking out. The audience gasps. You can practically hear the air being sucked out of the tent. It only lasts a second. Then the people applaud like you wouldn't believe. They go crazy. And the reflection steps through the mirror."

"So?" Sally said. "He and Ike learned a new trick. What about it?"

"Yes," Flip said distantly, looking at the night sky above the rooftops. "But see, then an assistant pulled another long, high mirror out onto the stage. It was the same as the first—like a school chalkboard on wheels. And the two Tarks, they took turns playing with *their* reflections. They did more routines together. Held hands and passed objects back and forth. Then they turned to face the audience. . . and once again, the reflections *didn't*. You could have heard a pin drop, Sally. A woman in the front row actually fainted. Then people went crazy all over again—clapping, hooting, cheering to beat the band. It was a standing ovation. The two reflections stepped out of the mirror, and they all stood on the stage together. All four, hand in hand. All absolutely identical. Then they took a bow."

The expression on Flip's face showed he was deeply troubled by what he had just described. That there was a bewildering terror to it.

Sally, in contrast, clucked as though Flip were a child who had worked himself into a tizzy over nothing.

"That could have been done a thousand different ways, and you know it," she told him. "With makeup or costumes. Or maybe the Tarks are identical quadruplets. Ike had gone down to Indiana to stay with family, right? Maybe he brought two more up with him. Did you ever think of that?"

"I went and waited by Tark's caravan after the show," Flip said. "He came out of the tent very late, bottle already in his hand. He looked surprised to see me. At first he was cheerful. Excited. Asked if I'd seen his new finale, like he was proud of it. I wanted to slap him across the face. I told him the things Nash had said to me. About the magic ramp along the shoreline, and a thing in the lake with triangle eyes. I asked if he remembered playing on the beach when he was a little boy, with Ike. I asked if the ramp had given him powers. Real powers. He went stone still. Then I asked if he understood that the thing he sometimes sees and talks to when he's drunk—a great insect beast—is connected to it. I believe that's the thing he stole from, Sally. I told Tark that whatever he took, that thing wants it back. I told Tark the thing was never going to stop. That it was going to send another Rotney Nash to prey on him. Then another. It would keep happening and happening until he was dead. His brother too."

"And what did Tark say?" Sally asked.

"He was quiet for a long spell," Flip told her. "Then he asked me what *I* thought he should do."

"And what did you say?"

"I told him he should do what Du Sable did after *he* was touched by the ramp. Leave town for good. Never come back to Chicago. Dis-a-fucking-pear."

"And?" Sally asked after a moment.

"And he said he would. And you and I ain't seen him since."

"Yes," Sally said, pondering. "I thought that *was* strange, the way he just evaporated. I figured he would have stopped by here, after it all happened. At least to drink some gin, or ask if he could see the girls, now that we weren't working together. I always wondered why he didn't. I figured the circus must have gone on a long tour. Then, to be honest, it kind of slipped from my mind. Last couple of years, now and then I'd meet someone who'd seen the Singling Brothers Circus. I'd ask about a magician, and they'd say there wasn't one in the show anymore. I wondered about that. I worried Tark had died, maybe drank himself to death. Do you know what became of him? Where he is?"

Flip inclined his head and gave a little pout, like a physician about to make a 'probably' diagnosis.

"About a year ago I saw a newspaper from Portland, Oregon," Flip said. "There was a piece about a travelling Negro magic act that'd come through. Said the performer did animal tricks and card tricks, but that he was best known for disappearing and reappearing all the way across a room. Went by the name of Cornelius Mack. Wasn't a photo, but the way they described him, it sure did sound like Tark."

Sally nodded thoughtfully.

Out in the street, the flapping drunk was beginning to accost passersby. In the doorway of an illegal tavern—they were all illegal now, of course—a man in a straw porkpie looked at Flip imploringly. Private drunkenness was one thing, but if you acted up in public, people were going to wonder where you had got so soused. It was not uniformed police that concerned the proprietor. It was the reformers and do-gooders who might be patrolling South State to see if that new laws were actually being enforced. And who might, depending on what they saw, insist the municipality perform a *proper* disinfecting of the area, as opposed to the cursory papering-over that had occurred.

Flip waved his hand to indicate that he would be on it in a moment.

"Duty calls," he said to Sally.

"It certainly does," she replied, glancing back to the Italian gents who lingered at her door.

Sally began to retreat inside, and Flip marched down the brothel's front steps.

Then a voice. Her voice.

"Flip. . ."

He turned back.

"Flip. . . help me not to forget Ursula Green, all right?" she said. "I want to remember her. I want to remember all of this. I don't ever want to forget her. Or Tark, either. Ursula used to tell me that there were many people in me. Other versions of me. And they were in other places, doing other things. . ."

Flip nodded.

"That does sound like Ursula," he said.

"These past two, three years, I feel like I've stepped into a world where I'm one of those different me's. Where I don't exist as I once did. Like I'm a train car sent down the wrong track, and now I'm in the wrong place. But I want to stay in *my* place, Flip. You know? This place. And I want to remember all the things that happened. Ursula, Tark. . . you."

"I know," Flip told her. "Tell you what, Sally; I'll help you. I'll help you keep all this in your mind. We'll both remember Ursula, all right? We'll do it together."

Something like relief crossed Sally's face. She nodded down at Flip. Her eyes and her smile radiated relief.

Flip smiled too. Then he turned back around to handle the flapping drunk. He walked a few paces into the street, and began to roll up his sleeves.

Unobserved now, he relaxed . . . and his face fell.

His words to Sally had been a lie.

In truth, Flip wanted only to forget.

And on those lonely midnights when he crept back to the promontory jutting out into Lake Michigan, when he sat there alone, silently watching the swaying, sentient ramp riffle like playing cards while the full moon shone overhead, when he gazed up into the sky a thousand feet above the lake at two small, triangular pinpoints that seemed to hover there—sentient, furious, and suspended in the empty ether. . .

That was when he wanted to forget most of all.

AUTHOR'S NOTE

Historians will find that I have taken some liberties with particulars regarding the Bucket of Blood—as, it should be remembered, the proprietors of the Bucket themselves did, so many years ago.

ABOUT THE AUTHOR

Born in New York and educated at Kenyon College and Columbia University, **Scott Kenemore** is the national best-selling author of *Lake of Darkness*, *The Grand Hotel*, and *Zombie Ohio*, as well as numerous other works of horror and satire. He lives in Evanston, IL.